Deoris Crouched on the Sands in Wildly Unreasoning Horror.

The half-human idiots were mewling more loudly now, grimacing at her . . .

Deoris looked madly around for a way of escape. To one side, a high wall of needled rock bristled away; to the other, a quicksand marsh of reeds and rushes stretched on to the horizon. She was hemmed in.

But how did I come here? Was there a boat?

She spun around, and saw only the empty, rolling sea. She began to run, in terror-stricken panic. Behind her the groping pad-pad-pad of the pursuit was like a merciless incoming tide.

Her feet splashed in the surf as she turned, whirling like a cornered animal. She stumbled, ran on, stumbled again—and fell. She struggled to rise, scratching at the wet sands, clawing to free herself from groping, scrabbling hands. Something hit her hard in the face. Her brain exploded in fire and she sank down . . . and down . . . and down . . .

Books by Marion Zimmer Bradley

Colors of Space
The Ruins of Isis
Web of Light

Published by POCKET BOOKS

WEB OF LIGHT

MARION ZIMMER BRADLEY

PUBLISHED BY POCKET BOOKS NEW YORK

Another *Original* publication of POCKET BOOKS

POCKET BOOKS, a division of Simon & Schuster, Inc.
1230 Avenue of the Americas, New York, N.Y. 10020

Published by arrangement with Starblaze Editions
of the Donning Company/Publishers

ISBN: 0-671-44875-7

First Pocket Books printing October, 1984

10 9 8 7 6 5 4 3

POCKET and colophon are registered trademarks
of Simon & Schuster, Inc.

Printed in the U.S.A.

Acknowledgments

First, to my dear friend and mentor Dorothy G. Quinn, who, more years ago than I like to think about, explored the past with me, and wrote, with me, a thin sheaf of handwritten scenes exploring the characters of Domaris and Micon. The book has been through four rewritings since, and Dorothy would probably not recognize her brainchild; but it was in her company that I first trod this path, and the debt is inestimable.

Second, to David R. Bradley, my son, who prepared the final draft of this manuscript for publication and who provided, from various sources, including the unpublished writings of his late father, Robert A. Bradley, the philosophical excerpts which appear at the head of each section.

—Marion Zimmer Bradley

Contents

BOOK ONE
Micon

"All events are but the consummation of preceding causes, clearly seen but not distinctly apprehended. When the strain is sounded, the most untutored listener can tell that it must end with the keynote, although he cannot see why each successive bar must lead at last to the concluding chord. The law of Karma is the force which leads all chords to the keynote, which spreads the ripples from the tiny stone dropped into a pool, until the tidal waves drown a continent, long after the stone has sunk from sight and been forgotten.

"This is the story of one such stone, dropped into the pool of a world which was drowned long before the Pharaohs of Egypt piled one stone upon another."

—*The Teachings of Rajasta the Mage*

Chapter One

EMISSARIES

I

At the sound of sandaled feet upon stone, the Priest Rajasta raised his face from the scroll he held open on his knee. The library of the Temple was usually deserted at this hour, and he had come to regard it as his peculiar privilege to study here each day undisturbed. His forehead ridged a little, not with anger, for he was not given to anger, but with residual annoyance, for he had been deep in thought.

However, the two men who had entered the library had aroused his interest, and he straightened and watched them; without, however, laying aside the scroll, or rising.

The elder of the two was known to him: Talkannon, Arch-Administrator of the Temple of Light, was a burly, cheerful-faced man, whose apparent good nature was a shrewd dissemblance for an analytical temperament which could turn cold and stern and even ruthless. The other was a stranger, a man whose graceful dancer's body moved slowly and with effort; his dark smile was slightly wry, as if lips shut tight on pain could grimace more easily. A tall man, this stranger, deeply tanned and handsome, clad in white robes of an unfamiliar pattern, which glimmered with faint luminescence in the sunlit shadows of the room.

"Rajasta," the Arch-Administrator said, "our brother

desires further knowledge. He is free to study as he will. Be he your guest." Talkannon bowed slightly to the still-seated Rajasta, and, turning back to the stranger, stated, "Micon of Ahtarrath, I leave you with our greatest student. The Temple, and the City of the Temple, are yours, my brother; feel free to call upon me at any time." Again Talkannon bowed, then turned and left the two men to further their acquaintance.

As the door scraped slowly shut behind the Arch-Administrator's powerful form, Rajasta frowned again; he was used to Talkannon's abrupt manners, but he feared that this stranger would think them all lacking in civility. Laying down his scroll, he arose and approached the guest with his hands outstretched in courteous welcome. On his feet, Rajasta was a very tall man, long past middle age; his step and manner disciplined and punctilious.

Micon stood quite still where Talkannon had left him, smiling still that grave, one-sided smile. His eyes were deeply blue as storm-skies; the small creases around them spoke of humor, and a vast tolerance.

This man is one of us, surely, thought the Priest of Light, as he made a ceremonious bow, and waited. Still the stranger stood and smiled, unheedful. Rajasta's frown returned, faintly. "Micon of Ahtarrath—"

"I am so called," said the stranger formally. "I have come here to ask that I may pursue my studies among you." His voice was low and resonant, but held an overlay of effort, as if kept always in careful control.

"You are welcome to share in what knowledge is mine," Rajasta said with grave courtesy, "and you are yourself welcome—" He hesitated, then added, on a sudden impulse, "Son of the Sun." With his hand he made a certain Sign.

"A fosterling, only, I fear," said Micon with a brief, wry smile, "and overly proud of the relationship." Nevertheless, in answer to the ritual identifying phrase, he raised his hand and returned the archaic gesture.

Rajasta stepped forward to embrace his guest; they were bound, not only by the bonds of shared wisdom and search, but by the power behind the innermost magic of the Priesthood of Light: like Rajasta, Micon was one of their highest initiates. Rajasta wondered at this—Micon seemed so young! Then, as they stepped apart, Rajasta saw what he had not noticed before. His face shadowed with sorrow and pity, and he took Micon's emaciated hands in his and led him to a seat, saying, "Micon, my brother!"

"A fosterling, as I said," Micon nodded. "How did you know? I was—told—that there is no outward scarring, nor—"

"No," Rajasta said. "I guessed. Your stillness—something in your gestures. But how did this come upon you, my brother?"

"May I speak of that at another time? What is—" Micon hesitated again, and said, his resonant voice strained, "—cannot be remedied. Let it suffice that I—returned the Sign."

Rajasta said, his voice trembling with emotion, "You are most truly a Son of Light, although you walk in darkness. Perhaps—perhaps the only Son of that Light who can face His splendor."

"Only because I may never behold it," Micon murmured, and the blank eyes seemed to gaze intently on the face they would never see. Silence, while that twisted and painful smile came and went upon Micon's face.

At last Rajasta ventured, "But—you returned the Sign—and I thought surely I was mistaken—that surely you saw—"

"I think—I can read thoughts, a little," Micon said. "Only a little; and only since there was need. I do not know, yet, how much to trust to it. But with you—" Again the smile lent brilliance to the dark, strained face. "I felt no hesitation."

Again the silence, as of emotions stretched too tightly for speech; then, from the passageway, a woman's young voice called, "Lord Rajasta!"

Rajasta's tense face relaxed. "I am here, Domaris," he called, and explained to Micon, "My disciple, a young woman —Talkannon's daughter. She is unawakened as yet, but when she learns, and is—complete, she holds the seeds of greatness."

"The Light of the Heavens grant knowledge and wisdom to her," said Micon with polite disinterest.

Domaris came into the room; a tall girl, and proudly erect, with hair the color of hammered copper that made a brightness in the dark spaces and shadows. Like a light bird she came, but paused at a little distance from the men, too shy to speak in the presence of a stranger.

"My child," Rajasta said kindly, "this is Micon of Ahtarrath, my brother in the Light, to be treated as myself in every respect."

Domaris turned to the stranger, in civil courtesy—then her eyes widened, a look of awe drew over her features, and with a gesture that seemed forced, as if she made it against her will, she laid her right hand over her breast and raised it slowly to forehead level, in the salute given only to the highest initiates of the Priesthood of Light. Rajasta smiled: it was a right instinct and he was pleased; but he let his voice break the spell, for Micon had gone grey with a deep pallor.

"Micon is my guest, Domaris, and will be lodged with me—if that is your will, my brother?" At Micon's nod of assent, he continued, "Go now, daughter, to the Scribe-Mother, and ask her to hold a scribe always in readiness for my brother."

She started and shivered a little; sent a worshipful glance at Micon; then inclined her head in reverence to her teacher and went on her errand.

"Micon!" Rajasta spoke with terse directness. "You are come here from the Dark Shrine!"

Micon nodded. "From their dungeons," he qualified immediately.

"I—I feared that—"

"I am no apostate," Micon reassured firmly. "I served not there. My service is not subject to compulsion!"

"Compulsion?"

Micon did not move, but the lift of his brows and the curl of his lip gave the effect of a shrug. "They would have compelled me." He held out his mutilated hands. "You can see that they were—eloquent in persuasion." Before Rajasta's gasp of horror, Micon drew back his hands and concealed their betrayal within the sleeves of his robe. "But my task is undone. And until it is completed, I hold death from me with these hands—though he companion me most closely."

Micon might have been speaking of last night's rain; and Rajasta bowed his head before the impassive face. "There are those we call Black-robes," he said bitterly. "They hide themselves among the members of the Magician's Sect, those who guard the shrine of the Unrevealed God—whom we call Grey-robes here. I have heard that these . . . Black-robes—torture! But they are secret in their doings. Well for them! Be they accursed!"

Micon stirred. "Curse not, my brother!" he said harshly. "You, of all men, should know the danger of that."

Rajasta said tonelessly, "We have no way of acting against

them. As I say, we suspect members of the Grey-robe sect.
Yet, all are—grey!"

"I know. I saw too clearly, so—I see nothing. Enough,"
Micon pleaded. "I carry my release within me, my brother,
but I may not yet accept it. We will not speak of this,
Rajasta." He arose, with slow carefulness, and paced deliberately to the window, to stand with his face uplifted to the
warm sunlight.

With a sigh, Rajasta accepted the prohibition. True, the
Black-robes always concealed themselves so well that no victim
could ever identify his tormentors. But why this? Micon was a
stranger and could hardly have incurred their enmity; and
never before had they dared meddle with so highly-placed a
personage. The knowledge of what had befallen Micon initiated a new round in a warfare as old as the Temple of Light.

And the prospect dismayed him.

II

In the School of Scribes, Mother Lydara was in the process of
disciplining one of her youngest pupils. The Scribes were the
sons and daughters of the Priest's Caste who showed, in their
twelfth or thirteenth year, a talent for reading or writing: and
thirty-odd intelligent boys and girls are not easy to keep in
order.

Mother Lydara felt that no child in all her memory had ever
been such a problem to her as the sullen little girl who faced
her just now: a thin angular girl, about thirteen, with stormy
eyes and hair that hung dishevelled in black, tumbled curls.
She held herself very stiff and erect, her nervous little hands
stubbornly clenched, taut defiance in her white face.

"Deoris, little daughter," the Scribe-Mother admonished,
standing rock-like and patient, "you must learn to control
both tongue and temper if you ever hope to serve in the Higher
Ways. The daughter of Talkannon should be an example and a
pattern to the others. Now, you will apologize to me, and to
your playmate Ista, and then you will make accounting to your
father." The old Priestess waited, arms crossed on her ample
breast, for an apology which never came.

Instead the girl burst out tearfully, "I won't! I have done

nothing wrong, Mother, and I won't apologize for anything!''
Her voice was plangent, vibrating with a thrilling sweetness
which had marked her, among the children of the Temple, as a
future Spell-singer; she seemed all athrob with passion like a
struck harp.

The Scribe-Mother looked at her with a baffled, weary
patience. "That is not the way to speak to an elder, my child.
Obey me, Deoris.''

"I will not!''

The old woman put out a hand, herself uncertain whether to
placate the girl or slap her, when a rap came at the door.
"Who is it?'' the Priestess called impatiently.

The door swung back and Domaris put her head around the
corner. "Are you at leisure, Mother?''

Mother Lydara's troubled face relaxed, for Domaris had
been a favorite for many years. "Come in, my child, I have
always time for you.''

Domaris halted on the threshold, staring at the stormy face
of the little girl in the scribe's frock.

"Domaris, I *didn't!*'' Deoris wailed, and, a forlorn little
cyclone, she flung herself on Domaris and wrapped her arms
around her sister's neck. "I didn't do anything,'' she hic-
coughed on a hysterical sob.

"Deoris—little sister!'' chided Domaris. Firmly she
disengaged the clinging arms. "Forgive her, Mother Lydara—
has she been in trouble again? No, be still, Deoris; I did not
ask *you*.''

"She is impertinent, impudent, impatient of correction and
altogether unmanageable,'' said Mother Lydara. "She sets a
bad example in the school, and runs wild in the dormitories. I
dislike to punish her, but—''

"Punishment only makes Deoris worse,'' said Domaris
levelly. "You should never be severe with her.'' She pulled
Deoris close, smoothing the tumbled curls. She herself knew so
well how to rule Deoris through love that she resented Mother
Lydara's harshness.

"While Deoris is in the Scribe-School,'' said the Scribe-
Mother with calm finality, "she will be treated as the others
are treated, and punished as they are punished. And unless she
makes some effort to behave as they behave she will not be
long in the School.''

Domaris raised her level brows. "I see . . . I have come

from Lord Rajasta. He has need of a scribe to serve a guest, and Deoris is competent; she is not happy in the school, nor do you want her here. Let her serve this man.'' She glanced at the drooping head, now snuggled into her shoulder; Deoris looked up with wondering adoration. Domaris always made everything right again!

Mother Lydara frowned, but was secretly relieved: Deoris was a problem quite beyond her limited capabilities, and the fact that this spoilt child was Talkannon's daughter complicated the situation. Theoretically, Deoris was there on an equal footing with the others, but the daughter of the Arch-Administrator could not be chastised or ruled over like the child of an ordinary priest.

"Have it as you will, Daughter of Light," said the Scribe-Mother gruffly, "but she must continue her own studies, see you to that!''.

"Rest assured, I shall not neglect her schooling," said Domaris coldly. As they left the squat building, she studied Deoris, frowning. She had seen little of her sister in these last months; when Domaris had been chosen as Rajasta's Acolyte, the child had been sent to the Scribe-School—but before that they had been inseparable, though the eight years difference in their ages made the relationship less that of sisters than of mother and daughter. Now Domaris sensed a change in her young sister that dismayed her. Always before, Deoris had been merry and docile; what had they done to her, to change her into this sullen little rebel? She decided, with a flare of anger, that she would seek Talkannon's permission to take Deoris again under her own care.

"Can I really stay with you?"

"I cannot possibly promise it, but we shall see." Domaris smiled. "You wish it?"

"Oh yes!" said Deoris passionately, and flung her arms about her sister again, with such intensity that Domaris's brow furrowed into lines of deep trouble. What had they *done* to Deoris?

Freeing herself from the clinging arms, Domaris admonished, "Gently, gently, little sister," and they turned their steps toward the House of the Twelve.

III

Domaris was one of the Twelve Acolytes: six young men and six young women, chosen every third year from the children of the Priest's Caste, for physical perfection, beauty, and some especial talent which made them archetypal of the Priest's Caste of the Ancient Land. When they reached maturity, they dwelt for three years in the House of the Twelve, studying all the ancient wisdom of the Priest's Caste, and preparing themselves for service to the Gods and to their people. It was said that if some calamity should destroy all of the Priest's Caste save only the Twelve, all the wisdom of the Temples could be reconstructed from these Twelve Acolytes alone. At the end of this three-year term, each married his or her allotted mate, and so carefully were these six young couples chosen that the children of Acolytes rarely failed to climb high in the Priesthood of their caste.

The House of the Twelve was a spacious building, crowning a high green hill apart from the clustered buildings of the precinct; surrounded by wide lawns and green enclosed gardens, and cool fountains. As the sisters sauntered along the path which climbed, between banks of flowering shrubs, toward the white walls of the retreat, a young woman, barely out of childhood, hurried across the lawns toward them.

"Domaris! Come here, I want you—oh Deoris! Have you been freed from the Scribe's prison?"

"I hope so," said Deoris shyly, and the girls hugged one another. The newcomer was between Domaris and Deoris in age; she might almost have been another sister, for the three were very much alike in form and feature, all three very tall and slender, finely-boned, with delicate hands and arms and the molded, incised features of the Priest's Caste. Only in coloring did they differ: Domaris the tallest, her fiery hair long and rippling, her eyes cool, shadowed grey. Deoris was slighter and smaller, with heavy black ringlets and eyes like crushed violets; and Elis's curls were the glossy red-brown of polished wood, her eyes merry and clear blue. Of all those in the House of the Twelve, or in all the Temple, the daughters of Talkannon loved their cousin Elis the most.

"There are envoys here from Atlantis," Elis told them eagerly.

"From the Sea Kingdom? Truly?"

"Yes, from the Temple at Ahtarrath. The young Prince of Ahtarrath was sent here with his younger brother, but they never arrived. They were kidnapped, or shipwrecked, or murdered, and now they're searching the whole seacoast for them or their bodies."

Domaris stared, startled. Ahtarrath was a formidable name. The Mother-Temple, here in the Ancient Land, had little contact with the Sea Kingdoms, of which Ahtarrath was the most powerful; now, twice in one day, had she heard of it.

Elis went on excitedly, "There's some evidence that he landed, and they're talking of Black-robes! Has Rajasta spoken of this, Domaris?"

Domaris frowned. She and Elis were of the Inner Circle of the Priest's Caste, but they had no right to discuss their elders, and the presence of Deoris should restrain such gossip in any case. "Rajasta does not confide in me; nor should an Acolyte listen to the gossip of the Gates!"

Elis turned pink, and Domaris relented a little. "There is no swarm that does not start with a single bee," she said pleasantly. "Rajasta has a guest from Ahtarrath. His name is Micon."

"Micon!" Elis exclaimed. "That is like saying that a slave's name is Lia! There are more Micons in the Sea Kingdoms than leaves on a songtree—" Elis broke off as a tiny girl, barely able to stand alone, clutched at her skirt. Elis looked down, impatient, then bent to take up the child; but the dimpled baby laughed, scampered toward Deoris, then tumbled down and lay squalling. Deoris snatched her up, and Elis glanced with annoyance at the little brown-skinned woman who scuttled after her refractory charge. "Simila," she rebuked, "cannot you keep Lissi from under our feet—or teach her *how* to fall?"

The nurse came to take the child, but Deoris clung to her. "Oh, Elis, let me hold her, I haven't seen her in so long, why she couldn't even creep, and now she's walking! Is she weaned yet? No? How do you endure it? There, Lissi love, you *do* remember me, don't you?" The baby girl shrieked with delight, plunging both hands into Deoris's thick ringlets. "Oh, you fat little darling!" Deoris gurgled, covering the chubby cheeks with kisses.

"Fat little nuisance." Elis looked at her daughter with a bitter laugh; Domaris gave Elis an understanding little pat. Because the women of the Acolytes were given in marriage without any regard for their own wishes, they were free until the very day of their marriage; and Elis, taking advantage of this freedom, had chosen a lover and borne him a child. This was perfectly allowable under the laws of the Temple, but, what was *not* allowable, her lover had failed to come forward and acknowledge paternity. Terrible penalties were visited on an unacknowledged child; to give her child caste, Elis had been forced to throw herself on the mercy of her allotted husband, an Acolyte like herself, called Chedan. Chedan had shown generosity, and acknowledged Lissi, but everyone knew he was not the father; not even Domaris knew who had fathered little Lissi. The real father would have suffered a severe penalty for his cowardice, had Elis denounced him; this she steadfastly refused to do.

Domaris said, gently, before Elis's bitter eyes, "Why don't you send the child away, Elis, since Chedan dislikes her so much? She cannot be important enough to disturb the peace of the Acolytes this way, and you will have other children—"

Elis's mouth twisted briefly, cynically. "Wait until you know what you are talking about before you advise me," she said, reaching out to reclaim her child from Deoris. "Give me the little pest, I must go back."

"We're coming, too," Domaris said, but Elis tucked Lissi under her arm, beckoned to the nurse and hurried away.

Domaris looked after her, troubled. Until this moment her life had moved in orderly, patterned channels, laid out as predictably as the course of the river. Now it seemed the world had changed: talk of Black-robes, the stranger from Ahtarrath who had so greatly impressed her—her quiet life seemed suddenly filled with strangeness and dangers. She could not imagine why Micon should have made such a deep impression on her.

Deoris was looking at her, her violet eyes disturbed, doubtful; Domaris returned, with relief, to the world of familiar duties, as she arranged for her sister's stay in the House of the Twelve.

Later in the day, a courteously worded request came from Micon, that she might bring the scribe to him that evening.

IV

In the library, Micon sat alone by a casement, shadowed; but the white robes he wore were faintly luminescent in the dimness. Except for his silent form, the library was deserted, with no light except that slight luminescence.

Domaris sang a low-toned note, and a flickering, golden light sprang up around them; another note, more softly pitched, deeped the light to a steady radiance with no apparent source.

The Atlantean turned at the sound of her voice. "Who is there? Is it you, Talkannon's daughter?"

Domaris came forward, Deoris's little hand nestled shyly in hers. "Lord Micon, I bring you the scribe-student Deoris. She has been assigned for your convenience at all times and will attend you." Encouraged by Micon's warm smile, she added, "Deoris is my sister."

"Deoris." Micon repeated the name with a soft, slurred accent. "I thank you. And how are you called, Acolyte to Rajasta? Domaris," he recalled, his softly vibrant voice lingering on the syllables. "And the little scribe, then, is your sister? Come here, Deoris."

Domaris withdrew as Deoris went timidly to kneel before Micon. The Atlantean said, disturbed, "You must not kneel to me, child!"

"It is customary, Lord."

"Doubtless, a Priest's daughter is well schooled." Micon smiled. "Yet if I forbid it?"

Deoris rose obediently and stood before him.

"Are you familiar with the contents of the library, little Deoris? You seem very young, and I shall have to depend on you wholly, for writing as well as reading."

"Why?" Deoris blurted out uncontrollably. "You speak our language as one born to it! Can you not read it as well?"

Just for a moment a tormented look flitted across the dark, drawn face. Then it vanished. "I thought that your sister had told you," he said quietly. "I am blind."

Deoris stood for a moment in dumb surprise. A glance at Domaris, who stood off to one side, showed her that her sister had gone chalky white; she had not known, either.

There was a moment of awkward silence; then Micon picked up a scroll which lay near him. "Rajasta left this for me. I should like to hear you read." He handed it to Deoris with a courteous gesture, and the child, wrenching her eyes from Domaris, unfastened it, seating herself upon the scribe's stool which was placed at the foot of Micon's chair. She began to read, in the steady and poised voice which never failed a trained scribe, whatever her emotions.

Left to herself, Domaris recovered her composure: she retired to a niche in the wall and murmured the soft note which lighted it brilliantly. She tried to become absorbed in a page of text, but, try as she might to fix her attention on her own tasks, her eyes kept returning, as with separate will of their own, to the man who sat motionless, listening to the soft monotonous murmur of the child's reading. She had not even guessed! So normal his movements, so beautiful the deep eyes—why should it affect her so? Had *he*, then, been the prisoner of the Black-robes? She had seen his hands, the gaunt twisted travesties of flesh and bone that had once, perhaps, been strong and skillful. Who and what was this man?

In the strange confusion of her emotions, there was not a shred of pity. Why could she not pity him, as she pitied others who were blinded or tortured or lamed? For a moment she felt sharp resentment—how dared he be impervious to her pity?

But I envy Deoris, she thought irrationally. *Why should I?*

Chapter Two

OF DISTANT STORMS

I

There was no thunder, but the insistent flicker of summer lightning came and went through the opened shutters. Inside it was damply hot. The two girls lay on narrow pallets placed side by side on the cool brick floor, both nearly naked beneath a thin linen sheet. The thinnest of net canopies hung unstirring above them. The heat clung like thick robes.

Domaris, who had been pretending to sleep, suddenly rolled over and freed one long plait of her loosened hair from Deoris's outflung arm. She sat up. "You needn't be so quiet, child. I'm not asleep either."

Deoris sat up, hugging her lanky knees. The thick curls clung heavily to her temples: she tossed them impatiently back. "We're not the only ones awake, either," she said with conviction. "I've been hearing things. Voices, and steps, and, somewhere, singing. No—not singing, chanting. Scary chanting, a long way off, a very long way off."

Domaris looked very young as she sat there in her filmy sleeping garment, limned in sharp patches of black and white by the restless lightning; nor, on this night, did she feel much older than her little sister. "I think I heard it too."

"Like this." Deoris hummed a thread of melody, in a whisper.

Domaris shuddered. "Don't! Deoris—where did you hear that chanting?"

"I don't know." Deoris frowned in concentration. "Far away. As if it came from under the earth—or in the sky—no, I'm not even sure whether I heard it or dreamed it." She picked up one of her sister's plaits and began listlessly to unravel it. "There's so much lightning, but no thunder. And when I hear the chanting, the lightning seems to brighten—"

"Deoris, *no!* That is impossible!"

"Why?" asked Deoris fearlessly. "Singing a note in certain rooms will bring light there; why should it not kindle a different light?"

"Because it is blasphemous, evil, to tamper with nature like that!" A coldness, almost fear, seemed to have clamped about her mind. "There is power in the voice. When you grow older in the Priesthood you will learn of this. But you must not speak of those evil forces!"

Deoris's quick thoughts had flitted elsewhere. "Arvath is jealous, that I may be near you when he may not! Domaris!" Her eyes held merry laughter that bubbled over into sound. "Is *that* why you wanted me to sleep in your apartments?"

"Perhaps." A faint stain of color etched the older sister's delicate face with crimson.

"Domaris, are you in love with Arvath?"

Domaris turned her eyes from the searching glances of her sister. "I am betrothed to Arvath," she said gravely. "Love will come when we are ready. It is not well to be too eager for life's gifts." She felt sententious, hypocritical, as she mouthed these sentiments; but her tone sobered Deoris. The thought of parting from her sister, even for marriage, filled her with jealousy which was partly jealousy for the children she knew Domaris would have . . . . All her life *she* had been Domaris's baby and pet.

As if to avoid that loss, Deoris said imploringly, "Don't ever make me go away from you again!"

Domaris slipped an arm around the meager shoulders. "Never, unless you wish it, little sister," she promised; but she felt troubled by the adoration in the child's voice. "Deoris," she said, squirming her hand beneath the small chin and turning Deoris's face up to hers, "you mustn't idolize me this way, I don't like it."

Deoris did not answer, and Domaris sighed. Deoris was an

odd child: mostly reserved and reticent, a few she loved so wildly that it scared Domaris; she seemed to have no moderation in her loves and hates. Domaris wondered: *Did I do that? Did I let her idolize me so irrationally when she was a baby?*

Their mother had died when Deoris was born. The eight-year-old Domaris had resolved, on that night, that her new-born sister would never miss a mother's care. Deoris's nurse had tried to enforce some moderation in this, but when Deoris was weaned, her influence was ended: the two were inseparable. For Domaris, her baby sister replaced the dolls Domaris had that day discarded. Even when Domaris grew older, and had lessons, and later duties in the world of the Temple, Deoris tagged continually at her heels. They had never been parted for a single day until Domaris had entered the House of the Twelve.

Domaris had been only thirteen when she had been betrothed to Arvath of Alkonath. He also was an Acolyte: the one of the Twelve whose Sign of the Heavens was opposite to and congenial to her own. She had always accepted the fact that one day she would marry Arvath, just as she accepted the rising and setting of the sun—and it affected her just about as much. Domaris really had not the slightest idea that she was a beautiful woman. The Priests among whom she had been fostered all treated her with the same, casual, intimate affection; only Arvath had ever sought a closer bond. To this, Domaris reacted with mixed emotions. Arvath's own youth and love of life appealed to her; but real love, or even conscious desire, there was none. Too honest to pretend an acquiescence she did not feel, she was too kind to repulse him utterly, and too innocent to seek another lover. Arvath was a problem which, at times, occupied her attention, but without gravely troubling it.

She sat, silent, beside Deoris, vaguely disturbed. Lightning flickered and glimmered raggedly like the phrases of a broken chant, and a coldness whispered through the air.

A long shiver ripped through Domaris then, and she clung to her sister, shuddering in the sudden, icy grip of fear. "Domaris, what is it, what is it?" Deoris wailed. Domaris's breath was coming in gasps, and her fingers bit sharply into the child's shoulder.

"I don't . . . I wish I knew," she breathed in terror. Suddenly, with deliberate effort, she recovered herself.

Rajasta's teaching was in her mind, and she tried to apply it.

"Deoris, no force of evil can harm us unless we permit it. Lie down—" She set the example, then reached in the darkness for her sister's hands. "Now, we'll say the prayer we used to say when we were little children, and go to sleep." Despite her calm voice and reassuring words, Domaris clasped the little cold fingers in her own firm ones a little too tightly. This was the Night of Nadir, when all the forces of the earth were loosed, good and evil alike, in balance, for all men to take as they would.

"Maker of all things mortal," she began in her low voice, now made husky with strict self-control. Shakily, Deoris joined in, and the sanctity of the old prayer enfolded them both. The night, which had been abnormally quiet until then, seemed somehow less forbidding, and the heat did not cling to them so oppressively. Domaris felt her strained muscles unlock, taut nerves relax.

Not so Deoris, who whimpered, cuddling closer like a scared kitten. "Domaris, talk to me. I'm so frightened, and those voices are still—"

Domaris cut her off, chiding, "Nothing can harm you here, even if they chant evil music from the Dark Shrine itself!" Realizing she had spoken more harshly than was wise in the circumstances, she quickly went on, "Well, then, tell me about Lord Micon."

Deoris brightened at once, speaking almost with reverence. "Oh, he is so kind, and good—but not *inhuman*, Domaris, like so many of the Initiates; like Father, or Cadamiri!" She went on, in a hushed voice, "And he suffers so! He seems always in pain, Domaris, though he never speaks of it. But his eyes, and his mouth, and his hands tell me. And sometimes— sometimes I pretend to be tired, so that he will send me away and go to his own rest."

Deoris's little face was transparent with pity and adoration, but for once Domaris did not blame her. She felt something of the same emotion, and with far less cause. Though Domaris had seen Micon often, in the intervening weeks, they had not exchanged a dozen words beyond the barest greetings. Always there was the strange sense of something half-perceived, felt rather than known. She was content to let it ripen slowly.

Deoris went on, worshipfully, "He is good to everyone, but he treats me like—almost like a little sister. Often when I am reading, he will stop me simply to explain something I have read, as if I were his pupil, his chela. . . ."

"That is kind," Domaris agreed. Like most children, she had served as a reader in her childhood, and knew how unusual this was: to treat a little scribe as anything more than an impersonal convenience, like a lamp or a footstool. But one might expect the unexpected of Micon.

As Rajasta's chosen Acolyte, Domaris had heard much of the Temple talk. The lost Prince of Ahtarrath had not been found, and the envoys were planning to return home, their mission a failure. By devious paths, Domaris had discovered that Micon had kept himself from their knowledge, that he had not even let them guess his presence within the Temple of Light. She could not fathom his motives—but no one could attribute any motive, other than the highest, in connection with Micon. Although she had no proof of it, Domaris felt sure that Micon was one whom they sought; perhaps the young brother of the Prince. . . .

Deoris's thoughts had drifted to still another tangent. "Micon speaks often of you, Domaris. Know what he calls you?"

"What?" breathed Domaris, her voice hushed.

"Woman-clothed-with-the-sun."

The grateful darkness hid the glimmer of the woman's tears.

II

Lightning flickered and went dark over the form of a young man who stood outlined in the doorway. "Domaris?" questioned a bass voice. "Is all well with you? I was uneasy—on such a night."

Domaris focussed her eyes to pierce the gloom. "Arvath! Come in if you like, we are not sleeping."

The young man advanced, lifting the thin netting, and dropped cross-legged on the edge of the nearer pallet, beside Domaris. Arvath of Alkonath—an Atlantean, son of a woman of the Priest's Caste who had gone forth to wed a man of the Sea Kingdoms—was the oldest of the chosen Twelve, nearly two years older than Domaris. The lightning that flared and darkened showed chastened, tolerant features that were open and grave and still loved life with a firm and convinced love. The lines about his mouth were only partly from self-discipline; the remainder were the footprints of laughter.

Domaris said, with scrupulous honesty, "Earlier, we heard chanting, and felt a—a wrongness, somehow. But I will not permit that sort of thing to frighten or annoy me."

"Nor should you," Arvath agreed vigorously. "But there may be more disturbance in the air. There are odd forces stirring; this is the Night of Nadir. No one sleeps in the House; Chedan and I were bathing in the fountain. The Lord Rajasta is walking about the grounds, clad in Guardian-regalia, and he —well, I should not like to cross his path!" He paused a moment. "There are rumors—"

"Rumors, rumors! Every breeze is loaded with scandal! Elis is full of them! I cannot turn around without hearing another!" Domaris twitched her shoulders. "And has even Arvath of Alkonath nothing better to do than listen to the clatter of the market-place?"

"It is not all clatter," Arvath assured her, and glanced at Deoris, who had burrowed down until only the tip of one dark curl was visible above the bedclothing. "Is she asleep?"

Again Domaris shrugged.

"No sails stir without wind," Arvath went on, shifting his weight a little, leaning toward Domaris. "You have heard of the Black-robes?"

"Who has not? For days, in fact, I seem to have heard of little else!"

Arvath peered at her, silently, before saying, "Know you, then, they are said to be concealed among the Grey-robes?"

"I know almost nothing of the Grey-robes, Arvath; save that they guard the Unrevealed God. We of the Priest's Caste are not admitted into the Magicians."

"Yet many of you join with their Adepts to learn the Healing Arts," Arvath observed. "In Atlantis, the Grey-robes are held in great honor. . . . Well, it is said, down there beneath the Grey Temple, where the Avatar sits, the Man with Crossed Hands, there is a story told of a ritual not performed for centuries, of a rite long outlawed—a Black Ritual—and an apostate in the Chela's Ring. . . ." His voice trailed into an ominous whisper.

Domaris, her fears stirred by the unfamiliar phrases with their hints of unknown horrors, cried out, "Where did you hear such things?"

Arvath chuckled. "Gossip only. But if it comes to Rajasta's ears—"

"Then there will be trouble," Domaris assured him primly, "for the Grey-robes, if the tale is true; for the gossips, if it be false."

"You are right, it concerns us not." Arvath pressed her hand and smiled, accepting the rebuke. He stretched himself on the pallet beside her, but without touching the girl—he had learned that long ago. Deoris slept soundly beside them, but her presence enabled Domaris to steer the conversation into the impersonal channels she wished; to avoid speaking of their personal affairs, or of Temple matters. And when Arvath slipped away to his own chambers, very late, Domaris lay wakeful, and her thoughts were so insistent that her head throbbed.

For the first time in the twenty-two summers of her young life, Domaris questioned her own wisdom in electing to continue as Priestess and student under Rajasta's guidance. She would have done better, perhaps, to have withdrawn from the Priesthood; to become simply another woman, content with dwelling as a Priest's wife in the Temple where she had been born, one of the many women in the world of the Temple; wives and daughters and Priests, who swarmed in the city without the faintest knowledge of the inner life of the great cradle of wisdom where they dwelled, content with their homes and their babies and the outward show of Priestly doings. . . . *What is the matter with me?* Domaris wondered restlessly. *Why can't I be as they are? I will marry Arvath, as I must, and then—*

And then what?

Children, certainly. Years of growth and change. She could not make her thoughts go so far. She was still vainly trying to imagine it when she fell asleep.

Chapter Three

THE LOOM OF FATE

I

The Temple of Light, set upon the shores of the Ancient Land, was near the sea; it was set high above the City of the Circling Snake, which ringed it like a crescent moon. The Temple, lying between the spread horns of the crescent, at the focus of certain natural forces which the walls were built to intercept and conduct, was like a woman in the encircling glow of a lover's arm.

It was afternoon; summer and sun lay like smooth butter on the city, and like topaz on the gilded sea, with the dream of a breeze and the faint, salt-sweet rankness of tidewaters.

Three tall ships lay lifting to the swell of sails and sea, in the harbor. A few yards from the wharves, merchants had already set up their stalls and were crying their wares. The coming of the ships was an event alike to city-folk and farmer, peasant and aristocrat. In the crowded streets, Priests in luminous robes rubbed elbows uncaring with stolid traders and ragged mendicants; and a push or chance blow from some unwary lout, that would have meant a flogging on another day, now cost the careless one only a sharp look; tatterdemalion boys ran in and out of the crowd without picking the scrip of a single fat merchant.

One little group, however, met with no jostling, no familiarities: awed smiles followed Micon as he moved through the streets, one hand resting lightly on Deoris's arm. His luminous robes, fashioned of a peculiarly stainless white, cut and girdled in an unusual style, marked him no ordinary Priest come to bless their children or energize their farmlands; and, of course, the daughters of the powerful Talkannon were known to all. Many a young girl in the crowd smiled as Arvath passed; but the young Priest's dark eyes were jealously intent on Domaris. He resented Micon's effect on his betrothed. Arvath had almost forced himself on them, today.

They paused atop a sandy ridge of dunes, looking out over the sea. "Oh!" Deoris cried out in childish delight, "the ships!"

From habit, Micon turned to her. "What ships are they? Tell me, little sister," he asked, with affectionate interest. Vividly and eagerly, Deoris described to him the tall ships: high and swaying above the waves, their serpent banners brilliantly crimson at the prow. Micon's face was remote and dreamy as he listened.

"Ships from my homeland," he murmured wistfully. "There are no ships in all the Sea Kingdoms like the ships of Ahtarrath. My cousin flies the serpent in crimson—"

Arvath said bluntly, "I too am of the Golden Isles, Lord Micon."

"Your lineage?" queried Micon with interest. "I am homesick for a familiar name. Have you been in Ahtarrath?"

"I spent much of my youth beneath the Star-mountain," the younger man said. "Mani-toret, my father, was Priest of the Outer Gates in the New Temple; and I am son by adoption to Rathor in Ahtarrath."

Micon's face lighted, and he stretched his gaunt hands joyfully to the young man. "You are my brother indeed, then, young Arvath! For Rathor was my first teacher in the Priesthood, and guided me first to Initiation!"

Arvath's eyes widened. "But—are you *that* Micon?" he breathed. "All my life have I been told of your—"

Micon frowned. "Let be," he warned. "Speak not of that."

In uneasy awe, the young man said, "You *do* read minds!"

"That took not much reading, younger brother," Micon said wryly. "Do you know these ships?"

Arvath looked at him steadily. "I know them. And if you wish to conceal yourself, you should not have come here. You have changed, indeed, for I did not recognize you; but there are those who might."

Mystified and intrigued, the two girls had drawn together, alternately gazing at the two men and exchanging glances with one another.

"You do not—" Micon paused. "Recognize me? Had we met?"

Arvath laughed ringingly. "I would not expect you to know me again! Listen, Domaris, Deoris, and I will tell you about this Micon! When I was a little boy, not seven years old, I was sent to the home of Rathor, the old hermit of the Star-mountain. He is such a man as the ancients call saint; his wisdom is so famed that even here they do reverence to his name. But at that time, I knew only that many sober and serious young men came to him to study; and many of them brought me sweets and toys and petted me. While Rathor taught them, I played about on the hills with a pet cat. One day, I fell on a slide of rocks, and rolled down, and twisted my arm under me—"

Micon smiled, exclaiming, "Are you *that* child? Now I remember!"

Arvath continued, in a reminiscent tone, "I fainted with the pain, Domaris, and knew no more until I opened my eyes to see a young Priest standing beside me, one of those who came to Rathor. He lifted me up and set me on his knee, and wiped the blood from my face. There seemed to be healing in his hands—"

With a spasmodic movement, Micon turned away. "Enough of this," he said, stifled.

"Nay, I shall tell, elder brother! When he cleaned away the blood and dirt, I felt no pain, even though the bones had pierced through the flesh. He said, 'I have not the skill to tend this myself,' and he carried me in his arms to Rathor's house, because I was too bruised to walk. And then, because I was afraid of the Healer Priest who came to set the broken bone, he held me on his knees while the bone was set and bandaged; and all that night, because I was feverish and could not sleep, he sat by me, and fed me bread and milk and honey, and sang and told me stories until I forgot the pain. Is that so terrible a tale?" he asked softly. "Are you afraid these maidens might think you womanish, to be kind to a sick child?"

"Enough, I say," Micon pleaded again.

Arvath turned to him with a disbelieving stare; but what he

saw in the dark blind face made his own expression alter into a gentler pattern. "So be it," he said, "but I have not forgotten, my brother, and I shall not forget." He pulled back the sleeve of his Priestly robe, showing Domaris a long livid streak against the tanned flesh. "See, here the bone pierced the flesh—"

"And the young Priest was Micon?" Deoris asked.

"Yes. And he brought me sweets and playthings while I was abed; but since that summer I had not seen him again."

"How strange, that you should meet so far from home!"

"Not so strange, little sister," said Micon, in his rich and gentle voice. "Our fates spin their web, and our actions bear the fruits they have sown. Those who have met and loved cannot be parted; if they meet not in this life, they meet in another."

Deoris accepted the words without comment, but Arvath asked aggressively, "Do you believe, then, that you and I are bound to one another in such manner?"

The trace of a wry smile touched Micon's lips. "Who can tell? Perhaps, when I picked you up from the rocks that day, I merely redeemed an old service done me by you before these hills were raised." He gestured, with a look of amusement, toward the Temple behind them. "I am no seer. Ask of your own wisdom, my brother. Perhaps the service remains to be met. The Gods grant we both meet it like men."

"Amen to that," Arvath said soberly. Then, because he had been deeply moved, his quick emotions swung in another direction. "Domaris came to the city to make some purchases; shall we return to the bazaar?"

Domaris came alive out of deep preoccupation. "Men have no love for bright cloth and ribbons," she said gaily. "Why do you not remain here upon the docks?"

"I dare not let you from my sight in the city, Domaris," Arvath informed her, and Domaris, piqued, flung her proud head high.

"Think not that you can direct my steps! If you come with me—you *follow!*" She took the hand of Deoris, and the two walked ahead, turning toward the market-place.

II

The sleepy bazaar, wakened into life by the ships from the
Sea Kingdoms, hummed with the bustle of much buying and
selling. A woman was selling singing birds in cages of woven
rushes; Deoris stopped, enchanted, to look and listen, and
with an indulgent laugh Domaris directed that one should be
sent to the House of the Twelve. They walked slowly on,
Deoris bubbling over with delight.

A drowsy old man watched sacks of grain and glistening clay
jugs of oil; a naked urchin sat cross-legged between casks of
wine, ready to wake his master if a buyer came. Domaris
paused again at a somewhat larger stall, where lengths of brilliantly patterned cloth were displayed; Micon and Arvath, following slowly, listened for a moment to the absorbed girlish
voices, then grinned spontaneously at one another and strolled
on together past the flower-sellers, past the old country-
woman. Chickens squawked in coops, vying with the cries of
the vendors of dried fish and fresh fish, or plump fruits from
the groves behind the city, as they moved past crones who sold
cakes and sweetmeats and cheap sour beer, the stalls of bright
rugs and shining ornaments, and the more modest stalls of
pottery and kettles.

A little withered Islandman was selling perfumes under a
striped tent, and as Micon and Arvath passed, his shrivelled
face contracted with keen interest. He sat upright, dipping a
miniature brush into a flask and waving it in air already honey-
sweet with mingled fragrances. "Perfumes from Kei-lin,
Lords," he cried out in a rumbling, wheezy bass, "spices of
the West! Finest of flowers, sweetest of spice-trees. . . ."

Micon halted; then, with his usual deliberate step, went
carefully toward the striped tent. The scent-seller, recognizing
Temple nobility, was awed and voluble. "Fine perfumes and
essences, Lords, sweet spices and unguents from Kei-lin, scents
and oils for the bath, all the fine fragrances of the wide world
for your sweetheart—" The garrulous little man stopped and
amended quickly, "For your wife or sister, Lord Priest—"

Micon's twisted grin came reassuringly. "Neither wife nor
sweetheart have I, Old One," he commented dryly, "nor will I
trouble you for unguents or lotions. Yet you may serve us.

There is a perfume made in Ahtarrath and only there, from the crimson lily that flowers beneath the Star-mountain."

The scent-seller looked curiously at the Initiate before he reached back into his tent and searched for a long time, fumbling about like a mouse in a heap of straw. "Not many ask for it," he muttered in apology; but, finally, he found what was wanted, and wasted no time in extolling its virtues, but merely waved a scented droplet in the air.

Domaris and Deoris, rejoining them, paused to breathe in the spicy fragrance, and Domaris's eyes widened.

"Exquisite!"

The fragrance lingered hauntingly in the air as Micon laid down some coins and picked up the small flask, examining it closely with his hands, drawing his attenuated fingers delicately across the filigree carving. "The fretwork of Ahtarrath—I can identify it even now." He smiled at Arvath. "Nowhere else is such work done, such patterns formed . . ." Still smiling, he handed the phial to the girls, who bent to exclaim over the dainty carven traceries.

"What scent is this?" Domaris asked, lifting the flask to her face.

"An Ahtarrath flower, a common weed," said Arvath sharply.

Micon's face seemed to share a secret with Domaris, and he asked, "You think it lovely, as I do?"

"Exquisite," Domaris repeated dreamily. "But strange. Very strange and lovely."

"It is a flower of Ahtarrath, yes," Micon murmured, "a crimson lily which flowers beneath the Star-mountain; a wild flower which workmen root up because it is everywhere. The air is heavy with its scent. But I think it lovelier than any flower that grows in a tended garden, and more beautiful. Crimson—a crimson so brilliant it hurts to look on it when the sun is shining, a joyous, riotous color—a flower of the sun." His voice sounded suddenly tired, and he reached for Domaris's hand and put the flask into it with finality, gently closing the fingers around it with his own. "No, it is for you, Domaris," he said with a little smile. "You too are crowned with sunlight."

The words were casual, but Domaris swallowed back unbidden tears. She tried to speak her thanks, but her hands were trembling and no words came. Micon did not seem to expect them, for he said, in a low voice meant for her ears alone, "Light-crowned, I wish I might see your face . . . flower of brightness. . . ."

Arvath stood squarely, frowning ferociously, and it was he who broke the silence with a truculent, "Shall we go on? We'll be caught by night here!" But Deoris went swiftly to the young man and clasped his arm in a proprietary grip, leaving Domaris to walk ahead with Micon—a privilege which Deoris usually claimed jealously for herself.

"I will fill her arms with those lilies, one day," Arvath muttered, staring ahead at the tall girl who walked at Micon's side, her flaming hair seeming to swim in sunlight. But when Deoris asked what he had said, he would not repeat it.

Chapter Four

THE HEALER'S HANDS

I

Rajasta, glancing from the scroll that had occupied his attention, saw that the great library was deserted. Only moments ago, it seemed, he had been virtually surrounded by the rustle of paper, the soft murmurings of scribes. Now the niches were dark, and the only other person he could see was a librarian, androgynously robed, gathering various scrolls from the tables where they had been left.

Shaking his head, Rajasta returned the scroll he had been poring over to its protective sheath and laid it aside. Although he had no appointments to keep that day, he found it faintly annoying that he had spent so long reading and re-reading a single scroll—one which, moreover, he could have recited phrase for phrase. A little exasperated, he rose to his feet and began to leave—only then discovering that the library was not so empty as he had thought.

Micon sat at a gloomy table not far away, his habitual wry smile almost lost in the shadows falling across his face. Rajasta stopped beside him and stood for a moment, looking down at Micon's hands, and what they betrayed: strange hands, with an attenuated look about them, as if the fingers had been forcibly elongated; they lay on the table, limp but also somehow tense, and twisted. With a deft gentleness, Rajasta

37

gathered up the strengthless fingers into his own, cradling them lightly in his strong grasp. Questioningly, Micon raised his head.

"They seemed—such a living pain," the Priest of Light heard himself say.

"They would be, if I let them." Micon's face was schooled to impassivity, but the limp fingers quivered a little. "I can, within certain limits, hold myself aloof from pain. I feel it—" Micon smiled tiredly. "But the essential *me* can hold it away—until I tire. I hold away my death, in the same manner."

Rajasta shuddered at the Atlantean's calm. The hands in his stirred, carefully and deliberately, to free themselves. "Let be," Rajasta pleaded. "I can give you some ease. Why do you refuse my strength?"

"I can manage." The lines around Micon's mouth tightened, then relaxed. "Forgive me, brother. But I am of Ahtarrath. My duty is undone. I have, as yet, no right to die—being sonless. I must leave a son," he went on, almost as if this were but the spoken part of an argument he had often had with himself. "Else others with no right will seize the powers I carry."

"So be it," said Rajasta, and his voice was gentle, for he, too, lived by that law. "And the mother?"

For a moment Micon kept silent, his face a cautious blank; but this hesitancy was brief. "Domaris," he answered.

"Domaris?"

"Yes." Micon sighed. "That does not surprise you, surely?"

"Not altogether," said Rajasta at last. "It is a wise choice. Yet, she is pledged to your countryman, young Arvath. . . ." Rajasta frowned, thoughtful. "Still, it is hers to choose. She has the right to bear another's child, if she wishes. You—love her?"

Micon's tense features brightened, relaxing, and Rajasta found himself wondering what those sightless eyes beheld. "Yes," Micon said softly. "As I never dreamed I could love—" The Atlantean broke off with a groan as Rajasta's clasp tightened.

Chastened, the Priest of Light released Micon's abused hands. There was a long and faintly uneasy silence between them, as Micon conquered the pain once again, patiently, and Rajasta stood watching, helpless so long as Micon refused his aid.

"You have attained greatly," said Rajasta suddenly. "And I am not, as yet, truly touched by the Light. For the time allotted you—will you accept me as disciple?"

Micon lifted his face, and his smile was a transcendent thing. "What power of Light I can give, will surely shine in you despite me," he promised. "But I accept you." Then, in a lower, more sober tone, Micon continued, "I think—I hope I can give you a year. It should suffice. And if not, you will be able to complete the Last Seal alone. That I vow to you."

Slowly, as he did everything, Micon rose up and stood facing Rajasta. Tall and thin, almost translucent in the shadowy sunlight that shone upon them through the library windows, the Atlantean laid his twisted hands lightly on the Priest's shoulders and drew him close. With one hand he traced a sign upon Rajasta's forehead and breast; then, with a feather-touch, ran his expressive fingers over the older man's face.

Rajasta's eyes were wet. This was an incredible thing to him: he had called a stranger to that most meaningful of relationships; he, Rajasta, Priest of Light, son of an ancient line of Priests, had asked to be a disciple to an alien from a Temple referred to, contemptuously, among the Priest's Caste, as *"that upstart backwoods chantry in the middle of the ocean!"*

Yet Rajasta felt no regret—only, for the first time in his life, true humility. *Perhaps my caste has become too proud*, the Priest thought, *and so the Gods show themselves through this blind and tortured foreigner, to remind us that the Light touches not only those ordained by heredity. . . . This man's simplicity, his courage, will be as talismans to me.*

Then Rajasta's lips tightened, stern and grim. "Who tortured you?" he demanded, as Micon released him. "Warrior of Light—*who?*"

"I do not know." Micon's voice was wholly steady. "All were masked, and in black. Yet, for a moment, I saw too clearly. And so, I see no more. Let it be. The deed will carry its own vengeance."

"No, that may be so, but vengeance delayed only gives time for further deeds. Why did you beg me to let you remain concealed while the envoys from Ahtarrath were among us?" Rajasta pressed.

"They would have slain many, tortured more, to avenge me —thus setting a worse evil in motion."

Rajasta started to make reply, but hesitated, again wondering at the strength of this man. "I will not question your wisdom, but—is it right to let your parents grieve needlessly?"

Micon, once more sitting down, laughed lightly. "Do not let that disturb you, my brother. My parents died before I was out of childhood. And I have written that I live, and how, and for how long, and sealed it with—with that my grandsire cannot mistake. My message travels on the same ship with the news of my death. They will understand."

Rajasta nodded approvingly, and then, remembering that although the Atlantean seemed to gaze into the Priest's very soul, Micon could not see him, said aloud, "That is as it should be, then. But what was done to you? And for what reason? Nay," he went on, more loudly, overriding Micon's protest, "it is my right—even more, my *duty*, to know! I am Guardian here."

Unknown to Rajasta, and all but forgotten by Micon, Deoris perched on the edge of her scribe's stool not far away from them. Silent as a little white statue, she had listened to all that they had said in mute absorption. She understood almost nothing of it, but Domaris had been mentioned, and Deoris was anxious to hear more. The fact that this conversation was not intended for her ears bothered her not at all; what concerned Domaris, she felt, was her affair as well. Fervently, Deoris hoped that Micon would continue forgetful of her presence. Domaris must know of this! Deoris's hands clenched into small fists at the thought of her sister as the mother of a baby. . . . A smothered and childish jealousy, of which Deoris was never to be wholly aware, turned her dismay into hurt. Why should Micon have chosen *Domaris?* Deoris knew that her sister was betrothed to Arvath—but that marriage was some time in the future. This was now! How could Micon and Rajasta dare to talk of her sister this way? How could Micon dare to love Domaris? If only they did not notice her!

They did not. Micon's eyes had grown dark, their queer luminosity veiled with suppressed emotion. "The rack, and rope," he said, "and fire, to blind, because I ripped away one mask before they could bind me." His voice was low and hoarse with exhaustion, as if he and Rajasta were not robed Priests in an ancient and sacred place, but wrestlers struggling on a mat. "The reason?" Micon went on. "We of Ahtarrath have an inborn ability to use—certain forces of nature: rain, and thunder, lightning, even the terrible power of the earthquake and volcano. It is—our heritage, and our truth, without which life in the Sea Kingdoms would be impossible, perhaps. There are legends . . ." Micon shook his head suddenly, and smiling, said lightly, "These things you must know, or have guessed. We use these powers for the benefit of all, even those who style themselves our enemies. But the ability to control this power can be—stolen, and bastardized into the filthiest kind of sorcery! But from me they gained nothing. I am not apostate—and I had the strength to defeat their ends, although not to save myself . . . I am not certain what befell my half-brother, and so I must force myself to live, in this body, until I am certain it is safe to die."

"Oh, my brother," said Rajasta in a hushed voice, and found himself drawing nearer Micon again.

The Atlantean bent his head. "I fear Reio-ta was won over by the Black-robes. . . . My grandsire is old, and in his dotage. The power passes to my brother, at my death, if I die without issue. And I will not leave that power in the hands of sorcerers and apostates! You know the law! *That* is important; not this fragile body, nor that which dwells in it and suffers. I—the essential I—remain untouched, because nothing can touch that unless I allow!"

"Let me lend you strength," Rajasta pleaded, again. "With what I know—"

"Under necessity, I may do so," Micon returned, calm again, "but now I need only rest. The need may come without warning. In that event, I shall take you at your word. . . ." And then the timbre of Micon's rich voice returned, and his face lighted with his rare, wonderful smile. "And I do thank you!"

Deoris fixed her eyes studiously upon her scroll, to appear absorbed, but now she felt Rajasta's stern gaze upon the top of her head.

"Deoris," said the Priest severely. "What are you doing here?"

Micon laughed. "She is my scribe, Rajasta, and I forgot to dismiss her." Rising, he moved toward Deoris and put a hand upon her curly head. "It is enough for today. Run away, my child, and play."

II

Dismissed with Micon's one-sided smile, Deoris fled in search of Domaris, her young mind filled with entangled words: Black-robes, life, death, apostasy—whatever that was —torture, Domaris to bear a son. . . . Kaleidoscopic images twisted and glimmered in her dismayed young mind, and she burst breathlessly into their apartments.

Domaris was supervising the slave women as they folded and sorted clean garments. The room was filled with afternoon sunlight and the fragrance of fresh, smooth linens. The women —little dark women, with braided hair and the piquant features of the pygmy race of the Temple slaves—chattered in birdlike trills as their diminutive brown bodies moved and pattered restlessly around the tall girl who stood in their midst, gently directing them and listening to their shrill little voices.

Domaris's loose hair moved smoothly upon her shoulders as she turned, questioning, toward the door. "Deoris! At this hour! Is Micon—?" She broke off, and turned to an older woman; not a slave, but one of the townspeople who was her personal attendant. "Continue with this, Elara," Domaris requested gently, then beckoned Deoris to her. She caught her breath at sight of the child's face. "You're crying, Deoris! What is the matter?"

"No!" Deoris denied, raising a flushed but tearless face. "I just—have to tell you something—"

"Wait, not here. Come—" She drew Deoris into the inner room where they slept, and looked again at the girl's flushed cheeks with dismay. "What are you doing here at this hour? Is Micon ill? Or—" She stopped, unable to voice the thought that tortured her, unable even to define it clearly in her own mind.

Deoris shook her head. Now, facing Domaris herself, she hardly knew how to begin. Shakily, she said, "Micon and Rajasta, were talking about you . . . they said—"

"Deoris! Hush!" Shocked, Domaris put out a hand to cover the too-eager lips. "You must never tell me what you hear among the Priests!"

Deoris twisted free, stinging under the implied rebuke. "But they talked right in front of me, they both knew I was there!

And they were talking about you, Domaris. Micon said that you—''

"*Deoris!*"

Before her sister's blazing eyes, the child knew this was one of those rare occasions when she dared not disobey. She looked sulkily down at the floor.

Domaris, distressed, looked at the bent head of her little sister. "Deoris, you know that a scribe must never repeat anything that is said among the Priests. That is the first rule you should have learned!"

"Oh, leave me alone!" Deoris blurted out wrathfully, and ran from the room, her throat tight with angry sobs, driven by a fear she could neither control nor conceal. What right had Micon—what right had Rajasta—it wasn't right, none of it was right, and if Domaris wouldn't even listen, what could she do?

III

Deoris had no sooner left the library than Rajasta turned to Micon. "This matter must be brought to Riveda's attention."

Micon sighed wearily. "Why? Who is Riveda?"

"The First Adept of the Grey-robes. This touches him."

Micon moved his head negatively. "I would rather not disturb him with—"

"It must be so, Micon. Those who prostitute legitimate magic into foul sorcery must reckon with the Guardians of what they defile, else they will wreak havoc on us all, and more than we can undo, perhaps. It is easy to say, as you say, 'Let them reap what they sow'—and a bitter harvest it will be, I have no doubt! But what of those they have injured? Would you leave them free to torture others?"

Micon looked away, silenced, and his blind eyes moved randomly. Rajasta did not like the idea of what visions were in the Atlantean's mind then.

At last, Micon forced a smile, and a kind of laugh. "I thought I was to be the teacher, and you the pupil! But you are right," he murmured. Still, there was a very human protest in his voice as he added, "I dread it, though. The questioning. And all the rest. . . ."

"I would spare you, if I could."

Micon sighed. "I know. Let it be as you will. I—I only hope Deoris did not hear all we said! I had forgotten the child was there."

"And I never saw her. The scribes are pledged to silence about what they hear, of course—but Deoris is young, and it is hard for mere babies to keep their tongues in silence. Deoris! That child!"

The weary exasperation in Rajasta's voice prompted Micon to ask, in some puzzlement, "You dislike her?"

"No, no," Rajasta hastened to reassure him. "I love her, much as I love Domaris. In fact I often think Deoris the more brilliant of the two; but it is only cleverness. She will never be so—so *complete* as Domaris. She lacks—patience. Steadfastness is not Deoris's virtue!"

"Come now," Micon dissented, "I have been much with her, and found her to be very patient, and helpful. Also kind and tactful as well. And I would say that she *is* more brilliant than Domaris. But she is only a child, and Domaris is—" His voice trailed off abruptly, and he smiled. Then, recalling himself, "Must I meet this—Riveda?"

"It would be best, I think," Rajasta replied. About to say more, the Priest stopped and bent to peer closely at Micon's face. The deepening lines he saw etched there made the Priest turn and summon a servant from the hall. "I go to Riveda now," Rajasta said as the servant approached. "Guide Lord Micon to his apartments."

Micon yielded gracefully enough—but as Rajasta watched him go, the muscles in his face were tight with worry and doubt. He had heard that the Atlanteans held the Grey-robes in a kind of reverence that bordered on worship—and this was understandable, in a way, when one considered the illnesses and disease that constantly troubled the Sea Kingdoms. The Grey-robes had done wonders there in controlling plague and pestilence. . . . Rajasta had not expected Micon to react in quite this way, however.

Rajasta dismissed his faint misgivings swiftly. It could only be for the best. Riveda was the greatest of their Healers, and might be able to help Micon where Rajasta could not; that, perhaps, was why the Atlantean was disturbed. *After all,* Rajasta thought, *Micon is of a noble lineage; despite his humility, he has pride. And if a Grey-robe tells him to rest more, he will have to listen!*

Turning, Rajasta strode from the room, his white robes making sibilant whispers about his feet. Even before this, Rajasta had heard the rumours of forbidden rituals among the Grey-robes, of Black-clad sorcerers who worked in secret with the old and evil forces at the heart of nature, forces that took no heed of humanity and made their users less human by degrees.

The Priest paused in the hall and shook his head, wonderingly. Could it be Micon believed those rumours, and feared Riveda would open the way for the Black-robes to recapture him? Well, once they had met, any such doubts would surely melt away. Yes, surely Riveda, First Adept among the Grey-robes, was best fitted to handle this problem. Rajasta did not doubt, either, that justice would be done. He knew Riveda.

His mind made up, Rajasta strode down the hallway, through a covered passageway and into another building, where he paused before a certain door. He knuckled the wood in three firm and evenly-spaced knocks.

IV

The Magician Riveda was a big man, taller even than the tall Rajasta; firmly-knit and muscular, his broad shoulders looked, and were, strong enough to throw down a bull. In his cowled robe to rough grey frieze, Riveda was a little larger than life as he turned from contemplation of the darkling sky.

"Lord Guardian," he greeted, courteously, "what urgency brings you to me?"

Rajasta said nothing, but continued to study the other man quietly for a moment. The cowl, flung loose on Riveda's shoulders, revealed a big head, set well on a thick neck and topped with masses of close-clipped fair hair—silver-gilt hair, a strange color above a stranger face. Riveda was not of the true Priest's Caste, but a Northman from the kingdom of Zaiadan; his rough-hewn features were an atavism from a ruder age, standing out strangely in contrast to the more delicate, chiselled lineaments of the Priest's Caste.

Under Rajasta's silent, intense scrutiny, Riveda flung back his head and laughed. "The need must be great indeed!"

Rajasta curbed his irritation—Riveda had always had the power to exasperate him—and answered, in a level voice that

sobered the Adept, "Ahtarrath has sent a son to our Temple;
the Prince Micon. He was apprehended by Black-robes,
tortured and blinded—to the end that he serve their Illusion. I
am come to tell you: look to your Order."

The frigid blue of Riveda's eyes was darkened with
troubled shadows. "I knew nothing of this," he said. "I have
been deep in study . . . I do not doubt your word, Rajasta,
but what could the Hidden Ones hope to achieve?"

Rajasta hesitated. "What do you know of the powers of
Ahtarrath?"

Riveda's brows lifted. "Almost nothing," he said frankly,
"and even that little is no more than rumor. They say that
certain of that lineage can bring rain from reluctant clouds and
loose the lightning—that they ride the storm-wrack, and that
sort of thing." He smiled, sardonic. "No one has told me how
they do it, or why, and so I have reserved judgment, so far."

"The powers of Ahtarrath are very real," said Rajasta.
"The Black-robes sought to divert that power to—a spiritual
whoredom. Their object, his apostasy and—service to their
demons."

Riveda's eyes narrowed. "And?"

"They failed," Rajasta said tersely. "Micon will die—but
only when he chooses." Rajasta's face was impassive, but
Riveda, skilled in detecting involuntary betrayals, could see
the signs of emotion. "Blinded and broken as he is—the
Releaser of Man will not conquer until Micon wills it. He is a—
a Cup of Light!"

Riveda nodded, a trifle impatiently. "So your friend would
not serve the Dark Shrine, and they sought to force apostasy
upon him? Hmm . . . it *is* possible . . . I could admire this
prince of Ahtarrath," Riveda murmured, "if all you say is
true. He must be, indeed, a man." The Grey-robe's stern face
relaxed for a moment in a smile; then the lips were harshly
curled again. "I will find the truth of this business, Rajasta;
believe me."

"That I knew," said Rajasta simply, and the eyes of the two
men met and locked, with mutual respect.

"I will need to question Micon."

"Come to me then, at the fourth hour from now," Rajasta
said, and turned to go.

Riveda detained him with a gesture. "You forget. The ritual
of my Order requires me to make certain lengthy preparations.
Only when—"

"I have not forgotten," said Rajasta coolly, "but this matter is urgent; and you have some leeway in such cases." With this, Rajasta hurried away.

Riveda stood looking at the closed door, troubled, but not by Rajasta's arrogance; one expected such things of the Guardians, and circumstances generally justified them.

There were always—would always be, Riveda suspected—a few Magicians who could not be restrained from dabbling in the black and forbidden arts of the past; and Riveda knew all too well that his Order was automatically suspected in any Temple disturbance. It had been foolish to submerge himself in study, leaving the lesser Adepts to govern the Grey-robes; now even the innocent might suffer for the folly and cruelty of a few.

Fools, worse than fools, Riveda thought, *that they did not confine their hell's play to persons of no importance! Or, having dared so high, fools not to make certain their victims did not escape alive to carry tales!*

Riveda's austere face was grim and ruthless as he swiftly gathered up and stored away the genteel clutter of the studies which had so long preoccupied him.

It was, indeed, time to see to his Order.

V

In a corner of the room set aside for Rajasta's administrative work, the Arch-Priest Talkannon sat quietly, for the moment apparently altogether detached from humanity and its concerns. Beside him Domaris stood, motionless, and with sidelong glances watched Micon.

The Atlantean had refused a seat, and stood leaning against a table. Micon's stillness was uncanny—a schooled thing that made Rajasta uneasy. He knew what it concealed. With a thoughtful frown, Rajasta turned his gaze away and saw, beyond the window, the grey-robed figure of Riveda, easily identifiable even at a distance, striding along the pathway toward them.

Without moving, Micon said, "Who comes?"

Rajasta started. The Atlantean's perceptivity was a continuing source of wonder to him; although blind, Micon had discerned what neither Talkannon nor Domaris had noticed.

"It is Riveda, is it not?" Micon said, before Rajasta could reply.

Talkannon raised his head, but he did not speak. Riveda entered, saluting the Priests carelessly but with enough courtesy. Domaris, of course, was ignored completely. She had never seen Riveda before, and now drew back in something like wonder. Her eyes met the Adept's for a moment; then she quickly lowered her head, fighting unreasoning fear and immediate dislike. In an instant she knew that she could hate this man who had never harmed her—and also that she must never betray the least sign of that hatred.

Micon, touching Riveda's fingers lightly with his own, thought, *This man could go far.* . . . Yet the Atlantean was also uneasy, without knowing why.

"Welcome, Lord of Ahtarrath," Riveda was saying, with an easy deference devoid of ceremony. "I deeply regret that I did not know, before—" He stopped, and his thoughts, running in deep channels, surfaced suddenly. This man was signed to Death; signed and sealed. It spoke in everything about Micon: the fitfully-fanned, forced strength; the slow, careful movements; the banked fires of his will; the deliberate husbanding of energy—all this, and the almost-translucence of Micon's thin body, proclaimed that this man had no strength to spare. And yet, equally clearly, the Atlantean was an Adept —as the high Mysteries made Adepts.

Riveda, with his thirst for knowledge and the power that was knowledge, felt a strange mixture of envy and regret. *What terrible waste!* he thought. *This man would better serve himself—and his ideals—by turning to Light's darker aspects!* Light and Dark, after all, were but balanced manifestations of the Whole. There was a kind of strength to be wrested from the struggle with Death that the Light could never show or grant. . . .

Micon's greetings were meaningless sounds, forms of polite speech, and Riveda attended them with half an ear; then, amazed and disbelieving, the Grey-robe realized just what Micon was saying.

"I was incautious." The Atlantean's resonant voice rang loud in the closed room. "What happened to me is of no importance. But there was, and is, one who must return to the Way of Light. Find my half-brother if you can. As for the rest —I could not, now, point out the guilty to you. Nor would I."

Micon made a slight gesture of finality. "There shall be no vengeance taken! The deed carries its own penalty."

Riveda shook his head. "My Order must be cleansed."

"That is for you to decide. I can give you no help." Micon smiled, and for the first time Riveda felt the outpouring warmth of the man. Micon turned his head slightly toward Domaris. "What say you, light-crowned?" he asked, while Riveda and Talkannon stood scandalized at this appeal to a mere Acolyte—and a woman at that!

"You are right," Domaris said slowly, "but Riveda is right, too. Many students come here in search of knowledge. If sorcery and torture go unpunished, then evil-doers thrive."

"And what say you, my brother?" Micon demanded of Rajasta. Riveda felt a surge of envious resentment; he too was Adept, Initiate, yet Micon claimed no spiritual kinship with him!

"Domaris is wise, Micon." Rajasta's hand closed very gently on the Atlantean's thin arm. "Sorcery and torture defile our Temple. Duty demands that others must not face the peril you have tasted."

Micon sighed, and with a helpless gesture said, "You are the judges, then. But I have, now, no way of knowing those involved. . . . They took us at the sea-wall, treating us with courtesy, and lodged us among Grey-robes. At nightfall we were led to a crypt, and certain things demanded of us under threat of torture and death. We refused. . . ." A peculiar smile crossed the lean, dark features. Micon extended his emaciated hands. "You can see their threats were no idle ones. And my half-brother—" He broke off again, and there was a brief, sorrowful silence before Micon said, almost in extenuation, "He is little more than a boy. And him they could use, although not fully. I broke free from them for a moment, before they bound me, and ripped the mask from one face. And so—" a brief pause, "I saw nothing more. After that— later, much later I think—I was freed; and men of kindliness, who knew me not, brought me to Talkannon's house, where I was reunited with my servants. I know not what tale was told to account for me." He paused, then added quietly, "Talkannon has told me that I was ill for a long time. Certainly there is a period which is wholly blank to me."

Talkannon's iron grip forced quiet on his daughter.

Riveda stood, with clasped hands, looking at Micon in

thoughtful silence; then asked, "How long ago was this?"

Micon shrugged, almost embarrassed. "I have no idea. My wounds were healed—what healing was possible—when I awakened in Talkannon's house."

Talkannon, who had said almost nothing so far, now broke his silence and said heavily, "He was brought to me, by commoners—fishermen, who said they found him lying on the shore, insensible and almost naked. They knew him for a Priest by the ornaments he still wore about his throat. I questioned them. They knew nothing more."

"*You* questioned!" Riveda's scorn was withering. "How do you know they told truth?"

Talkannon's voice lashed, whiplike and stern: "I could not, after all, question them under torture!"

"Enough of this," Rajasta pleaded, for Micon was trembling.

Riveda bit off his remarks unvoiced and turned to Micon. "Tell me more of your brother, at least."

"He is only my half-brother," Micon replied, a bit hesitant. Gone now was the uncanny stillness; his twisted, strengthless fingers twitched faintly at his sides, and he leaned more heavily against the table. "Reio-ta is his name. He is many years younger than I, but in looks we are not—were not—very dissimilar." Micon's words trailed away, and he wavered where he stood.

"I will do what I can," said Riveda, with a sudden and surprising gentleness. "If I had been told before—I cannot say how much I regret—" The Grey-robe bowed his head, maddened by the futility of his words. "After so long, I can promise nothing—"

"And I ask nothing, Lord Riveda. I know you will do what you must. But I beg you—do not ask for my aid in your—investigations." Micon's voice was an apology beyond words. "I have not the strength; nor could I be of much use, having now no way to—"

Riveda straightened, scowling: the intent look of a practical man. "You told me you saw one face. Describe him!"

Everyone in the room bent slightly toward Micon, waiting. The Atlantean drew himself erect and said clearly, "That is a secret which shall die with me. I have said, *there will be no vengeance taken!*"

Talkannon settled back in his seat with a sigh, and

Domaris's face betrayed her conflicting emotions. Rajasta did not question Micon even in his mind; of them all he knew the Atlantean best and had come to accept Micon's attitude, although he did not really agree.

Riveda scowled fiercely. "I beg you to reconsider, Lord Micon! I know your vows forbid you to take vengeance for your personal hurt, but—" He clenched his fists. "Are you not also under oath to protect others from evil?"

Micon, however, was inflexible. "I have said that I will not speak or testify."

"So be it!" Riveda's voice was bitter. "I cannot force you to speak against your will. For the honor of my Order, I must investigate—but be sure I shall not trouble you again!"

The anger in Riveda's voice penetrated deep; Micon slumped, leaning heavily on Rajasta, who instantly forgot all else and helped the Atlantean into the seat he had previously refused.

Swift pity dawned in the stern features of the Adept of the Grey-robes. Riveda could be gracious when it suited him, and his urge now was to conciliate. "If I have offended, Lord Micon," he said earnestly, "let this excuse me: this thing that has befallen you touches the honor of my Order, which I must guard as carefully as you guard your vows. I would root out this nest of evil birds—feather, wing and egg! Not for you alone, but for all who will follow you to our Temple's doors."

"With those aims I can sympathize," Micon said, almost humbly, his blind eyes staring up at Riveda. "What means you employ are none of my affair." He sighed, and his drawn nerves seemed to relax a little. Perhaps no one there except the abnormally sensitive Domaris had known how much the Atlantean had dreaded this interview. Now, at least, he knew that Riveda himself had not been among his tormentors. Tensed to this possibility, and prepared to conceal it if it had been so, relief left him limp with weariness. "My thanks are worth nothing, Lord Riveda," he said, "but accept my friendship with them."

Riveda clasped the racked fingers in his own, very lightly, secretly examining them with a Healer's eye to see how long they had been healed. Riveda's hands were big and hard, roughened by manual work done in childhood, yet sensitive as Micon's own. The Atlantean felt that Riveda's hands held some strong force chained—a defiant strength harnessed and made powerful. The strengths of the two Initiates met; but even the briefest contact with so much vitality was too much for Micon, and swiftly he withdrew his hand, his face ashen-pale. Without another word, trembling with the effort to seem calm, Micon turned and went toward the door.

Rajasta took a step to follow, then stopped, obeying some inaudible command that said, plainly, *No*.

VI

As the door scraped shut, Rajasta turned to Riveda. "Well?"

Riveda stood, looking down at his hands, frowning. Uneasily, he said, "The man is a raw, open channel of power."

"What do you mean?" Talkannon demanded roughly.

"When our hands touched," Riveda said, almost muttering, "I could feel the vital strength leaving me; he seemed to draw it forth from me—"

Rajasta and Talkannon stared at the Grey-robe in dismay. What Riveda described was a secret of the Priest's Caste, invoked only rarely and with infinite caution. Rajasta felt unreasoningly infuriated: Micon had refused such aid from him, with a definiteness that left no room for argument. . . . Abruptly, Rajasta realized that Riveda had not the slightest understanding of what had happened.

The Grey-robe's harsh whisper sounded almost frightened. "I think he knew it too—he drew away from me, he would not touch me again."

Talkannon said hoarsely, "Say nothing of this, Riveda!"

"Fear not—" Uncharacteristically, Riveda covered his face with his hands and shuddered as he turned away from them. "I could not—could not—I was too strong, I could have killed him!"

Domaris was still leaning against her father, her face as white as Talkannon's robes; her free hand gripped the table so tautly that the knuckles were white knots.

Talkannon jerked up his head. "What ails you, girl!"

Rajasta, his stern self-control reasserted at once, turned to her in concern. "Domaris! Are you ill, child?"

"I—no," she faltered. "But Micon—" Her face suddenly

streamed with tears. She broke away from her father and fled the room.

They watched her go, nonplussed; the room was oppressively silent. At last Riveda crossed the room and closed the door she had left open in her flight, remarking, with sarcastic asperity, "I note a certain lack of decorum among your Acolytes, Rajasta."

For once Rajasta was not offended by Riveda's acerbic manner. "She is but a girl," he said mildly. "This is harsh business."

"Yes," said Riveda heavily. "Let us begin it, then." Fixing his ice-blue eyes on Talkannon, the Adept proceeded to question the Arch-Administrator with terse insistence, demanding the names of the fishermen who had "discovered" Micon, the time when it all had happened, probing for the smallest revealing circumstance, the half-forgotten details that might prove significant. He had hoped to fuse overlooked bits of information into a cohesive basis for further investigation. He learned, however, little more than he had known already.

The Grey-robe's cross-examination of Rajasta was even less productive, and Riveda, whose temper was at the best of times uncertain, at last grew angry and almost shouted, "Can I work in the dark! You'd make me a blind man, too!"

Yet, even as his bafflement and irritation ignited, Riveda realized that he had truly plumbed the limits of their knowledge of the matter. The Adept flung back his head, as if to a challenge. "So, then! If Priests of Light cannot illuminate this mystery for me, I must learn to see black shapes moving in utter blackness!" He turned to go, saying over his shoulder, "I thank you for the chance to refine my perceptions!"

VII

In his secluded apartments, Micon lay stretched on his narrow bed, his face hidden in his arms, breathing slowly and with deliberation. Riveda's vitality, flooding in through Micon's momentary incaution, had disturbed the precarious control he held over his body, and the surging imbalance left the Atlantean dumbly, rigidly terrified. It was paradoxical that what, in a less critical situation, would have speeded Micon's recovery, in this instance threatened him with a total relapse, or worse. He was almost too weak to master this influx of strength!

Micon found himself thinking, with grim sureness, that his initial torture and what he suffered now were only the preliminaries of a long-drawn-out and bitter punishment—and for what? Resisting evil!

Priest though he was, Micon was young enough to be bitterly bewildered. *Integrity*, he thought, in a sudden fury, *is far too expensive a luxury!* But he arrested the questing feelers of this mood, knowing such thoughts for a sending of the Dark Ones, insinuating further sacrilege through the pinholes that their tortures had opened. Desperately, he fought to still the mental rebellion that would diminish the already-fading control he barely held, and must keep, over his body's torment.

A year. I thought I could bear this for a year!

Yet he had work to finish, come what might. He had made certain promises, and must keep them. He had accepted Rajasta as disciple. And there was Domaris. *Domaris . . .*

Chapter Five

THE NIGHT OF
THE ZENITH

I

The night sky was a silent vault of blues piled up on blues, purple heaped high on indigo, dusted with a sprinkle of just-blossoming stars. A tenuous luminescence, too dim for star-light, too wispy for any light belonging to earth, hovered faintly around the moonless path; by its glimmer Rajasta moved unerringly, and Micon, at his side, walked with a quiet deliberation that missed no step.

"But why go we to the Star Field tonight, Rajasta?"

"Tonight—I thought I had told you—is the night when Car-atra, the Star of the Woman, touches the Zenith. The Twelve Acolytes will scan the heavens, and each will interpret the omens according to their capability. It should interest you." Rajasta smiled at his companion. "Domaris will be there, and, I expect, her sister. She asked me to bring you." Taking Micon's arm, he guided the Atlantean gently as the path began to ascend the rim of a hill.

"I shall enjoy it." Micon smiled, without the twist of pain that so frequently marred his features. Where Domaris was, was forgetfulness; he was not so constantly braced. She had somehow the ability to give him a strength that was not wholly physical, the overflowing of her own abundant vitality. He wondered if this were deliberate; that she was capable of just such outpouring generosity, he never doubted. Her gentleness and graciousness were like a gift of the Gods. He knew she was beautiful, with a faculty that went beyond seeing.

Rajasta's eyes were sad. He loved Domaris; how dearly, he had never realized until now, when he saw her peace threatened. This man, whom Rajasta also loved, walked ever more closely with death; the emotion he sensed between Micon and Domaris was a fragile and lovely thing to hold such seeds of grief. Rajasta, too, knew that Domaris would give so generously as to rob herself. He would not and could not forbid, but he was saddened by the inevitable end he foresaw with such clarity.

Micon said, with a restraint that gave point to his words, "I am not wholly selfish, my brother. I too can see something of the coming struggle. Yet you know, too, that my line must be carried on, lest the Divine Purpose strive against too great odds. That is not pride." He trembled, as if with cold, and Rajasta was quick to support him with an unobtrusive arm.

"I know," said the Priest of Light, "we have discussed this often. The cause is already in motion, and we must ensure that it does not turn against us. All this I understand. Try not to think of it, tonight. Come, it is not far now," he assured. Rajasta had seen Micon when he surrendered to his pain, and the memory was not a good one.

To eyes accustomed to the starshine, the Star Field was a place of ethereal beauty. The sky hovered like folded wings, brushed with the twinklings of numberless stars; the sweet fragrance of the breathing earth, the rumor of muted talk, and the deep velvet of black shadows, made dreamy fantasy around them, as if a harsh word would dissolve the whole scene and leave an emptiness.

Rajasta said in a low tone, "It is—beyond words— lovely."

"I know." Micon's dark unquiet face held momentary torment. "I feel it."

Domaris, her pale robes gleaming silver as if with frost, seemed to drift toward them. "Come and sit with us, Teachers of Wisdom," she invited, and drew Deoris closely against her.

"Gratefully," Rajasta answered, and led Micon after the tall and lovely shape.

Deoris abruptly freed herself from the arm that encircled her waist, and came to Micon, her slender immaturity blending into the fantastic imagery of the place and the hour.

"Little Deoris," the Atlantean said, with a kindly smile.

The child, with a shy audacity, tucked her hand into his arm. Her own smile was blissful and yet, somehow, protective; the dawning woman in Deoris frankly took notice of all that the wiser Domaris dared not admit that she saw.

They stopped beside a low, sweet-smelling shrub that flowered whitely against the night, and Domaris sat down, flinging her cloak of silver gossamer from her shoulders. Deoris pulled Micon carefully down between them, and Rajasta seated himself beside his Acolyte.

"You have watched the stars, Domaris; what see you there?"

"Lord Rajasta," the girl said formally, "Caratra takes a strange position tonight, a conjunction with the Harpist and the Scythe. If I were to interpret it . . ." She hesitated, and turned her face up to the sky once again. "She is opposed by the Serpent," Domaris murmured. "I would say—that a woman will open a door to evil, and a woman will bar it. The same woman; but it is another woman's influence that makes it possible to bar the door." Domaris was silent again for a moment, but before her companions could speak, she went on, "A child will be born; one that will sire a line to check this evil, forever."

With an unguarded movement, the first one anyone had seen him make, Micon caught clumsily at her shoulders; "The stars say that?" he demanded hoarsely.

Domaris met his unseeing eyes in an uneasy silence, almost glad for once of his blindness. "Yes," she said, her voice controlled but husky. "Caratra nears the Zenith, and her Lady, Aderes, attends her. The Seven Guardians ring her about—protecting her not only from the Serpent but the Black Warrior, El-cherkan, that threatens from the Scorpion's claws . . ."

Micon relaxed, and for a space of minutes leaned weakly against her. Domaris held him gently, letting him rest against her breast, and in a conscious impulse poured her own strength into him. It was done unobtrusively, graciously, in response to a need that was imperative, and in the instinctive act she placed herself in rapport with Micon. The vistas that opened to her from the Initiate's mind were something far and away beyond her experience or imaginings, Acolyte of the Mysteries though she was; the depth and surety of his perceptions, the profundity of his awareness, filled her with a reverence she was never to lose; and his enduring courage and force of purpose moved her to something like worship. The very limitations of the man proclaimed his innate humanity, his immense humility blending with a kind of pride which obliterated the usual meaning of the word. . . . She saw the schooled control inhibiting emotions which would have made another savage or rebellious—and suddenly she started. She was foremost in his thoughts! A hot blush, visible even in the starlight, spread over her face.

She pulled out of the rapport quickly, but with a gentleness that left no hurt around the sudden vacancy. The thought she had surprised was so delicately lovely that she felt hallowed, but it had been so much his own that she felt a delicious guilt at having glimpsed it.

With a comprehending regret, Micon drew himself away from her. He knew she was confused; Domaris was not given to speculation about her effect upon men.

Deoris, watching with mingled bewilderment and resentment, broke the filmy connection that still remained. "Lord Micon, you have tired yourself," she accused, and spread her woolly cloak on the grass for him.

Rajasta added, "Rest, my brother."

"It was but a moment's weakness," Micon murmured, but he let them have their way, content to lie back beside Domaris; and after a moment he felt her warm hand touch his, with a feather-soft clasp that brought no pain to his wrecked fingers.

Rajasta's face was a benediction, and seeing it, Deoris swallowed hard. *What's happening to Domaris?* Her sister was changing before her eyes, and Deoris, clinging to what had been the one secure thing in the fluid world of the Temple, was suddenly terrified. For a moment she almost hated Micon, and Rajasta's evident acceptance of the situation infuriated her. She raised her eyes, full of angry tears, and stared fiercely at the blurring stars.

II

A new voice spoke a word of casual greeting, and Deoris started and turned, shivering with a strange and unfamiliar excitement, half attraction and half fascinated fear. *Riveda!*

Already keyed to a fever pitch of nervousness, Deoris shrank away as the dark shadow fell across them, blotting out the starlight. The man was uncanny; she could not look away.

Riveda's courtly, almost ritualistic salute included them all, and he dropped to a seat on the grass. "So, you watch the stars with your Acolytes, Rajasta? Domaris, what say the stars of me?" The Adept's voice, even muted in courteous inquiry, seemed to mock at custom and petty ritual alike.

Domaris, with a little frown, came back to her immediate surroundings with some effort. She spoke with a frigid politeness. "I am no reader of fortunes, Lord Riveda. Should they speak of you?"

"Of me as well as any other," retorted Riveda with a derisive laugh. "Or as ill . . . Come, Deoris, and sit by me."

The little girl looked longingly at Domaris, but no one spoke or looked at her forbiddingly, and so she rose, her short, close-girdled frock a shimmer of starry blue about her, and went to Riveda's side. The Adept smiled as she settled in the grass beside him.

"Tell us a tale, little scribe," he said, only half in earnest. Deoris shook her head bashfully, but Riveda persisted. "Sing for us, then. I have heard you—your voice is sweet."

The child's embarrassment became acute; she pulled her hand from Riveda's, shaking her dark curls over her eyes. Still no one came to the rescue of her confusion, and Micon said softly in the darkness, "Will you not sing, my little Deoris? Rajasta also has spoken of your sweet voice."

A request from Micon was so rare a thing, it could not be refused. Deoris said timidly, "I will sing of the Seven Watchers —if Lord Rajasta will chant the verse of the Falling."

Rajasta laughed aloud. "I, sing? My voice would startle the Watchers from the sky *again*, my child!"

"I will chant it," said Riveda with abrupt finality. "Sing, Deoris," he repeated, and this time there was that in his voice which compelled her.

The girl hugged her thin knees, tilted her face skyward, and began to sing, in a clear and quiet soprano that mounted, like a thread of smoky silver, toward the hushed stars:

> *On a night long ago, forgotten,*
> *Seven were the Watchers*
> *Watching from the Heavens,*

> *Watching and fearful*
> *On a black day when*
> *Stars left their places,*
> *Watching the Black Star of Doom.*
>
> *Seven the Watchers,*
> *Stealing a-tiptoe,*
> *Seven stars stealing*
> *Softly from their places,*
> > *Under the cover*
> > *Of the shielding sky.*
>
> *The Black Star hovers*
> *Silent in the shadows,*
> *Stealing through the shadows,*
> > *Waiting for the fall of Night;*
> *Over the mountain,*
> *Hanging, hovering,*
> *Darkly, a raven*
> > *In a crimson cloud.*
>
> *Softly the Seven*
> *Fall like shadows,*
> *Star-shadows, blotted*
> *In starless sunlight!*
> > *In a flaming shower,*
> > *Seven stars falling*
> > *Black on the Black Star of Doom!*

Others who had gathered on the Star Field to observe the omens, attracted by the song, drew nearer, hushed and appreciative. Now Riveda's deep and resonant baritone took up a stern and rhythmic chant, spinning an undercurrent of weird harmonies beneath the silvery treble of Deoris.

> *The mountain trembles!*
> *Thunder shakes the sunset,*
> *Thunder at the summit!*
> *As the Seven Watchers*
> *Fall in showers,*
> *Star-showers falling,*
> *Flaming comets falling*
> > *On the Black Star!*

The Ocean shakes in torment,
Mountains break and crumble!
Drowned lies the Dark Star
And Doomsday is dead!

In a muted, bell-like voice, Deoris chanted the lament:

Seven stars fallen,
Fallen from the heavens,
Fallen from the sky-crown,
Drowned where the Black Star fell!

Manoah the Merciful, Lord of Brightness,
Raised up the drowned ones,
The Black Star he banished
For endless ages,
          Till he shall rise in light.
The Seven Good Watchers
He raised in brightness.

Crowning the mountain,
High above the Star-mountain,
Shine the Seven Watchers,
          The Seven Guardians
          Of the Earth and Sky.

The song died in the night; a little whispering wind murmured and was still. The folk that had gathered, some Acolytes and one or two Priests, made sounds of approval, and drifted away again, speaking in soft voices.

Micon lay motionless, his hand still clasped in Domaris's fingers. Rajasta brooded thoughtfully, watching these two he loved so much, and it was for him as if the rest of the world did not exist.

Riveda inclined his head to Deoris, his harsh and atavistic features softened in the starlight and shadows. "Your voice is lovely; would we had such a singer in the Grey Temple! Perhaps one day you may sing there."

Deoris muttered formalities, but frowned. The men of the Grey-robe sect were highly honored in the Temple, but their women were something of a mystery. Under strange and secret vows, they were scorned and shunned, referred to contemptuously as *saji*—though the meaning of the word was not known to Deoris, it had a bleak and awful sound. Many of the Grey-robe women were recruited from the commoners, and some were the children of slaves; this in great part accounted for their being shunned by the wives and daughters of the Priest's Caste. The suggestion that Deoris, daughter of the Arch-Administrator Talkannon, might choose to join the condemned *saji* so angered the child that she cared little for Riveda's compliment to her singing.

The Adept only smiled, however. His charm flowed out to surround her again and he said, softly, "As your sister is too tired to advise me, Deoris, perhaps you would interpret the stars for me?"

Deoris flushed crimson, and gazed upward intently, mustering her few scraps of knowledge. "A powerful man—or something in masculine form—threatens—some feminine function, through the force of the Guardians. An old evil—either has been or will be revived—" She stopped, aware that the others were looking at her. Abashed at her own presumption, Deoris let her gaze fall downward once more; her hands twisted nervously in her lap. "But that can have little to do with you, Lord Riveda," she murmured, almost inaudibly.

Rajasta chuckled. "It is good enough, child. Use what knowledge you have. You will learn more, as you grow older."

For some reason, the indulgent tolerance in Rajasta's voice annoyed Riveda, who had felt some astonishment at the sensitivity with which this untaught child had interpreted a pattern ominous enough to challenge a trained seer. That she had doubtless heard the others discussing the omens that beset Caratra made little difference, and Riveda said sharply, "Perhaps, Rajasta, *you* can—"

But the Adept never finished his sentence. The stocky, heavy-set figure of the Acolyte Arvath had cast its shadow across them.

III

"The story goes," Arvath said lightly, "that the Prophet of the Star-mountain lectured in the Temple before the Guardians when he had not told his twelfth year; so you may well listen to the least among you." The young Acolyte

sounded amused as he bowed formally to Rajasta and Micon.
"Sons of the Sun, we are honored in your presence. And
yours, Lord Riveda." He leaned to twitch one of Deoris's
ringlets. "Do you now seek to be a Prophetess, puss?" He
turned to the other girl, saying, "Was it you singing,
Domaris?"

"It was Deoris," said Domaris curtly, ruffled. Was she
never to be free of Arvath's continual surveillance?

Arvath frowned, seeing that Micon was still almost in
Domaris's arms. Domaris was *his!* Micon was an intruder and
had no right between a man and his betrothed! Arvath's
jealousy kept him from thinking very clearly, and he clenched
his fists, furious with suppressed desire and the sense of in-
justice. *I'll teach this presumptuous stranger his manners!*

Arvath sat down beside them, and with a decisive movement
encircled Domaris's waist with his arm. At least he could show
this intruder that he was treading on forbidden ground! In a
tone that was perfectly audible, but sounded intimate and soft,
he asked her, "Were you waiting long for me?"

Half-startled, half-indignant, Domaris stared at him. She
was too well-bred to make a scene; her first impulse, to push
him angrily away from her, died unborn. She remained
motionless, silent: she was used to caresses from Arvath, but
this had a jealous and demanding force that dismayed her.

Irked by her unresponsiveness, Arvath seized her hands and
drew them away from Micon's. Domaris gasped, freeing herself quickly from both of them. Micon made a little startled
sound of question as she rose to her feet.

As if he had not seen, Rajasta intervened. "What say the
stars to you, young Arvath?"

The life-long habit of immediate deference to a superior pre-
vailed. Arvath inclined his head respectfully and said, "I have
not yet made any conclusions, Son of the Sun. The Lady of the
Heavens will not reach absolute zenith before the sixth hour,
and before then it is not possible to interpret correctly."

Rajasta nodded agreeably. "Caution is a virtue of great
worth," he said, mildly, but with a pointedness that made
Arvath drop his eyes.

Riveda, predictably, chuckled; and the tension slackened, its
focus diffused. Domaris dropped to the grass again, this time
beside Rajasta, and the old Priest put a fatherly arm about her
shoulders. He knew she had been deeply disturbed—and did

not blame her, even though he felt that she could have dealt more tactfully with both men. *But Domaris is still young—too young,* Rajasta thought, almost in despair, *to become the center of such conflict!*

Arvath, for his part, began to think more clearly, and relaxed. After all, he had really seen nothing to warrant his jealousy; and certainly Rajasta would not permit his Acolyte to act in opposition to the customs of the Twelve. Thus Arvath comforted himself, conveniently forgetting all customs but those he himself wished enforced.

Most powerful, perhaps, in alleviating Arvath's anger was the fact that he really liked Micon. They were, moreover, countrymen. Soon the two were engaged in casual, friendly conversation, although Micon, hypersensitive to Arvath's mood, answered at first with some reserve.

Domaris, no longer listening, hid herself from inner conflict in the earnest performance of her duty. Her eyes fixed on the stars, her mind intently stilled to meditation, she studied the portents of the night.

IV

Gradually, the Star Field quieted. One by one the little groups where the watchers clustered fell silent; only detached words rose now and then, curiously unearthly, from a particularly wakeful clique of young Priests in a far corner of the field. An idle breeze stirred the waving grasses, riffled cloaks and long hair, then dropped again; a cloud drifted across the face of the star that hovered near Caratra; somewhere a child wailed, and was hushed.

Far below them, a sullen flicker of red marked where fires had been built at the sea-wall, to warn ships from the rocks. Deoris had fallen asleep on the grass, her head on Riveda's knees and the Adept's long grey cloak tucked about her shoulders.

Arvath, like Domaris, sat studying the omens of the stars in a meditative trance; Micon, behind blind eyes, pursued his own silent thoughts. Rajasta, for some reason unknown even to himself, found his own gaze again and again turning to Riveda: still and motionless, his rough-cut head and sternly-straight back rising up in a blacker blackness against the starshine, Riveda sat in fixed reverie for hour after hour: the sight hypnotized Rajasta. The stars seemed to alternately fade and brighten behind the Adept. For an instant, past, present and future, all slid together and were one to the Priest of Light. He saw Riveda's face, thinner and more haggard, the lips set in an attitude of grim determination. The stars had vanished utterly, but a reddish-yellow, as of thousands of filmy, wind-blown strips of gossamer, danced and twisted about the Adept.

Suddenly and brilliantly, a terrible halo of fire encircled Riveda's head. *The dorje!* Rajasta started, and with a shudder that was at once within him and without, his actual surroundings reasserted themselves. *I must have slept*, he told himself, shaken. *That could have been no true vision!* And yet, with every blink of the Priest of Light's eyes, the awful image persisted, until Rajasta, with a little groan, turned his face away.

A wind was blowing across the quiet Star Field, turning the perspiration on the Priest of Light's brow to icy droplets as Rajasta wavered between lingering, mindless horror, and intermittent waves of reasoning thought. The moments that passed before Rajasta calmed himself were, perhaps, the worst of his life, moments that seemed an unending prison of time.

The Priest of Light sat, hunched over, still unable to look in Riveda's direction for simple fear. *It could only have been a nightmare*, Rajasta told himself, without much conviction. *But—if it was not?* Rajasta shuddered anew at this prospect, then sternly mastered himself, forcing his keen mind to examine the unthinkable.

I must speak with Riveda about this, Rajasta decided, unwillingly. *I must! Surely, if it was not a dream, it is meant for a warning—of great danger to him.* Rajasta did not know how far Riveda had gotten in his investigations, but perhaps—perhaps the Adept had gotten so close to the Black-robe sect that they sought to set their hellish mark on him, and so protect themselves against discovery.

It can only mean that, Rajasta reassured himself, and shivered uncontrollably. *Gods and spirits, protect us all!*

V

With tired and sleepless eyes, Domaris watched the sun rise, a gilt toy in a bath of pink clouds. Dawn reddened over the

Star Field slowly; the pale and pitiless light shone with a betraying starkness on the faces of those who slept there.

Deoris lay still, her regular breathing not quite a snore; Riveda's cloak remained, snuggled around her, although Riveda himself had gone hours ago. Arvath sprawled wide-limbed in the grass as if sleep had stolen up upon him like a thief in the night. Domaris realized how much like a sturdy small boy he looked—his dark hair tumbled around his damp forehead, his smooth cheeks glowing with the heavy, healthy slumber of a very young man. Then her eyes returned to Micon, who also slept, his head resting across her knees, his hand in hers.

After Rajasta had gone away, hurrying after Riveda with a pale and shaken look, she had returned to Micon's side, careless of what Arvath might say or think. All night Domaris had felt the Atlantean's thin and ruined hands twitch, as if even in sleep there remained an irreducible residue of pain. Once or twice, so ashen and strengthless had Micon's face appeared in the grey and ghastly light before dawn that Domaris had bent to listen to his breathing to be sure he still lived; then, her own breathing hushed to silence, she would hear a faint sigh, and be at once relieved and terrified—waking could only bring more pain for this man she was beginning to adore.

At the uttermost ebb-tide of the night, Domaris had found herself half-wishing Micon might drift out silently into the peace he so desired . . . and this thought had frightened her so much that she had but barely restrained herself from the sudden longing to clasp him in her arms and by sheer force of love restore his full vitality. *How can I be so full of life while Micon is so weak? Why,* she wondered rebelliously, *is he dying—and the devil who did this to him still walking around secure in his own worthless life?*

As if her thoughts disturbed his sleep, Micon stirred, murmuring in a language Domaris did not understand. Then, with a long sigh, the blind eyes opened and the Atlantean drew himself slowly upright, reaching out with a curious gesture—and drawing his hand back in surprise as he touched her dress.

"It is I, Micon—Domaris," she said quickly, addressing him by name for the first time.

"Domaris—I remember now. I slept?"

"For hours. It is dawn."

He laughed, uneasily but with that peculiar inner mirth

which never seemed to fail him. "A sorry sentry I should make nowadays! Is this how vigil is kept?"

Her instant laughter, soft and gentle, set him at ease. "Everyone sleeps after the middle hour of the night. You and I are likely the only ones awake. It is very early still."

When he spoke again, it was in a quieter tone, as if he feared he might wake the sleepers she had referred to so obliquely. "Is the sky red?"

She looked at him, bemused. "Yes. Bright red."

"I thought so," said Micon, nodding. "Ahtarrath's sons are all seamen; weather and storms are in our blood. At least I have not lost that."

"Storms?" Domaris repeated, dubiously glancing toward the distant, peaceful clouds.

Micon shrugged. "Perhaps we will be lucky, and it will not reach us," he said, "but it is in the air. I feel it."

Both were silent again, Domaris suddenly shy and self-conscious at the memory of the night's thoughts, and Micon thinking, *So I have slept at her side through the night. . . . In Ahtarrath, that would amount almost to a pledge.* He smiled. *Perhaps that explains Arvath's temper, last night . . . yet in the end we were all at peace. She sheds peace, as a flower its perfume.*

Domaris, meanwhile, had remembered Deoris, who still slept close by them, wrapped warm in Riveda's cloak. "My little sister has slept here in the grass all night," she said. "I must wake her and send her to bed."

Micon laughed lightly. "That seems a curiously pointless exercise," he remarked. "You have not slept at all."

It was not a question, and Domaris did not try to make any answer. Before his luminous face, she bent her head, forgetful that the morning light could not betray her to a blind man. Loosening her fingers gently from his, she said only, "I must wake Deoris."

VI

In her dream, Deoris wandered through an endless series of caverns, following the flickering flashes of light sparkling from the end of a strangely shaped wand held in the hand of a

robed and cowled figure. Somehow, she was not afraid, nor
cold, though she knew, in a way oddly detached from her
senses, that the walls and the floor of these caverns were icy
and damp. . . .

From somewhere quite nearby, a familiar but not immediately recognizable voice was calling her name. She came out of
the dream slowly, nestling in folds of grey. *"Don't,"* she
murmured drowsily, putting her fingers over her face.

With tender laughter, Domaris shook the child's shoulder.
"Wake up, little sleepyhead!"

The half-open eyes, still dream-dark, unclosed like bewildered violets; small fingers compressed a yawn. "Oh
Domaris, I meant to stay awake," Deoris murmured, and
scrambled to her feet, instantly alert, the cloak falling from
her. She bent to pick it up, holding it curiously at arm's length.
"What's this? This isn't mine!"

Domaris took it from her hands. "It is Lord Riveda's. You
went to sleep like a baby on his lap!"

Deoris frowned and looked sulky.

Domaris teased, "He left it, beyond doubt, so that he might
see you again! Deoris! Have you found your first lover so
young?"

Deoris stamped her foot, pouting. "Why are you so mean?"

"Why, I thought that would please you," said Domaris,
and merrily flung the cloak about the child's bare shoulders.

Deoris cast it off again, angrily. "I think you're—horrid!"
she wailed, and ran away down the hill to find the shelter of
her own bed and cry herself back to sleep.

Domaris started after her, then stopped herself; she felt too
ragged to deal with her sister's tantrums this morning. The
Grey-robe's cloak, rough against her arm, added to her feeling
of unease and apprehension. She had spoken lightly, to tease
the little girl, but now she found herself wondering about what
she had said. It was unthinkable that the Adept's interest in
Deoris could be personal—the child was not fourteen years
old! With a shudder of distaste, Domaris forced the thoughts
away as unworthy of her, and turned back to Micon.

The others were waking, rising, gathering in little groups to
watch what remained of the sunrise. Arvath came and put an
arm about her waist; she suffered it absent-mindedly. Her
calm grey eyes lingered dispassionately on the young Priest's
face. Arvath felt hurt, bewildered. Domaris had become so

different since—yes—since Micon had come into their lives! He sighed, wishing he could manage to hate Micon, and let his arm fall away from Domaris, knowing she was no more conscious of its removal than she had been of its presence.

Rajasta was coming up the pathway, a white figure faintly reddened in the morning light. Drawing near them, he stooped to pick up Micon's cloak of stainless white. It was a small service, but those who saw wondered at it, and at the caressing, familiar tone in Rajasta's normally stern voice. "Thou hast slept?" he asked.

Micon's smile was a blessing, almost beatific. "As I seldom sleep, my brother."

Rajasta's eyes moved briefly toward Domaris and Arvath, dismissing them. "Go, my children, and rest. . . . Micon, come with me."

Taking Domaris's arm, Arvath drew the girl along the path. Almost too weary to stand, she leaned heavily on his offered arm, then turned and laid her head for a moment against his chest.

"You are very tired, my sister," said Arvath, almost reproachfully—and, protective now, he led her down the hill, holding her close against him, her bright head nearly upon his shoulder.

Rajasta watched them, sighing. Then, his hand just touching Micon's elbow, he guided the Initiate unobtrusively along the opposite path, which led to the seashore. Micon went unerringly, as if he had no need whatsoever for Rajasta's guidance; the Atlantean's expression was dreamy and lost.

They paced in silence for some minutes before Rajasta spoke, without interrupting the slow rhythm of their steps. "She is that rarest of women," he said, "one born to be not only mate but comrade. You will be blessed."

"But she—accursed!" said Micon, almost inaudibly. The strange, twisted smile came again to his lips. "I love her, Rajasta, I love her far too much to hurt her; and I can give her nothing! No vows, no hope of real happiness, only sorrow and pain and, perhaps, shame . . ."

"Don't be a fool," was Rajasta's curt reply. "You forget your own teachings. Love, whenever and wherever it is found, though it last but a few moments, can bring only joy—if it is not thwarted! This is something greater than either of you. Do not stand in its way—nor in your own!"

They had stopped on a little rocky outcropping that over-looked the shore. Below, the sea crashed into the land, relent-less, insistent. Micon seemed to regard the Priest of Light with his sightless eyes, and Rajasta felt for a moment that he was looking at a stranger, so oddly changed did the Atlantean's face appear to him.

"I hope you are right," said Micon at last, still peering intently at the face he could not see.

BOOK TWO
Domaris

"If a scroll bears bad news, is it the fault of the scroll, or that which is described by the scroll? If the scroll is a bearer of good news, in what way does it differ from the scroll which bears the bad news?

"We begin life with a seemingly blank slate—and, though the writing that gradually appears on that slate is not our own, our judgment of the things written thereon determines what we are and what we will become. In much the same way, our work will be judged by the use to which other people put it. . . . Therefore, the question becomes, how can we control its use when it passes out of our control, into the hands of people over whom we have no control?

"The earliest teachings of the Priest's Caste have it that by performing our work with the wish and desire that it work for the betterment of man and the world, we endow it with our blessing which will reduce the user's desire to use it for destructive purposes. Doubtless this is not untrue—but reduction is not prevention."

—from the introduction to
The Codex of the Adept Riveda

Chapter One

SACRAMENTS

I

A heavy, soaking rain poured harshly down on the roofs and courts and enclosures of the Temple precinct; rain that sank roughly into the thirsty ground, rain that splashed with a musical tinkling into pools and fountains, flooding the flagged walks and lawns. Perhaps because of the rain, the library of the Temple was crowded. Every stool and table was occupied, each bench had its own bent head.

Domaris, pausing in the doorway, sought with her eyes for Micon, who was not in his usual recess. There were the white cowls of the Priests, the heavy grey hoods of Magicians, the banded filletings of Priestesses, bare heads of student-priests and scribes. At last, with a little joyous thrill, she saw Micon. He sat at a table in the farthest corner, deep in conversation with Riveda, whose smoky, deep-cowled robe and harsh, gaunt face made a curious contrast to the pallid and emaciated Initiate. Yet Domaris felt that here were two men who were really very much alike.

Pausing again, even as she directed her steps toward them, her intense, unreasoning dislike of Riveda surged back. She shuddered a little. *That man, like Micon?*

Riveda was leaning forward, listening intently; the Atlantean's blind, dark features were luminous with his smile.

Any casual observer would have sworn that they felt no emotion but comradeship—but Domaris could not dispel the feeling that here were two forces, alike in strength but opposite in direction, pitted against each other.

It was the Grey-robe who first became aware of her approach; looking up with a pleasant smile, Riveda said, "Talkannon's daughter seeks you, Micon." Otherwise, of course, he did not move or pay the least attention to the girl. Domaris was only an Acolyte, and Riveda a highly-placed Adept.

Micon rose painfully to his feet and spoke with deference. "How may I serve the Lady Domaris?"

Domaris, embarrassed by this public breach of proper etiquette, stood with her eyes cast down. She was not really a shy girl, but disliked the attention Micon's action called upon her. She wondered if Riveda was secretly scornful of Micon's evident ignorance of Temple custom. Her voice was hardly more than a whisper as she said, "I came on your scribe's behalf, Lord Micon. Deoris is ill, and cannot come to you today."

"I am sorry to hear that." Micon's wry grin was compassionate now. "Flower-of-the-Sun, tell her not to come to me again until she is quite well."

"I trust her illness is nothing serious," Riveda put in, casually but with a piercing glance from beneath heavy-lidded eyes, "I have often thought that these night vigils in the damp air do no good to anyone."

Domaris felt suddenly annoyed. This was none of Riveda's business! Even Micon could sense the chill in her voice as she said, "It is nothing. Nothing at all. She will be recovered in a few hours." As a matter of fact, although Domaris had no intention of saying so, Deoris had cried herself into a violent headache. Domaris felt disturbed and guilty, for she herself had brought on her sister's distress with her teasing remarks about Riveda that very morning. More, she sensed that Deoris was furiously jealous of Micon. She had begged and begged Domaris not to leave her, not to go to Micon, to send some slave to tell him of her illness. It had been difficult for Domaris to make herself leave the miserable little girl, and she had finally forced herself to do it only by reminding herself that Deoris was not really ill; that she had brought on the headache by her own crying and fussing, and that if Deoris once and for all learned that her tantrums and hysterics would not get her what she wanted, she would stop having them—and then there would be no more of these headaches, either.

Riveda rose to his feet. "I shall call to inquire further," he said definitely. "Many serious ills have their beginnings in a mild ailment." His words were far from uncourteous—they were indeed stamped with the impeccable manners of a Healer-Priest—but Riveda was secretly amused. He knew Domaris resented him. He felt no real malice toward Domaris; but Deoris interested him, and Domaris's attempts to keep him away from her sister impressed him as ridiculous maneuvers without meaning.

There was nothing Domaris could say. Riveda was a high Adept, and if he chose to interest himself in Deoris, it was not for an Acolyte to gainsay him. Sharply she reminded herself that Riveda was old enough to be their grandsire, a Healer-Priest of great skill, and of an austerity unusual even among the Grey-robes.

The two men exchanged cordial farewells, and as Riveda moved sedately away, she felt Micon's light groping touch against her wrist. "Sit beside me, Light-crowned. The rain has put me out of the mood for study, and I am lonely."

"You have had most interesting company," Domaris commented with a trace of asperity.

Micon's wry grin came and went. "True. Still, I would rather talk to you. But—perhaps it is not convenient just now? Or is it—improper?"

Domaris smiled faintly. "You and Riveda are both so highly-placed in the Temple that the Monitors have not reproved your ignorance of our restrictions," she murmured, glancing uneasily at the stern-faced scribes who warded the manuscripts, "but I, at least, may not speak aloud." She could not help adding, in a sharper whisper, "Riveda should have warned you!"

Micon, chagrined, chuckled. "Perhaps he is used to working in solitude," he hazarded, lowering his voice to match the girl's. "You know this Temple—where can we talk without restraint?"

II

Micon's height made Domaris seem almost tiny, and his rugged, wrenched features made a strange contrast to her smooth beauty. As they left the building, curious heads turned to gaze after them; Micon, unaware of this, was nevertheless affected by Domaris's shyness, and said no word as they went through a passageway.

Unobtrusively, graciously, Domaris slowed her light steps to match his, and Micon tightened his clasp on her arm. The girl drew back a curtain, and they found themselves in the anteroom to one of the inner courts. One entire wall was a great window, loosely shuttered with wooden blinds; the soft quiet fragrance of rain falling on glass and expectant flowers came faintly through the bars, and the dripping music of raindrops pouring into a pool.

Domaris—who had never before shared this favorite, usually-deserted nook even with Deoris—said to Micon, "I come here often to study. A crippled Priest who seldom leaves his rooms lives across the court, and this room is never used. I think I can promise you that we will be quite alone here." She found a seat on a bench near the window, and made room for him at her side.

There was a long silence. Outside, the rain fell and dripped; its cool, moist breath blowing lightly into their faces. Micon's hands lay relaxed on his knees, and the flicker of a grin, which never quite left his dark mouth, came and went like summer lightning. He was content just to be near Domaris, but the girl was restless.

"I find a place where we may talk—and we sit as dumb as the fish!"

Micon turned toward her. "And there is something to be said—Domaris!" He spoke her name with such an intensity of longing that the girl's breath caught in her throat. He repeated it again; on his lips it was a caress. "Domaris!"

"Lord Micon—Sir Prince—"

A sudden and quite unexpected anger gusted up in his voice. "Call me not so!" he ordered. "I have left all that behind me! You know my name!"

She whispered, like a woman in a dream, "Micon."

"Domaris, I—I am humbly your suitor." There was an oddly-muted tone in his voice, as of self-deprecation. "I have —loved you, since you came into my life. I know I have little to give you, and that only for a short time. But—sweetest of women—" He paused, as if to gather strength, and went on, in hesitant words, "I would that we might have met in a happier hour, and our—our love flowered—perhaps, slowly, into perfection. . . ." Once again he paused, and his dark intent features betrayed an emotion so naked that Domaris could not face it, and she looked away, glad for once that he could not see her face.

"Little time remains to me," he said. "I know that by Temple law you are still free. It is your—right, to choose a man, and bear his child, if you wish. Your betrothal to Arvath is no formal bar. Would you—will you consider me as your lover?" Micon's resonant voice was now trembling with the power of his emotions. "It is my destiny, I suppose, that I who had all things, commanding armies and the tribute of great families, should now have so little to offer you—no vows, no hope of happiness, nothing but a very great need of you—".

Wonderingly, she repeated, slowly, "You love me?"

He stretched questing hands toward her; found her slim fingers and took them into his own. "I have not even the words to say how great my love is, Domaris. Only—that life is unendurable when I am not near you. My—my heart longs for —the sound of your voice, your step, your—touch. . . ."

"Micon!" she whispered, still dazed, unable to comprehend completely. "You do love me!" She raised her face to look intently into his.

"This would be easier to say if I could see your face," he whispered—and, with a movement that dismayed the girl, he knelt at her feet, capturing her hands again and pressing them to his face. He kissed the delicate fingers and said, half stifled, "I love you almost too much for life, almost too much. . . . You are great in gentleness, Domaris. I could beget my child upon no other woman—but Domaris, Domaris, can you even guess how much I must ask of you?"

With a swift movement, Domaris leaned forward and drew him to her, pressing his head against her young breasts. "I know only that I love you," she told him. "This is your place." And her long red hair covered them both as their mouths met, speaking the true name of love.

III

The rain had stopped, although the sky was still grey and thickly overcast. Deoris, lying on a divan in the room she shared with her sister, was having her hair brushed by her maid; overhead, the little red bird, Domaris's gift, twittered and chirped, with gay abandon; Deoris listened and hummed softly to herself, while the brush moved soothingly along her hair, and outside the breeze fluttered the hangings at the window, the fringed leaves of the trees in the court. Inside, the room was filled with dim light, reflecting the polished shine of dark woods and the glint of silken hangings and of ornaments of polished silver and turquoise and jade. Into this moderate luxury, allotted to Domaris as an Acolyte and the daughter of a Priest, Deoris nestled like a kitten, putting aside her slight feeling of self-consciousness and guilt; the scribes and neophytes were curtailed to a strictness and austerity in their surroundings, and Domaris, at her age, had been forbidden such comforts. Deoris enjoyed the luxury, and no one had forbidden it, but under her consciousness she felt secretly shamed.

She twisted away from the hands of the slave girl. "There, that's enough, you'll make my head ache again," she said pettishly. "Besides, I hear my sister coming." She jumped up and ran to the door, but at seeing Domaris, the eager greeting died on her lips.

But her sister's voice was perfectly natural when she spoke. "Your headache is better, then, Deoris? I had expected to find you still in bed."

Deoris peered at Domaris dubiously, thinking, *I must be imagining things.* Aloud, she said, "I slept most of the afternoon. When I woke, I felt better." She fell silent as her sister moved into the room, then went on, "The Lord Riveda—"

Domaris cut her off with an impatient gesture. "Yes, yes, he told me he would call to inquire about you. You can tell me another time, can't you?"

Deoris blinked. "Why? Are you in a hurry? Is it your night to serve in the Temple?"

Domaris shook her head, then stretched her hand to touch her sister's curls in a light caress. "I'm very glad you are better," she said, more kindly. "Call Elara for me, will you, darling?"

The little woman came and deftly divested Domaris of her outer robes. Domaris then flung herself full-length upon a pile of cushions, and Deoris came and knelt anxiously beside her.

"Sister, is something wrong?"

Domaris returned an absent-minded "No," and then, with a sudden, dreamy decision, "No, nothing is wrong—or will be.'' She rolled over to look up, smiling, into Deoris's eyes. Impulsively, she started, ''Deoris—'' Just as suddenly, she stopped.

''What *is* it, Domaris?'' Deoris pressed, feeling again the inexplicable inner panic which had risen in her at her sister's return only moments ago.

''Deoris—little sister—I am going to the Gentle One.'' Abruptly she seized Deoris's hand, and went on, ''Sister—come with me?''

Deoris only stared, open-mouthed. The Gentle One, the Goddess Caratra—her shrine was approached only for particular rituals, or in moments of acute mental crisis. ''I don't understand,'' Deoris said slowly. ''Why—why?'' She suddenly put out her other hand to clasp Domaris's between both of her own. ''Domaris, what is happening to you!''

Confused and exalted, Domaris could not bring herself to speak. She had never doubted what answer she would bring Micon—he had forbidden her to decide at once—yet something deep within her heart was disturbed, and demanded comfort, and for once she could not turn to Deoris, for, close as they were, Deoris was only a child.

Deoris, who had never known any mother but Domaris, felt the new distance between them keenly, and exclaimed, in a voice at once wailing and strangled, *''Domaris!''*

''Oh, Deoris,'' said Domaris, freeing her hand with some annoyance, *''please* don't ask me questions!'' Then, not wanting the gap between them to widen any further, quickly added, gently, ''Just—come with me? Please?''

''Of course I will,'' murmured Deoris, through the peculiar knot in her throat.

Domaris smiled and sat up; embracing Deoris, she gave her a quick little kiss and was about to pull away, but Deoris clutched her tight, as if, with the bitter intuition of the young, she sensed that Micon had not so long ago rested there and wished to drive his lingering spirit away. Domaris stroked the silky curls, feeling the impulse to confide again; but the words would not come.

IV

The Shrine of Caratra, the Gentle Mother, was far away; almost the entire length of the Temple grounds lay between it and the House of the Twelve, a long walk under damp, flowering trees. In the cooling twilight, the scent of roses and of verbena hung heavily on the moist and dusky air. The two sisters were silent: one intent on her mission, the other for once at a loss for words.

The Shrine shone whitely at the further end of an oval pool of clear water, shimmering, crystalline, and ethereally blue beneath the high arch of clearing sky. As they neared it, the sun emerged from behind an intervening building for a few moments as it sank in the west, lightening the Shrine's alabaster walls. A pungent trace of incense wafted to them across the water; twinkling lights beckoned from the Shrine.

Noticing that Deoris was dragging her feet just the least bit, Domaris suddenly sat down on the grass to the side of the path. Deoris joined her at once; hand in hand they rested a little while, watching the unrippling waters of the holy pool.

The beauty and mystery of life, of re-creation, was embodied here in the Goddess who was Spring and Mother and Woman, the symbol of the gentle strength that is earth. To approach the Shrine of Caratra, they would have to wade breast-high through the pool; this sacred, lustral rite was undertaken at least once by every woman of the precinct, although only those of the Priest's Caste and the Acolytes were taught the deeper significance of this ritual: every woman came this way to maturity, struggling through reluctant tides, deeper than water, heavier and harder to pass. In pride or maturity, in joy or in sorrow, in childish reluctance or in maturity, in ecstasy or rebellion, every woman came one day to this.

Domaris shivered as she looked across the pale waters, frightened by the symbolism. As one of the Acolytes, she had been initiated into this mystery, and understood; yet she hung back, afraid. She thought of Micon, and of her love, trying to summon courage to step into those waters; but a sort of prophetic dread was on her. She clung to Deoris for a moment, in a wordless plea for reassurance.

Deoris sensed this, yet she looked sulkily away from her sister. She felt as if her world had turned upside down. She would not let herself know what Domaris was facing; and here, before the oldest and holiest shrine of the Priest's Caste into which they had both been born, she too was afraid; as if those waters would sweep her away, too, into the current of life, like any woman. . . .

She said moodily, "It is cruel—as all life is cruel! I wish I had not been born a woman." And she told herself that this was selfish and wrong, to force herself on Domaris's attention, seeking reassurance for herself, when Domaris faced this testing and her own was still far in the future. Yet she said, "Why, Domaris? Why?"

Domaris had no answer, except to hold Deoris tightly in her arms for a moment. Then all her own confidence flooded back. She was a woman, deeply in love, and she rejoiced in her heart. "You won't always feel that way, Deoris," she promised. Letting her arms drop, she said slowly, "Now I shall go to the Shrine. Will you come the rest of the way with me, little sister?"

For a moment, Deoris felt no great reluctance; she had once entered the Shrine beyond the pool, in the sacred rite undertaken by every young girl in the Temple when, at the first commencement of puberty, she gave her first service in the House of the Great Mother. At that time she had felt nothing except nervousness at the ritual's solemnity. Now, however, as Domaris rose from the grass, panic fixed chilly knuckles at Deoris's throat. If she went with Domaris, of her own free will, she felt she would be caught and trapped, handing herself over blindly to the violence of nature. Scared rebellion quivered in her denial. "No—I don't want to!"

"Not even—if I ask it?" Domaris sounded hurt, and was; she had wanted Deoris to understand, to share with her this moment which divided her life.

Deoris shook her head again, hiding her face behind her hands. A perverse desire to inflict hurt was on her: Domaris had left her alone—now it was *her* turn!

To her own surprise, Domaris found herself making yet another appeal. "Deoris—little sister—please, I want you with me. Won't you come?"

Deoris did not uncover her face, and her words, when they came, were barely audible—and still negative.

Domaris let her hand fall abruptly from her sister's shoulder. "I'm sorry, Deoris. I had no right to ask."

Deoris would have given anything to retract her words now, but it was too late. Domaris took a few steps away, and Deoris lay still, pressing her feverish cheeks into the cold grass, crying silently and bitterly.

Domaris, without looking back, unfastened her outer garments, letting them fall about her feet, and loosened her hair until it covered her body in a smooth cascade. She ran her hands through the heavy tresses, and suddenly a thrill went through her young body, from fingertips to toes: *Micon loves me!* For the first and only time in her life, Domaris knew that she was beautiful, and gloried in the knowledge of her beauty —although there was a chill of sadness in the knowledge that Micon could never see it or know it.

Only a moment the strange intoxication lasted; then Domaris divided her long hair about her neck and stepped into the pool, wading out until she stood breast-high in the radiant water, which was warm and tingling, somehow oddly not like water at all, but an effervescent, living light. . . . Blue and softly violet, it glowed and shimmered and flowed in smooth patterns around the pillar of her body, and she thrilled again with a suffocating ecstasy as, for an instant, it closed over her head. Then she stood upright again, the water running in scented, bubbling droplets from her glowing head and shoulders. Wading onward, toward the beckoning Shrine, she felt that the water washed away, drop by drop, all of her past life, with its little irritations and selfishness. Filled and flooded with a sense of infinite strength, Domaris became—as she had not on any earlier visit to Caratra's Shrine—aware that, being human, she was divine.

She came out of the water almost regretfully, and paused a moment before entering the Temple; solemnly, with sober, intent concentration, the young Priestess robed herself in the sacramental garments kept within the ante-room, carefully not thinking of the *next* time she must bathe here. . . .

Entering the sanctuary, she stood a moment, reverent before the altar, and bound the bridal girdle about her body. Then, arms wide-flung, Domaris knelt, her head thrown back in passionate humility. She wanted to pray, but no words came.

"Mother, lovely goddess," she whispered at last, "let me— not fail. . . ."

A new warmth seemed to envelop Domaris; the compassionate eyes of the holy image seemed to smile upon her, the eyes of the mother Domaris could barely remember. She knelt there for a long time, in a sober, listening stillness, while strange, soft, and unfocussed visions moved in her mind, indefinite, even meaningless, yet filling her with a calm and a peace that she had never known, and was never entirely to lose.

V

The sun was gone, and the stars had altered their positions considerably before Deoris, stirring at last, realized that it was very late. Domaris would have returned hours ago if she had intended to return at all.

Resentment gradually took the place of alarm: Domaris had forgotten her again! Unhappy and petulant, Deoris returned alone to the House of the Twelve, where she discovered that Elara knew no more than she—or, at least, the woman refused to discuss her mistress with Deoris. This did not sweeten her temper, and her snappish response, her fretful demands, soon reduced the usually patient Elara to silent, exasperated tears.

The servants, and several of the neighbors, had been made as miserable as Deoris was herself when Elis came in search of Domaris, and innocently made things even worse by asking her cousin's whereabouts.

"How would I know!" Deoris exploded. "Domaris never tells *me* anything anymore!"

Elis tried to placate the angry girl, but Deoris would not even listen, and at last Elis, who had a temper of her own, made herself clear. "Well, I don't see why Domaris *should* tell you anything—what concerns her is none of your business—and in any case, you've been spoilt until you are absolutely unbearable; I wish Domaris would come to her senses and put you in your place!"

Deoris did not even cry, but crumpled up, stricken.

Elis, already at the door, turned and came back swiftly, bending over her. "Deoris," she said, contritely, "I'm sorry, really, I didn't mean it quite like that. . . ." In a rather rare gesture of affection, for Elis was undemonstrative to a fault, she took Deoris's hand in hers, saying, "I know you are lonely. You have no one but Domaris. But that's your own fault, really. You could have many friends." Gently, she added, "Anyway, you shouldn't stay here alone and mope. Lissa misses you. Come and play with her."

Deoris's returning smile wavered. "Tomorrow," she said. "I'd—rather be by myself now."

Elis had intuitions that were almost clairvoyant at times, and now a sudden random impression almost as clear as sight made her drop her cousin's hand. "I won't try to persuade you," she said; then added, quietly and without emphasis, "Just remember this. If Domaris belongs to no one but herself— then you, too, are a person in your own right. Good night, puss."

After Elis had gone, Deoris sat staring at the closed door. The words, at first simple-seeming, had turned strangely cryptic, and Deoris could not puzzle out their meaning. At last she decided that it was just Elis being Elis again, and tried to put it out of her mind.

Chapter Two

THE FOOL

I

Unmarried Priests, above a certain rank, were housed in two dormitories. Rajasta and Micon, with several others of their high station, dwelt in the smaller and more comfortable of these. Riveda might have lived there as well—but, of his own free will, from humility or some inversion of pride, the Adept had chosen to remain among the Priests of lesser accomplishment.

Rajasta found him writing, in a room which doubled as sleeping-room and study, opening on a small, enclosed courtyard. The main room was sparsely furnished, with no hint of luxury; the court was laid simply with brick, without pools or flowers or fountain. A pair of smaller rooms to one side housed the Grey-robe's attendants.

The day was warm; throughout the dormitory most of the doors were wide open, to allow some circulation of the deadening air. So it was that Rajasta stood, unnoticed, gazing at the preoccupied Adept, for several moments.

The Priest of Light had never had any cause to distrust Riveda—and although the vision of the *dorje* sign still troubled Rajasta, courtesy demanded that he speak not again of the warning he had delivered to the Adept on the night of Zenith; to do so would have been an insulting lack of confidence.

Yet Rajasta was Guardian of the Temple of Light, and his responsibility no slight one. Should Riveda somehow fail to set his Order to rights, Rajasta would share the guilt in full, for by the strict interpretation of his duty, the Guardian should have persuaded, even forced Micon to give testimony about his ordeal at the hands of the Black-robes. The matter properly should have been laid before the High Council.

Now, thinking all these things over yet again, Rajasta sighed deeply. *Thus it is that even the best of motives ensnare us in karmic webs,* he thought tiredly. *I can spare Micon, but only at my own expense—so adding to his burdens, and binding us both more closely to this man. . . .*

Riveda, very straight at his writing-table—he said often that he had no liking for having some silly brat of a scribe running about after him—incised a few more characters in the heavy, pointed strokes which told so much about him, then abruptly flung the brush aside.

"Well, Rajasta?" The Adept chuckled at the Priest of Light's momentary discomfiture. "A friendly visit? Or more of your necessities?"

"Let us say, both," Rajasta answered after a moment.

The smile faded from Riveda's features, and he rose to his feet. "Well, come to the point—and then perhaps I shall have something to say, too. The people of my Order are restless. They say the Guardians intrude. Of course—" He glanced at Rajasta sharply. "Intrusion is the business of the Guardians."

Rajasta clasped his hands behind his back. He noticed that Riveda had not invited him to be seated, or even, really, to enter. The omission annoyed him, so that he spoke with a little more force than he had originally intended; if Riveda intended to discard the pretense of courtesy, he would meet the Adept half-way.

"There is more restlessness in the Temple precinct than that of your Order," Rajasta warned. "Day by day, the Priests grow more resentful. Rumors grow, daily, that you are a negligent leader who has allowed debased and decadent forms to creep into your ritual, so that it has become a thing of distortion. The women of your order—"

"I had wondered when we would come to them," Riveda interrupted in an undertone.

Rajasta scowled and continued, "—they are put to certain uses which frequently defy the laws even of your Order. It is known that you mask the Black-robes among yourselves—"

Riveda held up his hand. "Am I suspected of sorcery?"

The Guardian shook his head. "I have made no accusations. I repeat only the common talk."

"Does Rajasta, the Guardian, listen to the cackle of gate-gossip? That is not my idea of pleasant conversation—nor of a Priest's duty!" As Rajasta was silent, Riveda went on, the crackle of thunder in his deep voice. "Go on! Surely there is more of this! Who but the Grey-robes work with the magic of nature? Have we not been accused of blasting the harvests? What of my Healers who are the only men who dare to go into the cities when they are rotting with plague? Have they not yet been accused of poisoning the wells?"

Rajasta said tiredly, "There is no swarm that does not start with a single bee."

Riveda chuckled. "Then where, Lord Guardian, is the stinger?"

"That you care nothing for these things," Rajasta retorted sharply. "Yours is the responsibility for all these men. Accept it—or delegate it to another who will keep closer watch on the Order! Neglect it not—" Rajasta's voice deepened in impressive admonition: "—or their guilt may shape your destiny! The responsibility of one who leads others is frightful. See that you lead wisely."

Riveda, about to speak, instead swallowed the reproof in silence, staring at the brick floor; but the line of his jaw was insolent. At last he said, "It shall be seen to, have no fear of that."

In the silence which followed this, a faint, off-key whistling could be heard somewhere down the hall. Riveda glanced briefly at his open door, but his expression revealed little of his annoyance.

Rajasta tried another tack. "Your search for the Black-robes—?"

Riveda shrugged. "At present, all those of my Order can account for themselves—save one."

Rajasta started. "Indeed? And that one—?"

Riveda spread his hands. "A puzzle, in more ways than one. He wears chela's habit, but none claim him as their disciple; nor has he named anyone his master. I had never seen him before, yet there he was among the others, and, when challenged, he gave the right responses. Otherwise, he seemed witless."

"Micon's brother, perhaps?" Rajasta suggested.

Riveda snorted derision. "A halfwit? Impossible! Some runaway slave would be more like it."

Rajasta asked, using his privilege as Guardian of the Temple, "What have you done with him?"

"As yet, nothing," Riveda replied slowly. "Since he can pass our gates and knows our ritual, he is entitled to a place among our Order, even if his teacher is unknown. For the present, I have taken him as my own disciple. Although his past is a blanked slate, and he seems not to know even his own name, he has intervals of sanity. I think I can do much with him, and for him." A short space of silence passed. Rajasta said nothing, but Riveda burst out defensively, "What else could I have done? Forgetting for the moment that my vows pledge me to the aid of anyone who can give the Signs of my Order, should I have loosed the boy to be stoned and tormented, seized and put in a cage for fools to gape at as a madman—or taken again for evil uses?"

Rajasta's steady stare did not waver. "I have not accused you," he reminded Riveda. "It is your affair. But if Black-robes have tainted his mind—"

"Then I shall see that they make no evil use of him," Riveda promised grimly, and his face relaxed a little; "He has not the wit to be evil."

"Ignorance is worse than evil intent," Rajasta warned, and Riveda sighed.

"See for yourself, if you will," he said, and stepped to the open door, speaking in a low voice to someone in the court. After a moment, a young man came noiselessly into the room.

II

He was slight and small and looked very young, but on a second glance it could be seen that the features, though smooth as a boy's, were devoid of eyelashes as well as of beard. His brows were but the thinnest, light line, yet his hair was heavy and black, falling in lank locks which had been trimmed squarely at his shoulders. Light grey eyes gazed at Rajasta, unfocussed as if he were blind; and he was darkly tanned, although some strange pallor underlying the skin gave him a sickly look. Rajasta studied the haggard face intently, noting that the chela held himself stiffly erect, arms away from his body, thin hands hanging curled like a newborn child's at his sides. He had moved so lightly, so noiselessly, that Rajasta wondered, half-seriously, if the creature had pads like a cat's on his feet.

He beckoned the chela to approach, and asked kindly, "What is your name, my son?"

The dull eyes woke suddenly in an unhealthy glitter. He looked about and took a step backward, then opened his mouth once or twice. Finally, in a husky voice—as if unaccustomed to speaking—he said, "My name? I am . . . only a fool."

"Who are you?" Rajasta persisted. "Where are you from?"

The chela took another step backward, and the furtive swivelling of his sick eyes intensified. "I can see you are a Priest," he said craftily. "Aren't you wise enough to know? Why should I twist my poor brain to remember, when the High Gods know, and bid me be silent, be silent, sing silent when the stars glow, mooning driftward in a surge of light. . . ." The words slid off into a humming croon.

Rajasta could only stare, thunderstruck.

Riveda gestured to the chela in dismissal. "That will do," he said; and as the boy slipped from the room like a mumbling fog-wraith, the Adept added, in explanation to Rajasta, "Questions always excite him—as if at some time he'd been questioned until he—withdrew."

Rajasta, finding his tongue, exclaimed, "He's mad as a sea-gull!"

Riveda chuckled wryly. "I'm sorry. He does have intervals when he's reasonably lucid, and can talk quite rationally. But if you question—he slips back into madness. If you can avoid anything like a question—"

"I wish you had warned me of that," Rajasta said, in genuine distress. "You told me he gave the correct responses—"

Riveda shrugged this off. "Our Signs and counter-Signs are not in the form of questions," he remarked, "at least he can betray none of my secrets! Have you no secrets in the Temple of Light, Rajasta?"

"Our secrets are available to any who will seek sincerely."

Riveda's frigid eyes glittered with offense. "As our secrets are more dangerous, so we conceal them more carefully. The

harmless secrets of the Temple of Light, your pretty ceremonies and rites—no man could harm anyone even if he
meddled with the knowledge unworthily! But we work with
dangerous powers—and if one man know them and be unfit to
trust with such secrets, then such things come as befell young
Micon of Ahtarrath!" He turned savagely on Rajasta. "You
of all men should know why we have cause to keep our secrets
for those who are fit to use them!"

Rajasta's lips twisted. "Such as your crazy chela?"

"He knows them already; we can but make sure he does not
misuse them in his madness." Riveda's voice was flat and definite. "You are no child to babble of ideals. Look at
Micon . . . you honor him, I respect him greatly, your little
Acolyte—what is her name? Domaris—adores him. Yet what
is he but a broken reed?"

"Such is accomplishment," from Rajasta, very low.

"And at what price? I think my crazy boy is happier.
Micon, unfortunately—" Riveda smiled, "is still able to think,
and remember."

Sudden anger gusted up in Rajasta. "Enough! The man is
my guest, keep your mocking tongue from him! Look you to
your Order, and forbear mocking your betters!" He turned
his back on the Adept, and strode from the room, his firm
tread echoing and dying away on stone flooring; and never
heard Riveda's slow-kindled laughter that followed him all the
way.

Chapter Three

THE UNION

I

The sacred chamber was walled with tall windows fretted and overlaid with intricate stone-work casements. The dimmed moonlight and patterns of shadow bestowed an elusive, unreal quality upon the plain chairs and the very simple furnishings. A high-placed oval window let the silvery rays fall full on the altar, where glowed a pulsing flame.

Micon on one side, Rajasta on the other, Domaris passed beneath the softly shadowed archway; in silence, the two men each took one of the woman's hands, and led her to a seat, one of three facing the altar.

"Kneel," said Rajasta softly, and Domaris, with the soft sibilance of her robes, knelt. Micon's hand withdrew from hers, and was laid upon the crown of her head.

"Grant wisdom and courage to this woman, O Great Unknown!" the Atlantean prayed, his voice low-pitched, yet filling the chamber with its controlled resonances. "Grant her peace and understanding, O Unknowable!" Stepping back a pace, Micon permitted Rajasta to take his place.

"Grant purity of purpose and true knowledge to this woman," said the Priest of Light. "Grant her growth according to her needs, and the fortitude to do her duty in the fullest measure. O Thou which Art, let her be in Thee, and of Thee."

Rajasta took his hand from her head and himself withdrew.

The silence was complete. Domaris felt herself oddly alone upon the raised platform before the altar, though she had not heard the rustlings of robes, the slapping of sandals which would have accompanied Micon and Rajasta out of the room. Her heartbeats sounded dully in her ears, a muffled throbbing that slowed to a long drawn-out rhythm, a deep pulsing that seemed to take its tempo from the quivering flame upon the altar. Then, without warning, the two men raised her up and seated her between them.

Her hands resting in theirs, her face stilled to an unearthly beauty, Domaris felt as if she were rising, expanding to touch the far-flung stars. Even there a steady beat, a regular cadence that was both sound and light fused, filled and engulfed her. Domaris's senses shifted, rapidly reversing, painlessly twisting and contorting into an indescribable blending in which all past experience was suddenly quite useless. It was around her and in her and of her, a sustenance that, somehow, she herself fed, and slowly, very slowly, as if over centuries, the pulsing bright static of the stars gave way to the hot darkness of the beating heart of the earth. Of this, too, she was a part: it was she; she *was*.

With this realization, as if borne upward by the warm tides of the waters of life, Domaris came back to the surface of existence. About her, the sacred chamber was silent; to either side of her, she could see the face of a man transfigured even as Domaris had been. As one, the three breathed deeply, rose and went forth in silence from that place, newly consecrated to a purpose that, for a little time, they could almost understand.

Chapter Four

STORM WARNINGS

I

A cool breeze stirred the leaves, and what light penetrated the branches was a shimmering, shifting dance of golden and green. Rajasta, approaching along a shrubbery-lined path, thought the big tree and the trio beneath it made a pleasing picture: Deoris, with her softly curling hair, looked shadowy and very dark as she sat on her scribe's stool, reading from a scroll; before her, in contrast, Micon's pallor was luminous, almost translucent. Close by the Atlantean's side, yet not much more distant from her little sister, Domaris was like a stilled flame, the controlled serenity of her face a pool of quiet.

Because Rajasta's sandals had made no noise on the grass, he was able to stand near them unnoticed a little while, half-listening to Deoris as she read; yet it was Domaris and Micon on whom his thoughts focussed.

As Deoris paused in her reading, Micon abruptly raised his head and turned toward Rajasta, the twisted smile warm with welcome.

Rajasta laughed. "My brother, you should be Guardian here, and not I! No one else noticed me." There was a spreading ripple of laughter beneath the big tree as the Priest of Light moved closer. Gesturing to both girls to keep their seats, Rajasta stopped a moment, to touch Deoris's tumbled curls fondly. "This breeze is refreshing."

"Yes, but it is the first warning of the coming storm," said Micon.

There was a brief silence then, and Rajasta gazed thoughtfully upon Micon's uptilted face. *Which sort of storm, I wonder, does he refer to? There is more trouble ahead of us than bad weather.*

Domaris, too, was disturbed. Always sensitive, her new relationship with Micon had given her an awareness of him that was uncanny in its completeness. She could, with inevitable instinct, enter into his feelings; the result was a devotion that dwarfed all other relationships. She loved Deoris as much as ever, and her reverence for Rajasta had not altered in intensity or degree—but Micon's desperate need came first, and drew on every protective instinct in her. It was this which threatened to absorb her; for Domaris, of them all, had the faculty for an almost catastrophic self-abnegation.

Rajasta had, of course, long known this about his Acolyte. Now it struck him with renewed force that, as her Initiator, it was his duty to warn her of this flaw in her character. Yet Rajasta understood all too well the love that had given rise to it.

Nevertheless, he told himself sternly, *it is not healthy for Domaris to so concentrate all her forces on one person, however great the need!* But, before he had even quite completed this thought, the Priest of Light smiled, ruefully. *It might be well for me to learn that lesson, too.*

Settling on the grass beside Micon, Rajasta laid his hand over the Atlantean's lax and twisted one in a gently reassuring clasp. Scarcely a moment passed before his skilled touch found the slight, tell-tale trembling, and Rajasta shook his head sadly. Although the Atlantean seemed to have quite recovered his health, the truth was far otherwise.

But for the moment, the trembling lessened, then stilled, as if a door had slammed shut on sullen fury. Micon allowed the Guardian's strength to flow through his tortured nerves, comforting and reinforcing him. He smiled gratefully, then his face sobered.

"Rajasta—I must ask—make no further effort to punish on my behalf. It is an effort that will bear no, or bitter, fruit."

Rajasta sighed. "We have been over this so often," he said, but not impatiently. "You must know by now, I cannot let this rest as things stand; the matter is too grave to go unpunished."

"And it will not, be assured," said Micon, his blind eyes bright and almost glowing after the flow of new vitality. "But take heed that punishment for punishment not follow!"

"Riveda must cleanse his Order!" Domaris's voice was as brittle as ice. "Rajasta is right—"

"My gracious lady," Micon admonished gently, "when justice becomes an instrument of vengeance, its steel is turned to blades of grass. Truly, Rajasta must protect those to come —but he who takes vengeance will suffer! The Laws of Karma note first the act, and *then*—if at all—the intention!" He paused, then added, with emphasis, "Nor should we involve Riveda overmuch. He stands already at the crossroads of danger!"

Rajasta, who had been prepared to speak, gasped. Had Micon also been vouchsafed some vision or revelation such as Rajasta had had on the Night of Zenith?

The Priest of Light's reaction went unnoticed as Deoris raised her head, suddenly impelled to defend Riveda. Hardly had she spoken a word, though, before it struck her that no one had accused the Adept of anything, and she fell silent again.

Domaris's face changed; the sternness grew tender. "I am ungenerous," she acknowledged. "I will be silent until I know it is a love for justice, not revenge, that makes me speak."

"Flame-crowned," said Micon in softly ringing tones, "thou wouldst not be woman, wert thou otherwise."

Deoris's eyes were thunderclouds: Micon used the familiar "thou," which Deoris herself rarely ventured—and Domaris did not seem offended, but pleased! Deoris felt she would choke with resentment.

Rajasta, his misgivings almost forgotten, smiled now on Domaris and Micon, vast approval in his eyes. How he loved them both! On Deoris, too, he turned affectionate eyes, for he loved her well, and only awaited the ripening of her nature to ask her to follow in her sister's footsteps as his Acolyte. Rajasta sensed unknown potentialities in the fledgling woman, and, if it were possible, he greatly desired to guide her; but as yet Deoris was far too young.

Domaris, sensitive to his thought, rose and went to her sister, to drop with slender grace at her side. "Put up thy work, little sister, and listen," she whispered, "and learn. I have. And—I love thee, puss—very dearly."

Deoris, comforted, snuggled into the clasp of her sister's

arm; Domaris was rarely so demonstrative, and the unexpected caress filled her with joy. Domaris thought, with self-reproach, *Poor baby, she's lonely, I've been neglecting her so! But Micon needs me now! There will be time for her later, when I am sure . . .*

"—and still you know nothing of my half-brother?" Micon was asking, unhappily. "His fate is heavy on me, Rajasta; I feel that he still lives, but I know, I *know* that all is not well with him, wherever he may be."

"I shall make further inquiries," Rajasta promised, and loosed Micon's quiet hands at last, so that the Atlantean would not sense the half-deception in the words. Rajasta would ask—but he had little hope of learning anything about the missing Reio-ta.

"If he be but half-brother to thee, Micon," Domaris said, and her lovely voice was even softer than usual, "then he must find the Way of Love."

"I find that way not easy," Micon demurred gently. "To think always and only with compassion and understanding is —a difficult discipline."

Rajasta murmured, "Thou art a Son of Light, and hast attained—"

"Little!" An undertone of rebellion sounded clear in the Atlantean's resonant voice. "I was to be—Healer, and serve my fellows. Now I am nothing, and the service remains to be met."

For a long moment, all were silent, and Micon's tragedy stood stark in the forefront of every mind. Domaris resolved that every comfort of mind and body, every bit of service and love that was hers to give, should be given, no matter what the cost.

Deoris spoke at last, quietly but aggressively. "Lord Micon," she said, "you show us all how a man may bear misfortune, and be more than man. Is that wasted, then?"

Her temerity made Rajasta frown; at the same time, he inwardly applauded her sentiment, for it closely matched his own.

Micon pressed her small fingers lightly in his. "My little Deoris," he said gravely, "fortune and misfortune, worth and waste, these values are not for men to judge. I have set many causes in motion, and all men reap as they have sown. Whether a man meets good or evil lies with the Gods who have determined his fate, but every man—" His face twisted briefly in a smile. "And every woman, too, is free to make fortune or misfortune of the stuff that has been allotted him." The Atlantean's full, glorious smile came back, and he turned his head from Rajasta to Domaris in that odd gesture that gave almost the effect of sight. "You can say whether there is no good thing that has come of all this!"

Rajasta bowed his head. "My very great good, Son of Light."

"And mine, also," said Micon softly.

Deoris, surprise shadowed in her eyes, watched with vague discontent, and a jealousy even more vague. She drew her hand from Micon's light clasp, saying, "You don't want me any more today, do you, Lord Micon?"

Domaris said instantly, "Run along, Deoris, I can read if Micon wishes it." Jealousy never entered her head, but she resented anything which took Micon from her.

"But I must have a word with you, Domaris," Rajasta interposed firmly. "Leave Micon and the little scribe to their work, and you, Domaris, come with me."

II

The woman rose, sobered by the implied rebuke in Rajasta's tone, and went silently along the path at his side. Her eyes turned back for a moment to seek her lover, who had not moved; only now his bent head and his smile were for Deoris, who curled up at his feet: Domaris heard the clear ripple of her little sister's laughter.

Rajasta looked down at the shining crown of Domaris's hair, and sighed. Before he had made up his mind how to speak, Domaris felt the Priest's eyes, grave and kind but more serious than usual, bent upon her, and raised her face.

"Rajasta, I love him," she said simply.

The words, and the restraint of the emotion behind them, almost unmanned the Priest, disarming his intended rebuke. He laid his hands on her shoulders and looked down into her face, not with the severity he had planned, but with fatherly affection. "I know, daughter," he said softly. "I am glad. But you are in danger of forgetting your duty."

"My duty?" she repeated, perplexed. As yet she had no duties within the Priest's Caste, save for her studies.

Rajasta understood her confusion, but he knew also that she was evading self-knowledge. "Deoris, too, must be considered," he pointed out. "She, too, has need of you."

"But—Deoris knows I love her," Domaris protested.

"Does she, my Acolyte?" He spoke the term deliberately, in an attempt to recall her position to her mind. "Or does she feel that you have pushed her away, let Micon absorb all your attention?"

"She can't—she wouldn't—oh, I never meant to!" Reviewing in her mind the happenings of the last few weeks, Domaris found the reproof just. Characteristically, she responded to her training and gave her mentor's words strict attention, emblazoning them upon her mind and heart. After a time, she raised her eyes again, and this time they were shadowed with deep remorse. "Acquit me, at least, of intentional selfishness," she begged. "She is so dear and so close that she is like a part of myself, and I forget her concerns are not always as my own. . . . I have been negligent; I shall try to correct—"

"If it be not already too late." A shadow of deep trouble darkened the Priest's eyes. "Deoris may love you never the less, but will she ever trust you as much?"

Domaris's lovely eyes were clouded. "If Deoris no longer trusts me, I must accept the fault as mine," she said. "The Gods grant it be not too late. I have neglected my first responsibility."

And yet she knew she had been powerless to do otherwise, nor could she truly regret her exclusive concern with Micon. Rajasta sighed again as he followed her thoughts. It was hard to reprove her for a fault which was equally his own.

Chapter Five

THE SECRET CROWN

I

The rains were almost upon them. On one of the last sunny days they might reasonably expect, Domaris and Elis, with Deoris and her friend Ista, a scribe like herself, went to gather flowers; the House of the Twelve was to be decorated by the Acolytes for a minor festival that night.

They found a field of blossoms atop a hill overlooking the seashore. Faintly, from afar, came the salt smell of rushes and seaweed left by the receding tide; the scent of sweet grass, sun-parched, hung close about them, intermingled with the heavy, heady, honey-sweet of flowers.

Elis had Lissa with her. The baby was over a year old now, and scampering everywhere, to pull up flowers and trample in them, tumble the baskets and tear at skirts, until Elis grew quite exasperated.

Deoris, who adored the baby, snatched her up in her arms. "I'll keep her, Elis, I've enough flowers now."

"I've enough, too," said Domaris, and laid down her fragrant burden. She brushed a hand over her damp forehead. The sun was near-blinding even when one did not look toward it, and she felt dizzy with the heavy sickishness of breathing the mixed salt and sweet smells. Gathering her baskets of flowers together, she sat down in the grass beside Deoris, who had Lissa on her knees and was tickling her as she murmured some nonsensical croon.

"You're like a little girl playing with a doll, Deoris."

Deoris's small features tightened into a smile that was not quite a smile. "But I never liked dolls," she said.

"No." Her sister's smile was reminiscent, her eyes turned fondly on Lissa more than Deoris. "You wanted your babies alive, like this one."

Slender, raven-haired Ista dropped cross-legged on the grass, jerked at her brief skirts, and began delicately to plait the flowers from her basket. Elis watched for a minute, then tossed an armful of white and crimson blooms into Ista's basket. "My garlands are always coming untied," Elis explained. "Weave mine too, and ask me any favor you will."

Ista's dexterous fingers did not hesitate as she went on tying the stems. "I will do it, and gladly, and Deoris will help me—won't you, Deoris? But scribes work only for love, and not for favors."

Deoris gave Lissa a final squeeze and put her into Domaris's arms; then, drawing a basket toward her, began weaving the flowers into dainty festoons. Elis bent and watched them. "Shameful," she murmured, laughing, "that I must learn the Temple laws from two scribes!"

She threw herself down in the grass beside Domaris. From a nearby bush, she plucked a handful of ripe golden berries, put one into her own mouth, then fed the others, one by one, to the bouncing, crowing Lissa, who sat on Domaris's knees, plastering them both with juicy kisses and staining Domaris's light robe with berry juice. Domaris snuggled Lissa close to her, with a queer hungriness. *But my baby will be a son,* she thought proudly, *a straight little son, with dark-blue eyes. . . .*

Elis looked sharply at her cousin. "Domaris, are you ill—or only daydreaming?"

The older woman pulled her braid of coppery hair free from Lissa's fat, insistent fingers. "A little dizzy from the sun," she said, and gave Lissa to her mother. Once again she made a deliberate effort to stop thinking, to give up the persistent thought that the form of words, even in her own mind, might make untrue. *Perhaps this time, though, it* is *true. . . .* For weeks, she had secretly suspected that she now bore Micon's son. And yet, once before, her own wish and her own hope had betrayed her into mentioning a false suspicion which had ended in disappointment. This time she was resolved to be silent, even to Micon, until she was sure beyond all possible doubt.

Deoris, glancing up from her flowers, dropped her garland and leaned toward Domaris, her eyes wide and anxious. The change in Domaris had struck the world from under Deoris's feet. She knew she had lost her sister, and was ready to blame everyone: she was jealous of Arvath, of Elis, of Micon, and above all at times of Rajasta. Domaris, wrapped in the profound anesthesia of her love, saw nothing, really, of the child's misery; she only knew that Deoris was exasperatingly dependent these days. Her causeless childish clinging drove Domaris almost frantic. Why couldn't Deoris behave sensibly and leave her alone? Sometimes, without meaning it—for Domaris, although quick to irritation, and now tense with nervous strain, was never deliberately unkind—she wounded Deoris to the quick with a single careless word, only seeing what she had done when it was too late, if at all.

This time the tension slackened: Elis had taken Lissa, and the baby was pulling insistently at her mother's dress. Elis laughed, wrinkling her nose in pretended annoyance. "Little greedy pig, I know what she wants. I'm glad there are only a few months more of this nonsense!" She was unfastening her robe as she spoke, and gave Lissa a playful spank as the baby caught at her breast. "Then, little Mistress Mine, you must learn to eat like a lady!"

Deoris averted her eyes in something like disgust. "How do you endure it?" she asked.

Elis laughed merrily without troubling to answer; her complaints had been only in jest, and she thought Deoris's question equally frivolous. Babies were always nursed for two full years, and only an overworked slave-woman or a prostitute would have dreamed of shirking the full time of suckling.

Elis leaned back, cradling Lissa on her arm, and picked another handful of berries. "You sound like Chedan, Deoris! I sometimes think he hates my poor baby! Still—" She made a comical face and thrust another berry between her lips. "Sometimes I wonder, when she *bites* me—"

"And you will no sooner wean her," Ista remarked with gleeful gravity, "than she will begin to shed her baby teeth."

Domaris frowned: she alone knew that Deoris had not been joking. Lissa's eyes were closed, now, in sleepy contentment, and her face, a pink petal framed in sunny curls, lay like a curled bud on her mother's breast. Domaris felt a sudden stab of longing so great that it was almost pain. Elis, raising her eyes, met Domaris's glance; the intuitive wisdom of their caste was especially strong in Elis, and the girl guessed at a story that closely paralleled her own. Reaching her free hand to her cousin, Elis gave the narrow fingers a little squeeze; Domaris returned the pressure, furtively, grateful for the implied understanding.

"Little nuisance," crooned Elis, rocking the sleepy baby. "Fat little elf . . ."

The sun wavered, hiding itself behind a bank of cloud. Deoris and Ista nodded over their flower-work, still drowsily tying stems. Domaris suddenly shivered; then her whole body froze, tense, in an attitude of stilled, incredulous listening. And once again it came, somewhere deep inside her body, a faint and indescribable fluttering like nothing she had ever felt before, but unmistakable, like the beating of prisoned wings —it came and went so swiftly that she was hardly sure what she had felt. And yet she *knew*.

"What's the matter?" Elis asked in a low voice, and Domaris realized that she was still holding Elis's hand, but that her fingers had tightened, crushing her cousin's fingers together painfully. She let go of Elis, drawing back her hand quickly and in apology—but she did not speak, and her other hand remained resting lightly and secretly against her body, where once again that little instantaneous fluttering came and went and then was stilled. Domaris remembered to breathe; but she stayed very still, unable to think beyond that final, unmistakable surety that the concealed secret was now a confirmable truth, that there within her womb Micon's son—she dared not think that it was other than a son—stirred to life.

Deoris's eyes, large and somewhat afraid, met her sister's, and the expression in them was too much for the taut Domaris. She began to laugh, at first softly, then uncontrollably—because she dared not cry, she *would not* cry. . . . The laughter became hysterical, and Domaris scrambled to her feet and fled down the hill toward the seashore, leaving the three girls to stare at one another.

Deoris half rose, but Elis, on an intuitive impulse, pulled her back. "She would rather be alone for a while, I think. Here, hold Lissa for me, won't you, while I fasten my dress!" She plumped the baby into Deoris's lap, and carefully knotted the fastenings of her dress, taking her time, to avert a minor crisis.

II

At the edge of the salt-marshes, Domaris flung herself full-length into the long grass and lay hidden there, her face against the pungent earth, her hands clasped across her body in a wonder that was half fright. She lay moveless, feeling the long grasses wavering with the wind, her thoughts trembling as they did, but without stirring the surface of her mind. She was afraid to think clearly.

Noon paled and retreated, and Domaris, raising herself as if by instinct, saw Micon walking slowly along the shore. She got to her feet, her hair tumbling loose about her waist, her dress billowing in the wind, and began to run toward him on impatient feet. Hearing the quick, uneven steps, he stopped.

"Micon!"

"Domaris—where are you?" His blind face turned to follow the sound of her voice, and she darted to him, pausing —no longer even regretful that she could not throw herself into his arms—a careful step away, and lightly touching his arm, raised her face for his kiss.

His lips lingered an instant longer than usual; then he withdrew his face a little and murmured, "Heart of flame, you are excited. You bring news."

"I bring news." Her voice was softly triumphant, but failed her. She took the racked hands lightly in her own and pressed them softly against her body, begging him to understand without being told. . . . Perhaps he read her thoughts; perhaps he only guessed from the gesture. Whichever it may have been, his face grew bright with an inner brilliance, and his arms went out to gather her close.

"You bring light," he whispered, and kissed her again.

She hid her face on his breast. "It is sure now, beloved. This time it is sure! I have guessed it for weeks, and I would not speak of it, for fear that—but now there is no doubt! He—*our son*—stirred today!"

"Domaris—beloved—" The man's voice choked, and she felt burning tears drop from the blind eyes onto her face. His hands, usually so sternly controlled, trembled so violently that he could not raise them to hers, and as she held herself to him, loving him and almost drowning in the intensity of this love so closely akin to worship, she felt Micon's trembling as even a strong tree will tremble a little before a hurricane.

"My beloved, my blessed one . . ." With a reverence that hurt and frightened the girl, Micon dropped to his knees, in the sand, and managed to clasp her two hands, pressing them to his cheeks, his lips. "Bearer of Light, it is my life you hold, my freedom," he whispered.

"Micon! I love you, I love you," the girl stammered incoherently—because there was nothing else that she could possibly have said.

The Initiate rose, his control somewhat regained, though still trembling slightly, and gently dried her tears. "Domaris," he said, with tender gravity, "I—there is no way to tell you— I mean, I will try, but—" His mouth took on an even greater seriousness, and the twist of pain and regret and uncertainty there was like knives in Domaris's heart.

"Domaris," he said, and his voice rang in the deep and practiced tones that she recognized as the Atlantean's oath-voice. "I will—try," he promised solemnly, "to stay with you until our son is born."

And Domaris knew that she had pronounced the beginning of the end.

Chapter Six

IN THE SISTERHOOD

I

The Temple of Caratra, which overlooked the Shrine and the holy pool, was one of the most beautiful buildings of the entire Temple precinct. It was fashioned of milky stone, veined with shimmering, opalescent fires in the heart of the rock. Long gardens, linked by palisaded arbors covered with trailing vines, surrounded pool and Temple; cool fountains splashed in the courts where a profusion of flowers bloomed the year round.

Within these white and glistening walls, every child of the Temple was born, whether child to slave-maiden or to the High Priestess. Here, also, every young girl within the Temple was sent to render service in her turn (for all women owed service to the Mother of All Men); in assisting the Priestesses, in caring for the mothers and for the newly born, even (if she was of a satisfactory rank in the Priest's Caste) in learning the secrets of bringing children to birth. And every year thereafter she spent a certain assigned period—ranging from a single day for slave women and commoners, to an entire month for Acolytes and Priestesses—living and serving in the Temple of the Mother; and from this assigned yearly service, not the humblest slave nor the highest Initiate was ever exempted.

Over a year before, Deoris had been adjudged old enough to enter upon her time of service; but a severe, though brief, attack of fever had intervened, and somehow her name had been passed over. Now her name was called again; but although most of the young girls of the Priest's Caste looked on this service rather eagerly, as a sign of their own oncoming womanhood, it was with reluctance bordering on rebellion that Deoris made her preparations.

Once—almost two years earlier, at the time of her first approach to the Shrine—she had been given her initial lesson in the delivery of a baby. The experience had bewildered her. She dreaded a recurrence of the questions it raised in her mind. She had seen the straining effort, and the agony, and had been revolted at the seeming cruelty of it all—though she had also witnessed, after all that, the ecstatic welcome that the mother had given the tiny mite of humanity. Beyond the puzzlement she had felt at this contradictory behaviour, Deoris had been dismayed at her own feelings: the bitter hurt that she too must one day be woman and lie there in her turn, struggling to bring forth life. The eternal *"Why?"* beat incessantly at her brain. Now, when she had almost managed to forget, it would be before her again.

"I can't, I won't," she burst out in protest to Micon. "It's cruel—horrible—"

"Hush, Deoris." The Atlantean reached for her nervously twisting hands, catching and holding them despite his blindness. "Do you not know that to live is to suffer, and to bring life is to suffer?" He sighed, a faint and restrained sound. "I think pain is the law of life . . . and if you can help, dare you refuse?"

"I don't dare—but I wish I did! Lord Micon, you don't know what it's like!"

Checking his first impulse to laugh at her naivete, Micon reassured her, gently, "But I do know. I wish I could help you to understand, Deoris; but there are things everyone must learn alone—"

Deoris, flushed and appalled, choked out the question, "But how *can* you know—that?" In the world of the Temple, childbirth was strictly an affair for women, and to Deoris, whose whole world was the Temple, it seemed impossible that a man could know anything of the complexities of birth. Was it not everywhere a rigid, unalterable custom that no man might approach a childbed? No one, surely, could imagine this ultimate indecency! How could Micon, fortunate enough to have been born a man, even guess at it?

Micon could no longer restrain himself; his laughter only served to bruise Deoris's feelings even more. "Why, Deoris," he said, "men are not so ignorant as you think!" As her hurt silence dragged on, he tried to amend his statement. "Our customs in Atlantis are not like yours, child—you must remember—" He let an indulgent, teasing tone creep into his voice. "You must remember what barbarians we are in the Sea Kingdoms! And believe me, not all men are in ignorance, even here. And—my child, do you think I know nothing of pain?" He hesitated for a moment; could this be the right moment to tell Deoris that her sister bore his child? Instinct told him that Deoris, wavering on the balance between acceptance and rejection, might be swayed in the right direction by the knowledge. Yet it seemed to him it was Domaris's right, not his, to speak or be silent. His words blurred in sudden weariness. "Darling, I wish I could help you. Try to remember this: to live, you need every experience. Some will come in glory and in beauty, and some in pain and what seems like ugliness. But—they *are*. Life consists of opposites in balance."

Deoris sighed, impatient with the pious repetition—she had heard it before. Domaris, too, had failed her. She had tried, really tried, to make Domaris understand; Domaris had only looked at her, uncomprehending, and said, "But every woman must do that service."

"But it's so awful!" Deoris had wailed.

Domaris, stern-eyed, advised her not to be a silly little girl; that it was the way of nature, and that no one could change it. Deoris had stammered on, inclined to beg, cry, plead, convinced that Domaris *could* change it, if she only would.

Domaris had been greatly displeased: "You are being very childish! I've spoilt you, Deoris, and tried to protect you. I know now that I did wrong. You are not a child any longer. You must learn to take a woman's responsibilities."

II

Deoris was now fifteen. The Priestesses took it for granted that she had, like most girls of that age, completed the simpler preliminary tasks allotted to those who were serving for the first or second time. Too shy and too miserable to correct their mistake, Deoris found herself assigned an advanced task: as befitted a girl of her age who was the daughter of a Priest, she was sent to assist one of the midwife-Priestesses, a woman who was also a Healer of Riveda's Order; her name was Karahama.

Karahama was not of the Priest's Caste. She was the daughter of a Temple servant who, before her daughter was born, had claimed to be with child by Talkannon himself. Talkannon, then recently married to the highly-born Priestess who later became the mother of Deoris and Domaris, had most uncharacteristically refused to acknowledge the child. He admitted intimacy with the woman, but claimed that it was by no means sure that he was the father of her unborn child, and produced other men who had, in his opinion and theirs, a better claim.

Under such flagrant proofs of misconduct, the Elders had admitted that no one could be forced to acknowledge the child. The woman, stripped of her privileges as a Temple servant, was given only a minimum of shelter until the birth of her daughter, and then dismissed from the Temple altogether. Man and woman were free to live as they would before marriage, but promiscuity could not be tolerated.

The child Karahama, casteless and nameless, had been taken into the Grey-robe sect as one of their *saji*—and had grown up the very image of Talkannon. Eventually, of course, the Arch-Priest became aware of the jeers of the Temple slaves, the concealed gossip of his juniors. It was indeed a choice bit of scandal that the Temple's Arch-Priest should have a small replica of himself among the worst outcasts in the Temple. In self-defense, he at last succumbed to popular opinion. After doing lengthy penance for his error, he legally adopted Karahama.

As the Grey-robes had no caste laws, Karahama had been accepted by Riveda as a Healer-Priestess. Restored by Talkannon to her rightful caste and name, she had chosen to enter the Temple of Caratra, and was now an Initiate, entitled to wear the blue robe—a dignity as high as any in the Temple. No one could scorn or spit on the "nameless one" any more, but Karahama's uncertain beginnings had made her temperament a strange and uncertain thing.

At the realization that this girl assigned to her guidance was her own half-sister, Karahama felt oddly mixed emotions, which were soon resolved in Deoris's favor. Karahama's own children, born before her reclamation, were outcasts, nameless as she herself had been, and for them nothing could be done. Perhaps this was why Karahama tried to be particularly kind and friendly to this young and almost unknown kinswoman. But she knew that sooner or later she would have trouble with this child, whose sullen rebellion smouldered unspoken behind scared violet eyes, and whose work was carefully deliberate, as if Deoris made every movement against her will. Karahama thought this a great pity, for Deoris obviously had all the qualities of a born Healer: steady hands and a keen observation, a deft sure gentleness, a certain instinct for pain. Only the will was lacking—and Karahama quickly resolved that somehow she must make it her duty to find the hidden thing in Deoris which would win her over to the service of the Mother.

She thought she had found it when Arkati came to the House of Birth.

Arkati was the girl-wife of one of the Priests, a pretty thing scarcely out of childhood; younger, in fact, than Deoris herself. A fair-skinned, fair-haired, diminutive girl with sweet pleading eyes, Arkati had been brought to the Temple of Caratra a few weeks before the proper time, because she was not well; her heart had been damaged by a childhood illness, and they wished to strengthen her before her child was born. All of them, even the stern Karahama, treated the girl with tenderness, but Arkati was weak and homesick and would cry at nothing.

She and Deoris, it soon turned out, had known one another since childhood. Arkati clung to Deoris like a lost kitten.

Karahama used influence, and Deoris was given what freedom she wished to spend with Arkati. She noticed with pleasure that Deoris had a good instinct for caring for the sick girl; she followed Karahama's instructions with good sense and good judgment, and it seemed as if Deoris's hard rebellion gave the girl-mother strength. But there was restraint in their friendship, born of Deoris's fear.

More than fear, it was a positive horror. Wasn't Arkati afraid at all? She never tired of dreaming and making plans and talking about her baby; she accepted all the inconveniences, sickness and weariness, unthinkingly, even with laughter. How could she? Deoris did not know, and was afraid to ask.

Once, Arkati took Deoris's hand in hers, and put it against her swollen body, hard; and Deoris felt under her hand an odd movement, a sensation which filled her with an emotion she

could not analyze. Not knowing whether what she felt was
pleasure or acute annoyance, she jerked her hand roughly
away.

"What's wrong?" Arkati laughed. "Don't you like my
baby?"

Somehow this custom, speaking of an unborn child as if already a person, made Deoris uncomfortable. "Don't be foolish," she said roughly—but for the first time in her entire life,
she was consciously thinking of her own mother, the mother
they said had been gentle and gracious and lovely, and very
like Domaris, and who had died when Deoris was born.
Drowned in guilt, Deoris remembered that she had killed her
mother. Was that why Domaris resented her now?

She said nothing of all this, only attended to what she was
taught with a determination born of anger; and within a few
days Karahama saw, with surprise, that Deoris was already beginning to show something like skill, a deftness and intuitive
knowledge that seemed to equal years of experience. When the
ordinary term of service was ended, Karahama asked her—
rather diffidently, it is true—to stay on for another month in
the Temple, working directly with Karahama herself.

Somewhat to her own surprise, Deoris agreed, telling herself
that she had simply promised to Arkati to remain with her as
long as possible. Not even to herself would she admit that she
was beginning to enjoy the feeling of mastery which this work
gave her.

III

Arkati's child was born on a rainy night when will-o'-the-
wisps flitted on the seashore, and the wind wailed an ominous
litany. Karahama had no cause to complain of Deoris, but
somewhere in the dark hours the injured heart ceased to beat,
and the fight—pitifully brief, after all—ended in tragedy. At
sunrise, a newborn child wailed without knowing why, in an
upper room of the Temple, and Deoris, sick to the bone, lay
sobbing bitterly in her own room, her head buried in her
pillows, trying to shut out memory of the sounds and sights
that would haunt her in nightmares for the rest of her life.

"You mustn't lie here and cry!" Karahama bent over her,
then sat down at her side, gathering up Deoris's hands in hers.
Another girl came into the little dormitory, but Karahama

curtly motioned her to leave them alone, and continued, "Deoris, listen to me, child. There was nothing we could have done for—"

Deoris's sobs mixed with incoherent words.

Karahama frowned. "That is foolishness. The child did not kill her! Her heart stopped; you know she has never been strong. Besides—" Karahama bent closer and said, in her gently resolute voice, so like Domaris's and yet so different, "You are a daughter of the Temple. We know Death's true face, a doorway to further life, and not something to be feared—"

"Oh, leave me alone!" Deoris wailed miserably.

"By no means," said Karahama firmly. Self-pity was not in her category of permitted emotions, and she had no sympathy with the involved reasoning that made Deoris curl herself up into a forlorn little huddle and want to be left alone. "Arkati is not to be pitied! So stop crying for yourself. Get up; bathe and dress yourself properly, and then go and tend Arkati's little daughter. She is your responsibility until her father may claim her, and also you must say protective spells over her, to guard her from the imps who snatch motherless children—"

Rebelliously, Deoris did as she was told, assuming the dozen responsibilities which must be taken: arranging for a wet-nurse, signing the child with protective runes, and—because a child's true name was a sacred secret, written on the rolls of the Temple but never spoken aloud except in ritual—Deoris gave the child the "little name" by which she would be called until she was grown: *Miritas*. The baby squirmed feebly in her arms, and Deoris thought, with unhappy contempt, *Protective spells! Where was the spell that could have saved Arkati?*

Karahama watched stoically, more grieved than she would say. They had all known that Arkati would not live; she had been warned, when she married, that she should not attempt to bear a child, and the Priestesses had given her runes and spells and arcane teachings to prevent this. Arkati had willfully disobeyed their counsel, and had paid for this disobedience with her life. Now there was another motherless child to be fostered.

But Karahama had known something else, for she understood Deoris better even than Domaris. Unlike as they were, both Deoris and Karahama had inherited from Talkannon a rugged and stubborn determination. Resentment, more than triumph, would spur Deoris on; hating pain and death, she would vow to conquer it. Where being forced to witness such a tragedy might have lost another neophyte, driving her away in revulsion, Karahama felt that this would place a decisive hand on Deoris.

Karahama said nothing more, however; she was wise enough to let the knowledge ripen slowly. When all had been done for the newborn child, Karahama told Deoris that she might be excused from other duties for the remainder of the day. "You have had no sleep," she added dryly, when Deoris would have thanked her. "Your hands and eyes would have no skill. Mind that you rest!"

Deoris promised, in a strained voice; but she did not ascend the stairway to the dormitory reserved for the women who were serving their season in the Temple. Instead, she slipped out by a side entrance, and ran toward the House of the Twelve, with only one thought in her mind—the lifelong habit of carrying all her sorrows to Domaris. Her sister would certainly understand her now, she *must!*

A summer wind was blowing, moist with the promise of more rain; Deoris hugged her scarf closely about her neck and shoulders, and ran wildly across the lawns. Turning a sharp corner she almost tumbled against the stately form of Rajasta, who was coming from the House. Barely pausing to recover her balance, Deoris stammered breathless words of apology and would have run on, but Rajasta detained her gently.

"Look to your steps, dear child, you will injure yourself," he cautioned, smiling. "Domaris tells me you have been serving in Caratra's Temple. Have you finished with your service there?"

"No, I am only dismissed for the day." Deoris spoke civilly, but twitched with impatience. Rajasta did not seem to notice.

"That service will bring you wisdom and understanding, little daughter," he counselled. "It will make a woman of a child." He laid his hand for a moment, in blessing, on the tangled, feathering curls. "May peace and enlightenment follow thy footsteps, Deoris."

IV

In the House of Twelve, men and women mingled almost promiscuously, in a brother-and-sisterly innocence, fostered by the fact that all Twelve had been brought up together. Deoris, whose more impressionable years had been spent in the stricter confines of the Scribe's School, was not yet accustomed to this freedom, and when, in the inner courtyard, she discovered some of the Acolytes splashing in the pool, she felt confused and—in her new knowledge—annoyed. She did not want to seek her sister among them. But Domaris had often cautioned her, with as much sternness as Domaris ever showed, that while Deoris lived among the Acolytes she must conform to their customs, and forget the absurd strictures forced upon the scribes.

Chedan saw Deoris first, and shouted for her to strip and bathe with them. A merry boy, the youngest of the Acolytes, he had from the first treated Deoris with a special friendliness and indulgence. Deoris shook her head, and the boy splashed her until her dress was sopping and she ran out of reach. Domaris, standing under the fountain, saw this exchange and called to Deoris to wait; then, wringing the water from her drenched hair, Domaris went toward the edge of the pool. Passing Chedan, his bare shoulders and turned back tempted her to mischief; she scooped up a handful of water and dashed it into his eyes. Before the retaliating deluge, she dodged and squealed and started to run—then, remembering that it was hardly wise to risk a fall just now, slowed her steps to a walk.

The water fell away in shallows, and Deoris, waiting, looked at her sister—and her eyes widened in amazement. She didn't believe what she saw. Abruptly, Deoris turned and fled, and did not hear Domaris cry out as Chedan and Elis, screaming with mirth, caught Domaris at the very edge of the pool and dragged her back into the water, ducking her playfully, threatening to fling her into the very center of the fountain. They thought she was playing when she struggled to free herself of their rough hands. Two or three of the girls joined in the fun, and their shrieks of laughter drowned her pleas for mercy, even when, genuinely scared, Domaris began to cry in earnest.

They had actually swung her free of the water when Elis suddenly seized their hands and cried out harshly, "Stop it, stop it, Chedan, Riva! Let her go—take your hands from her, now, at once!"

The tone of her voice shocked them into compliance: they lowered Domaris to her feet and released her, but they were still too wild with mirth to realize that Domaris was sobbing. "She started it," Chedan protested, and they stared in disbelief as Elis encircled the shaken girl with a protecting arm, and helped her to the rim of the pool. Always before, Domaris had been a leader in their rough games.

Still crying a little, Domaris clung helplessly to Elis as her cousin helped her out of the water. Elis picked up a robe and tossed it to Domaris. "Put this on before you take a chill," she said, sensibly. "Did they hurt you? You should have told us —stop shaking, Domaris, you're all right now."

Domaris wrapped herself obediently in the white woolen robe, glancing down ruefully at the contours emphasized so strongly by the crude drapery. "I wanted to keep it to myself just a little longer . . . now I suppose everyone will know."

Elis slid her wet feet into sandals, knotting the sash of her own robe. "Haven't you even told Deoris?"

Domaris shook her head silently as they arose and went toward the passageway leading to the women's apartments. In retrospect, Deoris's face, shocked and disbelieving, was sharp in her memory. "I meant to," Domaris murmured, "but—"

"Tell her, right away," Elis ventured to advise, "before she hears it as gossip from someone else. But be gentle, Domaris. Arkati died last night."

They paused before Domaris's door, Domaris whispering distractedly, "Oh, what a pity!" She herself had barely known Arkati, but she knew Deoris loved her, and now—now, in such sorrow, Deoris could not come to see her without receiving a further shock.

Elis turned away, but over her shoulder she flung back, "Yes, and have a little more care for yourself! We could have hurt you badly—and suppose Arvath had been there?" Her door slammed.

V

While Elara dried and dressed her, and braided her wet hair, Domaris sat lost in thought, staring at nothing. There might be trouble with Arvath—no one knew that better than Domaris— but she could not spare any worry about that now. She had, as yet, no duty toward him; she acted within her rights under the law. Deoris was a more serious matter, and Domaris reproached herself for neglect. Somehow she must make Deoris understand. Warm and cozy after Elara's ministrations, she curled up on a divan and awaited her sister's return.

It was, in fact, not very long before Deoris returned, sullen fires burning a hectic warning in her cheeks. Domaris smiled at her joyously. "Come here, darling," she said, and held out her arms. "I have something wonderful to tell you."

Deoris, wordless, knelt and caught her sister close, in such a violent embrace that Domaris was dismayed, feeling the taut trembling of the thin shoulders. "Why, Deoris, Deoris," she protested, deeply distressed; and then, although she hated to, she had to add, "Hold me not so tightly, little sister— you'll hurt me—you can hurt us both, now." She smiled as she said it, but Deoris jerked away as if Domaris had struck her.

"It's true, then!"

"Why yes—yes, darling, you saw it when I came from the pool. You are a big girl now, I felt sure you would know without being told."

Deoris gripped her sister's wrist in a painful grasp, which Domaris endured without flinching. "No, Domaris! It can't be! Tell me you are jesting!" Deoris would disbelieve even the evidence of her own eyes, if Domaris would only deny it.

"I would not jest of a sacred trust, Deoris," the woman said, and a deep sincerity gave bell-tones to the reproach in her voice, and the near-disappointment.

Deoris knelt, stricken, gazing up at Domaris and shaking as if with intense cold. "Sacred?" she whispered, choking. "You, a student, an Acolyte, under discipline—you gave it all up for *this?*"

Domaris, with her free hand, reached down and unclasped Deoris's frantic grip from her wrist. The white skin showed discolorations where the girl's fingers had almost met in the flesh.

Deoris, looking down almost without comprehension, suddenly lifted the bruised wrist in her palm and kissed it. "I didn't mean to hurt you, I—I didn't know what I was doing," she said, her breath catching with contrition. "Only I—I can't stand it, Domaris!"

The older girl touched her cheek gently. "I don't understand you, Deoris. What have I given up? I am still student, still discipline; Rajasta knows and has given his blessing."

"But—but this will bar you from Initiation—"

Domaris looked down at her in absolute bewilderment. Taking Deoris's resisting hand in hers, by main force she pulled her up on the divan, saying, "Who has put these bats into your brain, Deoris? I am still Priestess, still Acolyte, even if—no, because I am a woman! You have served in Caratra's Temple a month or more now, you should know better than that! Surely they have taught you that the cycles of womanhood and of the universe itself are attuned, that—" Domaris broke off, shaking her head with a light laugh. "You see, I even *sound* like Rajasta sometimes! Deoris, dear, as a woman—and even more as an Initiate—I must know fulfillment. Does one offer an empty vessel to the Gods?"

Deoris retorted hysterically, "Or one soiled by use?"

"But that's absurd!" Domaris smiled, but her eyes were sober. "I must find my place, to go with life and—" She laid her slender, ringed hands across her body with a protective gesture, and Deoris saw again, with a shudder, the faint, almost negligible rounding there. "—accept my destiny."

Deoris twisted away from her. "So does a cow accept destiny!" destiny!"

Domaris tried to laugh, but it came out as a sob.

Deoris moved close to her again and threw her arms around her sister. "Oh, Domaris, I'm hateful, I know it! All I do is hurt you, and I don't want to hurt you, I love you, but, this, this desecrates you! It's awful!"

"Awful? Why?" Domaris smiled, a little mournfully. "Well, it does not seem so to me. You needn't be afraid for me, darling, I have never felt stronger or happier. And as for desecration—" The smile was not so sad now, and she took Deoris's hand in hers again, to hold it once more against her body. "You silly child! As if *he* could desecrate me— Micon's son!"

"Micon?" Deoris's hand dropped away and she stared at Domaris in absolute bewilderment, repeating stupidly, *"Micon's son?"*

"Why, yes, Deoris—didn't you know? What did you think?"

Deoris did not answer, only staring at Domaris with a stunned fixity. Domaris felt the sob trembling at her lips again as she tried to smile, saying, "What's the matter, Deoris? Don't you like my baby?"

"OH!" Stung by a twinge of horrified memory, Deoris wailed again, "Oh *no!*" and fled, sobbing, hearing the grieved cries of her sister follow her.

Chapter Seven

WHAT THE STARS REVEALED

I

On a couch in her room, Domaris lay watching the play of the rainclouds across the valley. Long, low waves of cloud, deep grey tipped with white vapor like foam capping the waves of the sea, shifted in the wild winds as they drove across the sky, scattering arrows of sunshine across the face of Micon, who half reclined on a heap of cushions nearby, his useless hands in his lap, his dark quiet face at peace. The silence between them was charged with restfulness; the distant rumble of thunder and the faraway drumming of the stormy surf seemed to accentuate the shadowy comfort and coolness within the room.

They both sighed at the knock on the door, but as the tall shadow of Rajasta crossed the threshold, Domaris's annoyance vanished. She rose, still slender, still moving as lightly as a dancing palm, but the Priest detected a new dignity in her bearing as she crossed the room.

"Lord Rajasta, you have read the stars for my child!"

He smiled kindly as she drew him toward a seat by the windows. "Do you wish me to speak before Micon, then, my daughter?"

"I most certainly do wish it!"

At her emphatic tone, Micon raised his head inquiringly.

"What means this, heart-of-flame? I do not understand—what will you tell us of our child, my brother?"

"I see that *some* of our customs are unknown in Atlantis." Rajasta smiled pleasantly, and he added, lightly, "Forgive my satisfaction that I can, for a change, make you *my* disciple."

"You teach me much, Rajasta," Micon murmured soberly.

"You honor me, Son of the Sun." Rajasta paused a moment. "Briefly, then—among the Priest's Caste, before your son can be acknowledged—and this must be done as soon as possible—the hour of his conception must be determined, from your stars and those of his mother. In this way, we shall know the day and the hour of his birth, and we may give your coming child a suitable name."

"Before even being born?" Micon asked in astonishment.

"Would you have a child born *nameless?*" Rajasta's own amazement verged on the scandalized. "As the Initiator of Domaris, this task is mine—just as, before Domaris was born, I read the stars for her mother. She, too, was my Acolyte, and I knew that her daughter, although fathered by Talkannon, would be the true daughter of my own soul. It was I who gave her the name of Isarma."

"Isarma?" Micon frowned in confusion. "I don't—"

Domaris laughed gleefully. "Domaris is but my baby name," she explained. "When I marry—" Her face changed abruptly, but she went on, in an even voice, "I shall use my true Temple name, Isarma. In our language that means *a doorway to brightness.*"

"So you have been to me, beloved," Micon murmured. "And Deoris?"

"Deoris means only—*little kitten*. She seemed no bigger than a kitten, and I called her so." Domaris glanced at Rajasta; to discuss one's own true name was permissible, but it was not common practice to speak of another's. The Priest of Light only nodded, however, and Domaris continued, "Her true name on the rolls of the Temple is Adsartha; *child of the Warrior Star.*"

Micon shuddered, a convulsive shiver that seemed to tear at his whole body. "In the name of all the Gods, why such a name of cruel omen for your sweet little sister?"

Rajasta's aspect was grave. "I do not know, for I did not read her stars; I was in seclusion at the time. I always meant to confer with Mahaliel, but—" Rajasta broke off. "This I know," he said, after a moment. "She was conceived upon the Nadir-night, and her mother, dying only a few hours after Deoris was born, told me almost with her last breath, that Deoris was foredoomed to much suffering." Rajasta paused again, regretful that in the rush of events following Deoris's birth he had not made time to inquire of Mahaliel, who had been greatly skilled; but the old Priest was many years dead now, and could be of no help anymore. Drawing a deep breath, Rajasta resumed, "And so we guard our little Deoris so tenderly, that her sorrows may be lessened by our love, and her weakness nurtured by our strength—although I sometimes think too much care does not diminish weakness enough—"

Domaris cried out impatiently, "Enough of all these omens and portents! Rajasta, tell me, shall I bear my lord a son?"

Rajasta smiled and forbore to rebuke her impatience, for indeed it was a subject he was happy to set aside. He drew from his robes a scroll covered with figures which Domaris could not read, although he had taught her to count and to write the sacred numbers. For everyday counting, everyone but the very highest Initiates reckoned on their fingers; numbers were the most sacredly guarded mystery, and were never used lightly or for any frivolous purpose, for by them Priests read the movements of the stars and reckoned the days and years on their great calendar-stones—even as the Adepts, through the sacred numbers, manipulated the natural forces which were the source of their power. In addition to the cryptic figures and their permutations, Rajasta had drawn the simpler symbols of the Houses of the Sky—and with these Domaris, as an Acolyte of the Twelve, was familiar; to these, therefore, he referred as he spoke.

"At such a time, in the Sign of the Scales, were you born, Domaris. Here, under the House of the Carrier, is Micon's day of birth. I will not read all of this now," Rajasta said, in an aside to the Atlantean, who stirred with interest, "but if you truly wish, I will read it to you later. At present, I am sure, the primary interest to you both is the date upon which your child will be born."

He went on, pedantically, to give himself opportunity to ignore the overtones in their voices as they murmured happily to one another, "In such an hour, so your stars tell me, under the signs of the moon which regulate these things in women, your womb must have received the seed of life—and on such a day," he tapped the chart, "in the sign of the Scorpion, you will be brought to bed of a son—if my calculations are perfectly correct."

"A son!" Domaris cried out in triumph.

But Micon looked troubled.

"Not—on the Nadir-night?"

"I trust not," Rajasta reassured him, "but surely soon thereafter. In any case, remember that the Nadir-night brings not only evil. As I have told you, Deoris was conceived upon the Nadir-night, and she is as clever and dear a child as one could desire. With the balancing effects of your child's conception date falling so closely between your birthdate and that of Domaris—"

Rajasta rattled on soothingly like this for a little while, and Micon showed definite signs of relief which, in truth, Rajasta did not altogether share. The Priest of Light had puzzled over this chart for many hours, troubled by the knowledge that Micon's son might, indeed, be born on that night of evil omen. Try as he had, though, Rajasta had been unable to wholly exclude this possibility, for it had proven impossible to fix the time of conception with any exactness. *Had I only instructed Domaris more completely,* he now thought, not for the first time, *she herself would have been able to determine the proper time!*

"In fact," Rajasta ended, with just the proper note of amused tolerance for parental worryings, "I should say the worst thing you have to fear for your son-to-be is that he will be perhaps over-fond of contests and strifes, and be sharp-tongued, as Scorpions often are." He put the chart aside, deliberately. "Nothing that proper instruction during his youth cannot correct. I have other news, as well, my daughter," he said, smiling at Domaris. She was, he thought, lovelier than ever; something of the glow and sanctity of motherhood was already in her face, a radiant joy undimmed by the shadow of grief. Yet that shadow lay there already, a menace formless as yet, but discernible even to the relatively unimaginative Rajasta, and the Priest felt a surge of protectiveness.

"The time has come when I may give thee work for the Temple," Rajasta said. "Thou art woman, no longer incomplete." Catching the expression of fleeting disquiet in Micon's face, he hastened to reassure him. "Have no fear, my brother. I will not permit her to exhaust herself. She is safe with me."

"Of that I have no doubt," said Micon, quietly.

Rajasta returned his attention to Domaris, whose thoughtful expression was tinged with a great curiosity. "Domaris—what know you of the Guardians?"

She hesitated to answer, considering. Rajasta himself, Guardian of the Outer Gates, was the only Guardian ever named in public. There were others, of course, but no one in the Temple knew their names, or even for certain that there were no more than the seven who sat veiled in Council on high occasions. A sudden suspicion widened her eyes.

Rajasta went on, without waiting for her answer, "My beloved daughter, you yourself have been chosen Guardian of the Second Circle, successor to Ragamon the Elder—who will remain at his post to teach and instruct thee until thou art mature in wisdom. You will be pledged to this duty as soon as your child has been acknowledged—although," he added, with another smile in Micon's direction, 'this will entail no arduous duties until you have fulfilled your responsibilities to the coming child. And, as I know women—" His face was filled with tender indulgence as he regarded his young Acolyte. "—the acknowledgment of your son will take precedence over the greater ceremony!"

Domaris lowered her eyes, color staining her cheeks. She knew that if she had received this high honor at any other time, she would have been almost overcome by the thought; now it seemed remote, a vague secondary consideration beside the thought of the ceremony which would admit her child into the life of the Temple. "It is even so," she admitted.

Rajasta's smile was a benediction. "No woman would have it otherwise."

Chapter Eight

THE NAMING
OF THE NAME

I

It was the responsibility of the Vested Five to keep the records of the Priest's Caste and, as Temple Elders, to investigate and ascertain all matters pertaining to the place assigned each child born within the precinct. Their voluminous robes were embroidered and imprinted with cryptic symbols of such antiquity that only the highest Initiates had even a foggy conception of their meanings.

Side by side, Domaris and Micon stood before them in meditative silence as the ceremonial sprinkling of incense burnt itself out in the ancient filigreed bowl, filling the air with its perfume. As the last smoky tendrils curled up and were gone, an Acolyte stepped forward to softly shut the bowl's metal lid.

For the first time, Domaris was robed in blue, the color sacred to the Mother; her beautiful hair was braided and bound into a fillet of blue. Her heart pounded with a vast joy, touched with pride, as Micon, alerted by the faint sound of the incense burner's closing, stepped forward to address the Vested Five. Robed in simple white, with a fine golden band about his head, the Atlantean took his place before them with a sureness of step that belied his blindness.

His trained tones filled the room proudly, without being loud.

"Fathers, I am come here with this woman, my beloved, to announce and acknowledge that my chosen lady is with child, and that this child of her body is sole son of my begetting, my firstborn, and the inheritor of my name, station, and estate. I make solemn declaration of the purity of this woman, and I now swear, by the Central Fire, the Central Sun, and the Three Wings Within the Circle, that the law has been observed."

The Atlantean now took a step back, turned, and with a deliberation and economy of movement which told the Vested Five much, he knelt at Domaris's feet. "This mother and this child," Micon said, "are acknowledged under the law, in gratitude and in reverence; this, that my love not be wasted, nor my life unblessed, nor my duty unfinished. This, that I may give all honor where honor is due."

Domaris placed her hand lightly upon the crown of Micon's head. "I am come," she said, her voice ringing defiantly clear in that centuried chamber, "to announce and acknowledge my coming child as the son of this man. I, Domar—Isarma, daughter of Talkannon, declare it." She paused, coloring, abashed at having stumbled in the ritual; but the Elders did not move an eyelash, and she continued, "I further make declaration that this is the child of virginity, and the child of love; in reverence, I declare this." She now knelt beside Micon. "I act within my right under the law."

The Elder who sat at the center of the Five asked gravely, "The child's name?"

Rajasta presented the scroll with a formal gesture. "This to be placed in the archives of the Temple; I, Rajasta, have read the stars for the daughter of Talkannon, and I name her son thus: O-si-nar-men."

"What means it?" whispered Micon to Domaris, almost inaudibly, and she returned, in an undertone, "Son of Compassion."

The Elders stretched forth their hands in a gesture older than humanity, and intoned, "The budding life is acknowledged and welcome, under the law. Son of Micon and Isarma, O-si-nar-men. Be thou blessed!"

Rising slowly, Micon put out his hand to Domaris, who clasped it in her own and rose. They stood together with bent heads, as the low-voiced cadenced blessing flowed on: "Giver of Life—Bearer of Life—be thou blessed. Now and ever, blessed thou art, and blessed thy seed. Go in peace."

Domaris raised her hand in the ancient Sign of honor, and after a moment Micon followed her lead, hearing the rustling of her sleeve and remembering the instructions he had received from Rajasta. Together, with quiet humility, they left the council room—but Rajasta remained behind, for the Vested Five would wish to question him regarding specifics of the unborn child's horoscope.

In the outer vestibule, Domaris leaned against Micon's shoulder for a moment. "It is done," she whispered. "And even as I spoke, our child stirred again within me! I—I would be much with you now!"

"Beloved, thou shalt be," Micon promised tenderly; yet a wistful note shadowed his voice as he bent to kiss her. "Would that I might see thy coming glory!"

Chapter Nine

A QUESTION OF SENTIMENT

I

Karahama, Priestess of Caratra, had judged Deoris well. In the days after Arkati's death, Deoris had indeed concentrated all her facilities upon this work she had formerly despised. Her intuitive knowledge grew into a deft sureness and skill and at the conclusion of her extra term of service, it was almost with reluctance that she prepared to leave the Temple.

Having completed the ritual purification, she went to Karahama to bid her goodbye. In the last weeks they had drawn as close as the older woman's reserve would allow, and in spite of Karahama's severe mannerisms, Deoris suddenly realized that she would miss Karahama.

After they had exchanged the usual formal exchanges, the Priestess detained Deoris a little longer. "I shall miss you," she said. "You have become skillful, my child." And while Deoris stood speechless with surprise—Karahama's praise was rare and difficult to earn—the Priestess took up a small silver disk on a fine chain. This ornament, inscribed with the sigil of Caratra, was a badge of service and achievement given eventually to every woman who served the Goddess—but it was rarely bestowed on anyone as young as Deoris. "Wear it in wisdom," said Karahama, and herself fastened the clasp about the girl's wrist. This done, she stood regarding Deoris as if she would speak further.

Karahama was a big woman, tall and deep-breasted, and imposing, with yellow cat-eyes and tawny hair. Like Talkannon, she gave the impression of an animal ferocity held in stern control; the blue robes of her rank added a certain arrogance to her natural dignity. "You are in the Scribe's school?" she asked at last.

"I left it many months ago. I have been assigned as a scribe to the Lord Micon of Ahtarrath."

Karahama's scorn withered Deoris's pride. "Any girl can do that work of reading and writing! Have you chosen to make *that* your life's work, then? Or is it your intention to follow the Lady Domaris into the Temple of Light?"

Until that very moment, Deoris had never seriously doubted that she would one day seek initiation into the Temple of Light, following in her sister's footsteps. Now, all at once, she knew that this was impossible, that it had always been impossible for her, and she said, with the first real decisiveness of her life, "No. I do not wish either of those things."

"Then," Karahama said quietly, "I believe your true place is here, in Caratra's Temple—unless you choose to join with Riveda's sect."

"The Grey-robes?" Deoris was shocked. "I, a *saji?*"

"Caratra guard you!" Karahama's hands wove a swift rune. "All Gods forbid I should send any child into that! No, my child—I meant as a Healer."

Deoris paused again, considering. She had not realized that women were admitted into the Healer sect. She said, tentatively, "I might—ask Riveda—"

Karahama chuckled lightly. "Riveda is not a very approachable man, child. Your own kinsman Cadamiri is a Healer-Priest, and it would be far easier to take up the matter with him. Riveda never troubles himself with the novices."

Her smile, for some reason, annoyed Deoris, who said, "Riveda himself once asked me whether I wished to enter the Grey Temple!"

This did have the desired effect, for Karahama's expression altered considerably, and she regarded Deoris in a curious silence before saying, "Very well then. If you wish, you may tell Riveda that I have pronounced you capable. Not that my word will carry much weight with him, but he knows my judgment to be sound on such matters."

Their talk turned to other matters; faltered and soon died away. But, watching Deoris go, Karahama began to be disturbed. *Is it really well,* she asked herself, *to send this child in Riveda's path?* The Priestess of Caratra knew Riveda better, perhaps, than his own novices did; and she knew his motives. But Karahama threw off the disturbing thought. Deoris was nearly grown up, and would not take it kindly if Karahama were to meddle, even with the best of intentions. Riveda aroused strong feelings.

II

In the House of the Twelve, Deoris put away the bracelet and wandered idly through her rooms, feeling lonely and neglected. She wanted to make up the quarrel with Domaris, slip back into her old life, forget—for a while, at least—everything that had happened in the last few months.

The emptiness of the rooms and courts bothered her obscurely. Suddenly she stopped, staring at the cage which held her red bird. The bird lay in a queer still heap on the floor of the cage, its crimson plumage matted and crumpled. With a gasp Deoris ran to unfasten the cage door and took up the tiny corpse, cradling it in her palm with a little cry of pain.

She turned the bird helplessly on her hand, nearly crying. She had loved it, it was the last thing Domaris had given her before she began to change so—but what had happened? There was no cat to tear it—and anyhow, the tiny thing had not been mauled. Looking into the now-empty cage, she saw that the little pottery bowl inside was empty of water and there were only one or two scattered husks of seeds in the dirty litter at the bottom.

The sudden entrance of Elara startled her and Deoris, turning around, flew at the little woman in a fury. "You forgot my bird and now it's dead, dead!" she charged passionately.

Elara took a fearful step backward. "What bird do you mean? Why—I did not know—"

"Don't lie to me, you miserable slut!" Deoris cried out, and in an uncontrollable rage, she slapped Elara across the face.

"Deoris!" Shock and anger were in the voice, and Deoris, with a catch of breath, whirled to see Domaris standing, white and astonished in the doorway. "Deoris, what is the meaning of this—this performance?"

She had never spoken so roughly to Deoris before, and the girl put her hand to her mouth in sudden guilt and fear, and stood scarlet and speechless as Domaris repeated, "What is going on? Or must I ask Elara?"

Deoris burst into a flood of angry tears. "She forgot my bird, and it's dead!" she stammered, choking.

"That is neither a reason nor an excuse," Domaris said, still angry, her voice taut. "I am very sorry, Elara. My sister will apologize to you."

"To her?" Deoris said incredulously. "I will not!"

Domaris made her words come steadily, with an effort. "If you were my own child and not my sister, you should be beaten! I have never been so ashamed in my life!" Deoris turned to flee, but before she had taken more than a few steps, Domaris had grasped her wrist and held it in a tense grip. "You stay here!" she commanded. "Do you think I am going to let you disobey me?"

Deoris twisted free, white and furious; but she did stammer out the required apology.

Elara raised her serene face, the print of fingers already reddening on the tanned cheek. Her voice had its own dignity, the unshakable poise of the humble. "I am truly sorry about your bird, little mistress, but its care was not entrusted to me; I knew nothing of it. Have I ever forgotten anything you asked of me?"

When Elara had left them alone, Domaris looked at her sister almost in despair. "What has come over you, Deoris?" she said at last. "I don't know you any more."

Deoris's eyes remained sullenly fixed on the paving-stones; she had not moved since muttering her "apology" to Elara.

"Child, child," Domaris said, "I am sorry about your bird, too, but you could have a dozen for the asking. Elara has never been anything but kind to you! If she were your equal it would be bad enough, but to strike a servant!" She shook her head. "What am I going to do with you?"

Still Deoris made no reply, and Domaris looked into the open cage, with a shake of her head. "I do not know who is responsible," she said quietly, glancing back at Deoris, "but if there was negligence here, you have no one to blame but yourself."

Deoris muttered sulkily, "I haven't been here."

"That does not lessen your fault." There was no mercy in

the older woman's voice. "Why did you not delegate its care directly to one of the women? You cannot blame them for neglecting a duty which no one had assigned to any one of them. Your own forgetfulness cost your pet its life! Have you no sense of responsibility?"

"Haven't I had enough to think about?" Pitiful tears began to trickle down the girl's face. "If you really cared about me, *you'd* have remembered!"

"Must I shoulder your responsibilities all your life?" Domaris retorted, in so furious a tone that Deoris actually stopped crying. Seeing her sister's shocked face, Domaris relented a little, taking the dead bird from Deoris's hands and laying it aside. "I meant what I said; you may have all the birds you wish," she promised.

"Oh, I don't care about the bird! It's *you!*" Deoris wailed, and flung her arms around Domaris, crying harder than ever. Domaris held her tight, feeling that Deoris was finally giving way to the frozen resentment she had been unable to speak before; that now perhaps they could cross that barrier which had lain between them since the night in the Star Field . . . but, finally, she had to remind her: "Gently, Deoris. Hold me not so tightly, you must not hurt us—"

Abruptly, Deoris's arms dropped to her sides and she turned away without a word.

Domaris stretched out her hand, pleading. "Deoris, don't draw away like that, I didn't mean—Deoris, can I say *nothing* that does not wound you?"

"You don't want me!" Deoris accused miserably. "You don't have to pretend."

"Oh, Deoris!" The grey eyes were misted now with tears. "How can you be jealous? How can you? Deoris, don't you know that Micon is dying? Dying! And I must stand between him and death!" Her hands clasped again, with that strange gesture, across her body. "Until our son is born—"

Blindly, Deoris caught her sister in her arms, hugging her close, anything to shut out that terrible, naked grief. Her self-pity fell away, and for the first time in her life she tasted a sorrow that was more than personal, knowing she could only try to comfort where there clearly could be no comfort, vainly try to say what she knew to be untrue . . . and for the first time, her own rebellion fell away, unimportant before her sister's tragedy.

Chapter Ten

MEN OF PURPOSE

I

With a definiteness that left no room for argument, Riveda at last informed Rajasta that his house had been set in order. Rajasta complimented him on work well done, and the Adept bowed and took his leave, a faintly derisive smile behind his heavy-lidded eyes.

The investigation into forbidden sorceries by members of his Order had lasted half a year. It had resulted in a round dozen of merited floggings for rather minor blasphemies and infringements: misuse of ceremonial objects, the wearing or display of outlawed symbols, and other similar offenses. There had also been two serious cases—not clearly connected—involving lesser Adepts who had been beaten and then expelled from the rolls of the Grey-robe sect. One had made use of certain alchemical potions to induce various otherwise blameless neophytes and *saji* to take part in acts of excessive sexual cruelty which, afterward, the victims could not even remember. In the other of these two cases, the culprit had broken into a locked shelf of the Order's private library and stolen some scrolls. This alone would have been bad enough, but it turned out that the man had been growing contagious disease cultures in his rooms. Decontamination procedures were still going on, so far with good hopes of a satisfactory outcome.

Still, all this had warned the undetected that Riveda was alert to their existence, and further progress was not likely to be easy.

For Riveda himself, the greatest reward, in some ways, was the discovery of a new field of experiment with tremendous potentials, which the Adept intended to test. The key to it was the stranger he had taken on as chela. Under hypnosis the lad revealed strange knowledge, and a stranger power—though hypnosis was necessary to make any impression on the odd apathy of the unknown, who existed (one could not say he lived) as in a shell of dark glass over which events passed as shadowy reflections, holding attention only a moment. His mind was locked away, as if from some recent horror and shame that had frozen him; but in his rare ravings he burst forth with oddly coherent words that sometimes gave Riveda clues to great things—long vistas of knowledge which Riveda himself could only glimpse were hidden in that seemingly damaged mind.

Whether the man was Micon's brother, Riveda did not know, nor did he care. He felt, quite sincerely, that any attempt to confront the two could only harm them both. Scrupulously he refrained from making serious inquiry into the chela's origin, or into the mystery of his coming to the Grey Temple.

However, Riveda did watch Micon—always casual, as became a Magician among Priests of Light; always detached, barely hovering on the edges of the Atlantean's circle of acquaintances, but studying them intently. Riveda quickly saw that for Domaris all had ceased to exist, save only Micon; he also discerned Rajasta's preoccupation with the blind Initiate, a relationship which transcended that of fellow-Priests and approached, at times, that of father and son. It was with somewhat less casualness that he watched Deoris.

Rajasta did not very often agree with Rajasta, but in this case, both sensed strange potentialities in the young girl. With the coming of her womanhood, Deoris might be powerful, if she were properly taught. Yet, though he had spent much time in meditation over the question, Riveda could not quite determine exactly what potentialities he saw in her—possibly because they were many, and varied.

She seemed to be, Riveda noticed, Micon's pupil as well as his scribe. Somehow this enraged the Adept, as if Micon were usurping a privilege which should be Riveda's own. The Atlantean's impersonal and diffident guidance of the girl's thoughts impressed Riveda as fumbling, overcautious, and incompetent. In his opinion, they were holding Deoris back, where she should be allowed—even, if necessary, compelled—to open and unfold.

He watched, with detached humor, the growth of her interest in him; and, with even more amusement, the childish and stormy progress of her relationship with Chedan, an Acolyte and the pledged husband of Elis. Temple gossip (to which Riveda was not as deaf as he tried to seem) often made reference to the strained relations between Elis and Chedan. . . .

Chedan's infatuation with Deoris may have begun as an attempt, pure and simple, to spite Elis. In any case, it was now more serious than that. Whether Deoris really cared for Chedan or not—and not even Domaris pretended to know that —she accepted his attentions with gravely mischievous pleasure. Micon and Domaris watched and welcomed this new state of affairs, believing that it might bring Deoris some understanding of their own predicament, and alleviate her hostility to their love.

Riveda happened upon them one morning in an outdoor garden: Deoris, seated on the grass at Micon's feet, was sorting and caring for her writing instruments; Chedan, a slender brown-eyed stripling in the robes of an Acolyte, bent over her, smiling. Riveda was too far away to hear their words, but the two children—they were hardly more, especially in Riveda's eyes—disagreed on something. Deoris sprang up, indignant; Chedan fled in pretended terror, and Deoris raced after him, laughing.

Micon looked up at Riveda's approaching steps, and stretched out his hand in welcome—but he did not rise, and Riveda was struck anew by the ravages of pain in the blind Initiate's face. As always, because he was smitten by devastating pity, he took refuge in the mocking deference with which he masked his deepest emotions.

"Hail, Lord of Ahtarrath! Have your disciples fled from teachings over-wise? Or are you ready with a birchen rod for your neophytes?"

Micon, sensing the sarcasm, was wearily perplexed. He had genuinely tried to conquer his first wariness of Riveda, and his own failure dismayed him. Superficially, of course, Riveda was an easy man to like; yet Micon thought he could almost as easily hate this man, if he would permit himself to do so.

Now, sternly disciplining himself, Micon shrugged off Riveda's sardonic mood and instead spoke of the fevers that regularly decimated the coastal hills, and of the famine that might rage if too many men were disabled by disease and could not harvest the crops. "It is your Healers who can do most to remedy that," he complimented, sincerely and deliberately. "I have heard of the fine work which you have done among them, Lord Riveda. These same Healers were, if I recall rightly, hardly more than corrupt charlatans, not ten years ago—"

"That would be something of an exaggeration." Riveda smiled, with the grim enjoyment of the reformer. "Yet it is true, there was much decadence in the Grey Temple when I came here. I am not of the Priest's Caste—as I would guess Rajasta has told you—I am a northman of Zaiadan; my people were common fisher folk, sea-farers after their fashion. In my land, we know that the right drugs are more efficient than the most earnest prayers, unless the illness be all in the brain. As a boy I learned the care of wounds, because I was lame in one leg and my family thought me fit for nothing else."

Micon seemed startled by this statement, and Riveda chuckled. "Oh, I was healed—never mind how—but I had learned by then there was more to the body than most Priests will ever admit—except in their cups." He chuckled again; then, sobering, went on, "And I had also learned just how much stronger the mind can be when the body is harnessed and brought under the discipline of the will. As, by that time, I had little fondness for the village of my birth, I took up my staff and wandered abroad, as they say. So I came to know of the Magicians; you call them Grey-robes here." Expressively, he shrugged, forgetful for a moment that Micon could not see him. "At last I came here, an Adept, and found among the local Order of Magicians a cult of lazy-minded mystics who masqueraded as Healers. They were not, as I have said, utter charlatans, for they had on their shelves most of the methods we employ today, but they had become decadent and careless, preferring chants and spells to honest work. So I threw them out."

"In anger?" Micon murmured, with a hint of deprecation.

"In good solid wrath," Riveda returned, with a laugh and a

relishing grin. "Not to mention a few well-placed kicks. Some, in fact, I threw out bodily, only stopping to talk about it afterward . . ." He paused a moment in reflection. "Then I gathered together the few who felt as I did—both Priests of Light and Grey-robes—men who believed, like me, that the mind has healing powers of a kind, but that the body needs its treatments too. The greatest help I had was from the Priestesses of Caratra, for they work with living women, not souls and ideals, and it is not so easy for them to forget that great truth, that bodies must be treated simply as suffering bodies. They have been using the correct methods for centuries; and now I have managed to return them to the world of men, where they are equally, if not more needed."

Micon smiled, somewhat sorrowfully. As a physician, at least, he knew he must admire Riveda; and the mental daring of Micon's own nature saluted like qualities in the Adept. *What a pity,* Micon thought, *that Riveda did not apply his high intelligence and his supreme good sense to his own life . . . what a pity that such a man must be wasted on the empty conquest of Magic!*

"Lord Riveda," he said suddenly, "your Healers are above all reproach, but some of your Grey-robes still practice self-torture. How can a man of your intelligence countenance that?"

Riveda countered, "You are of Ahtarrath; surely you know the value of—certain austerities?"

Micon's answer was to form a certain Sign with his right hand. Riveda pondered the value of returning this gesture to one who could not see—but went on, less guardedly, "Then you will know the value of sharpening the senses, raising certain mental and physical factors to a high level of awareness—without completing the pattern or releasing the tension. There are, of course, less extreme methods available, but in the end, you must concede that a man is his own master, and that which harms no one else—well, in the last analysis, there is not much one can do about it."

The Initiate's face betrayed his dissent; the thin lips seemed uncharacteristically stern. "I know that—results may be had from such procedures," he said, "but such results I call valueless. And—there is the question of your women, and the—uses—you make of them." He hesitated, trying to phrase his words in such a way as to give the least offense. "Perhaps what you do brings development, of a kind—but it can only be unbalanced, a violence to nature. You must always guard against madness within your walls, as a result.''

"Madness has many causes," Riveda observed. "Yet, we Grey-robes spare our women the brutality of bearing children to satisfy our pride!''

The Atlantean ignored the insult, only asking quietly, "Have you no sons, Riveda?''

There was an appreciable pause. Riveda lowered his head, unable to rid himself of the absurd notion that this man's blind eyes saw more than his own good ones.

"We believe," Micon continued quietly, "a man shirks duty who leaves no son to follow his name. And as for your Magicians, it may be that the good they do others shall at last outmeasure the harm they do themselves. Yet one day they may set in motion causes which they themselves cannot control or set right.'' The twisted grin came back to Micon's face. "Yet that is but a possibility. I would not quarrel with you, Lord Riveda.''

"Nor I with you," the Adept returned, and there was more than courtesy in his emphatic tone. He knew that Micon did not altogether trust him, and had no wish to make an enemy in so high a place as the Atlantean currently occupied. A word from Micon could bring the Guardians down upon the Grey Temple, and no one knew better than Riveda that certain of his Order's practices would not bear dispassionate investigation. Forbidden sorcery they might not be—but they would not meet with the approval of the stern Guardians. No, he did not want to quarrel with Micon. . . .

Deoris and Chedan, walking side by side and sedately now, rejoined them. Riveda greeted Deoris with a deference that made Chedan stare, his jaw suddenly loose and useless.

"Lord Micon," the Adept said, "I am going to take Deoris from you.''

Micon's dark sightless features went rigid with displeasure, and as he turned his face toward Riveda, some ominous instinct touched the Atlantean. Tightly, he said, "Why do you say that, Riveda?''

Riveda laughed loudly. He knew very well what Micon meant, but it pleased him to misunderstand. "Why, what think you I meant?" he asked. "I must speak with the little maiden for a few minutes, for Karahama of Caratra's Temple gave me her name for admission into the Healers." Riveda laughed again. "If you think so ill of me, I will gladly speak in your presence, Prince Micon!"

A deathly weariness crept into Micon, supplanting his anger by degrees. His shoulders sagged. "I—know not what I meant. I—" He broke off, still nervous but unable to justify it even to himself. "Yes, I had heard that Deoris was to seek Initiation. I am very glad. . . . Go, my Deoris."

II

Thoughtful, Riveda drew the girl along the pathway. Deoris was sensitive, fine-grained, all nerves; instinctively he felt she belonged, not among the Healers but among the Grey-robes themselves. Many of the women of the Grey Temple were only *saji*, despised or ignored—but now and then a woman might be accepted on the Magician's Path. A few, only a few, could seek attainment on the same footing as a man, and it would be hard to make a place for Deoris among them.

"Tell me, Deoris," said Riveda suddenly, "have you served long in the House of the Mother?"

She shrugged. "Only the preliminary services which all women must do." She glanced briefly into the Adept's eyes, but looked away again as she murmured, "I worked for a month with Karahama."

"She spoke of your skill." Riveda paused. "Perhaps you are not learning this for the first time, but recovering something which you once knew, in a previous life."

Deoris raised her eyes to his once more, wonder clear to read in her face. "What do you mean?"

"I am not permitted to speak of it to a daughter of Light," said Riveda, smiling, "but you will learn of this, as you rise in the Temple. Let us talk for a minute about practical things." Aware that her shorter legs were not accustomed to his own swift stride, Riveda turned aside onto a little plaza that overlooked one of the rivulets that ran through the Temple precinct. "Karahama," the Adept continued, "tells me that you wish admission into the Healers, but there are many reasons why I do not wish to accept you at this time." He watched her out of the corner of his eye as he said this, and was vaguely gratified at her discomfort. "As a Healer," he went on, "you would remain only a child of the Temple, not a Priestess. . . . Tell me, have you yet been bound into the Path of Light?"

So rapidly had Deoris's emotions vacillated in the last minutes that at first she could only shake her head, speechless. Then, recovering her composure, she clarified, "Rajasta has said I am still too young. Domaris took no vows until she was past seventeen."

"I would not have you wait so long," Riveda demurred, "but it is true that there is no need of haste—" He fell silent again, gazing off across the plaza and into the distances beyond. At last, turning to Deoris, he said, "This is what I advise you: first, to seek initiation into the lowest grade of the Priestesses of Caratra. As you grow older, you may decide that your true place is among the Magicians—" Riveda checked her question with an imperative gesture. "I know, you do not wish to be *saji*, nor do I suggest it. However, as an Initiated Priestess of Caratra, you could rise in Her service to the highest levels—or enter the Grey Temple. Most women are not fit to attain the grade of Adept, but I believe you have inborn powers." He smiled down at her and added, "I only hope you will use them as you should."

She returned his gaze earnestly. "I don't know how—"

"But you will learn." He laid one of his hands on her shoulder. "Trust me."

"I do," she said confidingly, with the sudden realization that it was true.

In perfect seriousness, Riveda warned her, "Your Micon puts no faith in me, Deoris. Perhaps I'm not a good man to trust."

Deoris looked unhappily down at the flagstones. "Micon—Lord Micon had been so cruelly treated—perhaps he trusts no one anymore," she hazarded, unable to face the idea that Micon might be right. She didn't want to believe anything unpleasant of Riveda.

The Adept let his hand fall away from her. "I will ask Karahama, then, to take you under her personal guidance," he said, with an air of dismissal. Deoris, accepting it, thanked him rather timidly and departed. Riveda stood watching her go, his arms folded on his chest, and though there was a trace of an ironic smile upon his lips, his eyes were thoughtful. Could Deoris be the woman he had visualized? No one knew better than he that the random memories of previous lives sometimes appear to one as presentiments of the future. . . . If he read this girl's character rightly, she was eager—over-eager, perhaps, even impetuous. Did she have any caution at all?

Unwilling to let his thoughts drift too far from current realities, Riveda turned on his heel and began to walk once more, his stride swiftly carrying him from the plaza. Deoris was still a little girl, and he must wait, perhaps for years, to be sure he was not mistaken—but he had made a beginning.

The Adept Riveda was not accustomed to waiting for what he wanted—but this once, it might prove worth the waiting!

Chapter Eleven

OF BLESSINGS AND CURSES

I

Her hands folded meekly before her, her hair simply braided, Deoris stood before the assembled Priestesses of Caratra. She wore, for the last time, her scribe's frock, and already it felt strange.

Even while she listened with serious attention to the grave admonitions of Karahama, Deoris was scared, even panicky, her thoughts running in wistful counterpoint to the Priestess's words. From this day and hour, she would no longer be "little Deoris," but a woman who had chosen her life's work—although for years to come she would be no more than an apprenticed Priestess, even this conferred upon her the responsibilities of an adult. . . .

And now Karahama beckoned her forward. Deoris stretched forth her hands, as she had been bidden.

"Adsartha, daughter of Talkannon, called Deoris, receive from my hands these ornaments it is now thy right to wear. Use them wisely, and profane them never," Karahama adjured. "Daughter thou art to the Great Mother; daughter and sister and mother to every other woman." Into the outstretched hands Karahama placed the sacred ornaments which Deoris must wear for the rest of her life. "May these hands be blessed for the Mother's work; may they be consecrated," said

Karahama, and closed Deoris's small fingers over the ritual gems, holding them closed for a moment, then Signing them with a protective gesture.

Deoris did not consider herself in any way a superstitious person, and yet she half-expected to feel the touch of some great, warm and mystic power flowing into her—or else, that the very walls would denounce her as unworthy. But she felt nothing, only a continuing nervous tension and a slight trembling in her calves from standing almost motionless throughout the long ceremony—which, clearly, was not yet ended.

Karahama raised her arms in yet another ritual gesture, saying, "Let the Priestess Deoris be invested as befits her rank."

Mother Ysouda, the old Priestess who had brought both Domaris and Deoris into the world and who had cared for them after the death of their mother, led her away; Domaris, in the place of her mother, accompanied them into the antechamber.

First the scribe's flaxen frock was taken from her and cast into the fire; Deoris stood naked, shivering on the stones. In prescribed silence, Mother Ysouda's face too forbidding to reassure either of them, Domaris unbraided her sister's heavy hair, and the ancient Priestesses sheared it off and cast the heavy dark ringlets into the flames. Deoris blinked back tears of humiliation as she watched them burn, but she did not utter a sound; it would have been unthinkable to weep during such a ceremony. While Mother Ysouda performed the elaborate rites of purification, and of dressing the shorn and chastened Deoris in the garments of a Priestess of the lowest grade, Domaris looked on with eyes shining. She was not sorry that Deoris had chosen a different service than herself; all were aspects of the hierarchy into which they had been born, and it seemed right that Deoris should choose the service of humanity, rather than her own choice of the esoteric wisdom of Light. Seeing Deoris in the simple novice's garments, Domaris's eyes filled and spilled over with tears of joy; she felt a mother's pride in a grown child, without a mother's sorrow that the child is grown past her control.

Once Deoris had been robed in the straight sleeveless garment of blue, cross-woven with white, they bound a plain blue girdle about her waist and fastened it with a single pearl— the stone of the Great Deep, brought from the womb of earth in danger and death, and thus symbolic of childbirth. About Deoris's throat was hung an amulet of carven crystal, which she would later learn to use as both hypnotic pendulum and psychic channel when this became necessary in her work.

Thus clothed and thus adorned, she was led back to the assembled Priestesses, who had broken their solemn circle and now crowded around the girl to welcome her to their order, kissing and embracing her, congratulating her, even teasing her a little about her shorn hair. Even Mother Ysouda, stern and bony, unbent enough to reminisce with the delighted Domaris—who stood apart from the throng of blue-clad women crowding about the newcomer.

"It hardly seems that it can have been fifteen years since I first laid her in your arms!"

"What was I like?" Deoris asked curiously.

Mother Ysouda straightened herself with a dignified air. "Very much like a little red monkey," she returned, but she smiled at Deoris and Domaris lovingly. "You have lost your little one, Domaris—but soon now I shall lay another child in your arms, shall I not?"

"In only a few months," Domaris said shyly, and the old lady pressed her hand with warm affection.

II

Since Deoris's formal duties would not begin until the next day, the sisters walked back together toward the House of the Twelve. Domaris put a hand to her sister's close-cropped head with hesitant compassion. "Your lovely hair," she mourned.

Deoris shook her head, sending the short ringlets flying. "I like it," she lied recklessly. "Now I need not spend all my time plaiting and combing it—Domaris, is it so very ugly?"

Domaris saw the tremble of her sister's mouth and laughed, reassuring her quickly, "No, no, little Deoris, you grow very lovely. I think the style suits you, really—but it does make you look very little," she teased. "Chedan may ask proof that you are a woman!"

"He is welcome to such proofs as he has had already," Deoris said negligently, "but I shall not imperil my friendship with Elis for the sake of that overgrown baby!"

Domaris laughed. "You might win Elis's undying gratitude

if you took Chedan from her altogether!" Her mirth evaporated as an annoyingly recurrent little thought came to trouble her again: she still did not know how Arvath really felt about the fact that she had invoked her legal freedom. Already there had been some unpleasantness, and Domaris anticipated more. She had seen how Chedan behaved when Elis had done the same thing. She hoped Arvath would be more generous, more understanding—but more and more she suspected that hope was only wishful thinking.

Frowning slightly, Domaris gave a little impatient shrug. She had made her choice, and if it involved unpleasantness, well, she would face it when the time came. Deliberately, she turned her thoughts to more immediate concerns. "Micon wished to see you after the ceremonies, Deoris. I will go and take off these tapestries," she joked, shaking the cumbersome robes which she had had to wear for the ritual, "and join you both afterward."

Deoris started. Inexplicably, the idea of confronting Micon without Domaris nearby disturbed her. "I'll wait for you," she offered.

"No," said Domaris lightly, "I think he wanted to see you alone."

III

Micon's Atlantean servants conducted her into a room which opened on a great series of terraced gardens, green with flowering trees and filled with the sound of falling waters and of the songs of many birds. These rooms were spacious and cool, as befitted apartments reserved for visitors of rank and dignity; Rajasta had spared no pains to insure the comfort of his guest.

Outlined against the window, Micon's luminous robes gave his erect, emaciated form an almost translucent look in the afternoon sunlight. As he turned his head, smiling brilliantly, Deoris caught a flash of radiant color, like an aura of sparkling, exploding brightness around his head—then it was gone, so swiftly that Deoris could only doubt the evidence of her own eyes. The instant of clairvoyant sight had made her a little dizzy, and she halted in the doorway; then regretted the pause, for Micon heard her and moved painfully toward her.

"Is it you, my little Deoris?"

At hearing his voice, her lingering nervousness vanished; she ran and knelt before him. He grinned down at her crookedly. "And I must not call you *little Deoris* now, they have told me," he teased, and laid his hand, thin and blue-veined, on her head; then moved it in surprise. "They have cut off your pretty hair! Why?"

"I don't know," she said shyly, rising. "It is the custom."

Micon smiled in puzzlement. "How odd," he murmured. "I have always wondered—are you like Domaris? Is your hair fiery, like hers?"

"No, my hair is black as night. Domaris is beautiful, I am not even pretty," said Deoris, without subterfuge.

Micon laughed a little. "But Domaris has said the same of you, child—that you are lovely and she is quite plain!" He shrugged. "I suppose sisters are always so, if they love one another. But I find it hard to picture you to myself, and I feel I have lost my little scribe—and indeed I have, for you will be far too busy to come to me!"

"Oh, Micon, truly I am sorry for that!"

"Never mind, puss. I am glad—not to lose you, but that you have found the work which will lead you to Light."

She corrected him hesitantly. "I am not to be a Priestess of Light, but of the Mother."

"But you are yourself a daughter of Light, my Deoris. There is Light in you, more than you know, for it shines clearly. I have seen it, though these eyes are blind." Again he smiled. "But enough of this; I am sure you have heard quite enough vague exhortations for one day! I know you may not wear ornaments while you are only an apprentice Priestess, but I have a gift for you . . ." He turned, and from a table beside him took up a tiny statuette: a little cat, carved from a single piece of green jade, sitting back on sleek haunches, topaz eyes winking comically at Deoris. About its neck was a collar of green stones, beautifully cut and polished. "The cat will bring you luck," he said, "and when you are the Priestess Adsartha, and no longer forbidden to wear gems and ornaments—" Deftly, Micon unclasped the collar of gems. "See, Master Cat will lend you his collar for a bracelet, if your wrist be still as dainty as now." Taking her slim hand in his, he slipped the circlet of stones for a moment over her wrist; then removed it, laughing. "But I must not tempt you to break your vow," he added, and clasped the ornament about the cat's throat again.

"Micon, it's lovely!" Deoris cried, enchanted.

"And therefore, it could only belong to you, little one—my beloved little sister," he repeated, his voice lingering for a moment on the words; then he said, "Until Domaris comes, let us walk in the garden."

The lawns were shadowy and cool, although the summer greens were parched now and yellow. The great tree where they had so often sat during the summer was dry, with clusters of hard bright berries among the branches—but the fine gritty dust did not penetrate to there, and the trees filtered out the burning glare of the sun somewhat. They found their old seat, and Deoris dropped to the dry grass, letting her head rest lightly against Micon's knees as she looked up at him. Surely the bronzed face was thinner—more drawn with pain.

"Deoris," he said, his odd smile coming and going like summer lightning, "your sister has missed you." His tone was not reproachful, but Deoris felt guilty crimsons bannering her cheeks.

"Domaris doesn't need me now," she muttered.

Micon's touch on her shorn curls was very tender. "You are wrong, Deoris, she needs you now more than ever—needs your understanding, and—your love. I would not intrude on what is personal between you—" He felt her stir jealously beneath his hand. "No, wait, Deoris. Let me tell thee something." He shifted restlessly, as if he would have preferred to speak standing; but an odd look crossed his mobile features, and he remained where he was. "Deoris, listen to me. I shall not live much longer."

"Don't say that!"

"I must, little sister." A shadow of regret deepened the Atlantean's resonant voice. "I shall live—perhaps—until my son is born. But I want to know that—afterward—Domaris will not be altogether alone." His mutilated hands, scarred but thin and gentle, touched her wet eyes. "Darling, don't cry—I love you very dearly, little Deoris, and I do feel I can trust Domaris to you. . . ."

Deoris could not force herself to speak, or move, but only gazed up into Micon's sightless eyes as if transfixed.

With a ghastly emphasis, the Atlantean went on, "I am not so much in love with life that I could not bear to leave it!" Then, as if conscious that he had frightened her, the terrible self-mockery slowly faded from his face. "Promise me, Deoris," he said, and touched her lips and breast in a curious symbolic gesture she did not understand for many years.

"I promise," she whispered, crying.

The man closed his eyes and leaned back against the great tree's broad trunk. Speaking of Domaris had weakened the fiercely-held control to which he owed his life, and he was human enough to be terrified. Deoris saw the shadow that crossed his face and gasping, sprang up.

"Micon!" she cried out, fearfully bending close to him. He raised his head, perspiration breaking out upon his brow, and choked out a few words in a language Deoris could not comprehend. "Micon," she said gently, "I can't understand—"

"Again it comes!" he gasped. "I felt it on the Night of Nadir, reaching for me—some deadly evil—" He leaned against her shoulder, heavy, limp, breathing with a forced endurance. *"I will not!"* he shrieked, as if in reply to some unseen presence—and the words were harsh, rasping, utterly like his usual tone, even in extremity.

As Deoris drew him into her arms, unable to think of anything else to do, she suddenly found herself supporting all of his weight. He slipped down, almost insensible but holding to consciousness with what seemed must be his last wisps of strength.

"Micon! What shall I do?"

He tried to speak again, but his command of her language had deserted him again, and he could only mutter broken phrases in the Atlantean tongue. Deoris felt very young, and terrified: she had had some training, of course, but nothing that prepared her for this—and the wisdom of love was not in her arms; the very strength of her frightened embrace was cruel to Micon's pain-wracked body. Moaning, he twitched away from her, or tried to; swaying, he would have fallen precipitously had the girl not held him upright. She tried to support him more gently, but fingers of freezing panic were squeezing at her throat; Micon looked as if he were dying, and she dared not even leave him to summon aid! The feeling of helplessness only added to her terror.

She uttered a little scream as a shadow fell across them, and another's arms lifted the burden of Micon's weight abruptly from her young shoulders.

"Lord Micon," said Riveda firmly, "how can I assist you?"

Micon only sighed, and went limp in the Grey-robe's arms. Riveda glanced at Deoris, his stern, sharp face appraising her coolly, as if to make certain she was not about to faint.

"Good Gods," the Adept murmured, "has he been this way for long?" He did not wait for her answer, but easily rose to his feet, bearing the wasted form of the blind man without apparent effort. "I had better take him at once to his rooms. Merciful Gods, the man weighs no more than you! Deoris, come with me; he may need you."

"Yes," Deoris said, the flush of her embarrassment at her previous terror fading. "I will show you the way," she said, rushing ahead of Riveda and up the path.

Behind them, Riveda's chela sought his master with dull, empty eyes. A flicker of life momentarily brightened their flatness as they observed Micon. Moving noiselessly at Riveda's heels, the chela's face was a troubled emptiness, like a slate wiped imperfectly with a half-dampened sponge.

As they entered Micon's suite, one of the Atlantean servants cried out, running to help Riveda lay the unconscious man upon his bed. The Grey-robe Adept gave a swift succession of low-voiced orders, then set about applying restoratives.

Mute and frightened, Deoris stood at the foot of the bed. Riveda had forgotten her existence; the Adept's whole intense attention was concentrated on the man he was tending. The chela ghosted into the room on feet more silent than a cat's, and stood uncertainly by the doorway.

The blind man stirred on the bed, moaned deliriously, and muttered something in the Atlantean tongue; then, quite suddenly, in a low and startlingly clear voice, he said, "Do not be afraid. They can only kill us, and if we submit to them we would be better dead—" He emitted another groan of agony, and Deoris, sickened, clutched at the high bed-frame.

The chela's staring eyes found Micon, and the dulled glance widened perceptibly. He made an odd sound, half gasp, half whimper.

"Be quiet!" Riveda snarled, "or get out!"

Beneath the Grey-robe's gently restraining hands, Micon moved: first a stir, as of returning consciousness—then he writhed, groping, his head jerking backward in a convulsive movement, his whole body arching back in horror as the twisted hands made terrible clutching movements; suddenly Micon screamed, a high shrill scream of agonized despair.

"Reio-ta! Reio-ta! Where are you? What are you? *They have blinded me!"*

The chela stood twitching, as if blasted by lightning and unable to flee. "Micon!" he shrieked. His hands lifted, clenched, and he took one step—then the impulse died, the spark faded, and the chela's hands fell, lax-fingered, to his sides.

Riveda, who had raised his head in sharp question, saw that the chela's face was secret with madness, and with a shake of his head, the Adept bent again to his task.

Micon stirred again, but this time less violently. After a moment he murmured, "Rajasta—"

"He will come," said Riveda, with unwonted gentleness, and raised his head to the Atlantean servant, who stood staring at the chela with wide, unbelieving eyes. "Find the Guardian, you fool! I don't care where or how, *go and find him!*" The words left no room for argument or hesitation; the servant turned and went at a run, only pausing to cast a furtive quick look at the chela.

Deoris, who had stood motionless and rigid throughout, suddenly swayed, clutching with wooden hands at the high bed-frame, and would have fallen—but the chela stepped swiftly forward and held her upright, his arm about her waist. It was the first rational action anyone had yet seen from him.

Riveda covered his start of surprise with harsh asperity. "Are you all right, Deoris? If you feel faint, sit down. I have no leisure to attend to you too."

"Of course I am all right," she said, and pulled herself away from the grey-clad chela in fastidious disgust. How dared this half-wit touch her!

Micon murmured, "My little Deoris—"

"I am here," she assured him softly. "Shall I send Domaris to you?"

He gave a barely perceptible nod, and Deoris went quickly before Riveda could make a move to prevent her; Domaris must be warned, she must not come unexpectedly upon Micon when he was like this!

Micon gave a restless sigh. "Is that—Riveda? Who else is here?"

"No one, Lord of Ahtarrath," Riveda lied compassionately. "Try to rest."

"No one else?" The Atlantean's voice was weak, but surprised. "I—I don't believe it. I felt—"

"Deoris was here, and your servant. They have gone now," said Riveda with quiet definiteness. "You were wandering in your mind, I think, Prince Micon."

Micon muttered something incomprehensible before the

weary voice faded again, and the lines of pain around his
mouth reappeared, as if incised there by words he could not
utter. Riveda, having done all he could, settled himself to
watch—glancing, from time to time, at the blank-faced chela.

It was not long before the rustling of stiff robes broke into
the near silence, and Rajasta practically brushed Riveda aside
as he bent over Micon. His face had a look no one else ever
saw. Wonder and question mingled in his voice as he spoke the
Adept's name.

"I would that I might do more," Riveda answered, with
grave emphasis, "but no living man can do that." Rising to his
feet, the Grey-robe added softly, "In his present state, he does
not seem to trust me." He looked down at Micon regretfully,
continuing, "But at any hour, night or day, I am at your
service—and his."

Rajasta glanced up curiously, but he was already alone with
Micon. Casting all other thoughts from his mind, the Priest of
Light knelt by the bedside, taking Micon's thin wrists carefully
in his hands, gently infusing his own strengthening energies
into the depleted and flickering spirit of the half-sleeping
Atlantean. . . . Hearing steps, Rajasta came out of his meditation, and motioned for Domaris to approach and take his
place.

As Rajasta lifted one hand, however, Micon stirred again,
whispering with an effort, "Was—someone else—here?"

"Only Riveda," said Rajasta in surprise, "and a half-wit he
calls his chela. Rest, my brother—Domaris is here."

At Rajasta's answer to his question, a frown had crossed
Micon's face—but at mention of Domaris, all other thoughts
fled. "Domaris!" he sighed, and his hand groped for hers, his
taut features relaxing.

Yet Rajasta had seen that frown, and immediately divined
its significance. The Priest of Light's nostrils flared wide in
disdain. There was something very wrong about Riveda's
chela, and Rajasta resolved to find out what it was at the
earliest opportunity.

IV

Micon slept, at last, and Domaris slipped down on the floor
beside his bed in a careful, listening stillness—but Rajasta bent
and gently raised her up, drawing her a little distance away,

where his whispered words would not disturb the sleeping man.

"Domaris, you must go, daughter. He would never forgive me if I let you spend your strength."

"You—you will send for me if he wakes?"

"I will not promise even that." He looked in her eyes, and saw exhaustion there. "For his son's sake, Domaris. Go!"

Thus admonished, the girl obediently departed; it was growing late, and the moon had risen, silvering the dried foliage and wrapping the fountains in a luminous mist. Domaris went carefully and slowly, for her body was heavy now, and she was not altogether free of pain.

Abruptly a pale shadow darkened the pathway, and the girl drew a frightened breath as Riveda's tall broad figure barred her way; then let it out, in foolish relief, as the Adept stepped aside to let her pass. She bowed her head courteously to him, but the man did not respond; his eyes, cold with the freezing fire of the Northern lights, were searching her silently and intently. Then, as if compelled, he uncovered his head and bent before her in a very ancient gesture of reverence.

Domaris felt the color drain from her face, and the pounding of her heart was very loud against her ribs. Again the Greyrobe inclined his head—this time in casual courtesy—and drew the long skirt of his cowled robe aside so that she might pass him with more ease. When she remained standing, white and shaken, in the middle of the pathway, the ghost of a smile touched Riveda's face, and he moved past her, and was gone.

It was perfectly clear to Domaris that the Adept's reverence had been directed, not toward her personally, nor even to the rank betrayed by her Initiate's robes, but to the fact of her incipient maternity. Yet this raised more questions than it answered: what had prompted Riveda to bestow upon her this high and holy salutation? It occurred to Domaris that she would have been less frightened if the Adept of the Grey-robes had struck her.

Slowly, thoughtfully, she continued on her way. She knew very little of the Grey Temple, but she had heard that its Magicians worshipped the more obvious manifestations of the lifeforce. Perhaps, standing like that in the moonlight, she had resembled one of their obscenely fecund statues! Ugh, what a thought! It made her laugh wildly, in the beginnings of hysteria, and Deoris, crossing the outer corridor of the House of the Twelve, heard the strained and unnatural laughter, and hurried to her in sudden fright.

"Domaris! What's wrong, why are you laughing like that?"

Domaris blinked, the laughter choking off abruptly. "I don't know," she said, blankly.

Deoris looked at her, distressed. "Is Micon—"

"Better. He is sleeping. Rajasta would not let me stay," Domaris explained. She felt tired and depressed, and longed for sympathetic companionship, but Deoris had already turned away. Tentatively, Domaris said, "Puss—"

The girl turned around and looked at her sister. "What is it?" she inquired, with a shade of impatience. "Do you want something?"

Domaris shook her head. "No, nothing, kitten. Good night." She leaned forward and kissed her sister's cheek, then stood watching as Deoris, released, darted lightly away. Deoris was growing very fast in these last weeks . . . it was only natural, Domaris thought, that she should grow away from her sister. Still she frowned a little, wondering, as Deoris disappeared down the passageway.

At the time when Deoris had made known her decision to seek initiation into Caratra's Temple, she had also been assigned—as befitted a girl her age—separate apartments of her own. Since she was still technically under the guardianship of Domaris, those apartments were here, in the House of the Twelve, and near those of Domaris, but not adjacent to them. Domaris took it for granted that all the Acolytes mingled casually, without considering the strictures usually accepted outside: there was an excellent reason for this freedom, and it really meant very little. Nothing could be kept secret from the Acolytes, and everyone knew that Chedan slept sometimes in Deoris's rooms. How little that meant, Domaris knew; since her thirteenth year Domaris had passed many nights, quite innocently, with Arvath, or some other boy at her side. It was acceptable behaviour, and Domaris detested herself for the malice of her suspicion. After all, Deoris was now fifteen . . . if the two *were* actually lovers, well, that too was permissible. Elis had been even younger when her daughter was born.

As if their minds ran along similar paths, Elis herself suddenly joined Domaris in the hallway. "Is Deoris angry with me?" Elis asked. "She passed me without a word just now."

Domaris, dismissing her worries, laughed. "No—but she does take growing up very seriously! I am sure that tonight she feels older than Mother Lydara herself!"

Elis chuckled in sympathy. "I had forgotten, her ceremony was today. So! Now she is a woman, and a postulant of Caratra's Temple; and perhaps Chedan—" At the look on her cousin's face, Elis sobered and said, "Don't look like that, Domaris. Chedan won't do her any harm, even if—well, you and I would have no right to criticize."

Domaris's face, in its halo of coppery hair, was pale and strained. "But Deoris is so very young, Elis!"

Elis snorted lightly. "You have always babied her much too much, Domaris. She is grown up! And—we both chose for ourselves. Why deny her that privilege?"

Domaris looked up, with a heartbreaking smile. "You do understand, don't you," she said; and it was not a question.

Brusquely, to hide her feelings (Elis did not often display emotion), she took Domaris by the wrist and half pulled, half pushed her cousin into her room, propelled Domaris to a divan and sat down beside her. "You don't have to tell me anything," she said. "Remember, I know what you are living through." Her gentle face recalled humiliation and tenderness and pain. "I have known it all, Domaris. It does take courage, to be a complete person. . . ."

Domaris nodded. Elis *did* understand.

A woman had this right, under the Law, and indeed, in the old days it had been rare for a woman to marry before she had proven her womanhood by bearing a child to the man of her choice. The custom had gradually fallen into disuse; few women these days invoked the ancient privilege, disliking the inevitable accompaniment of curious rumors and speculations.

Elis asked, "Does Arvath know yet?"

Domaris shivered unexpectedly. "I don't know—he hasn't spoken of it—I suppose he must," she said, with a nervous smile. "He's not stupid."

Arvath had maintained a complete and stony silence in the last weeks, whenever he came into the presence of his pledged wife. They appeared together when custom demanded, or as their Temple duties brought them into contact; otherwise he let her severely alone. "But I haven't told him in so many words—Oh, Elis!"

The dark girl, in a rare gesture of affection, laid her soft hand over Domaris's. "I—am sorry," she said shyly. "He can be cruel. Domaris . . . forgive me for asking. Is it Arvath's child?"

Silently, but indignantly, Domaris shook her head. That *was* forbidden. A woman might choose a lover, but if she and her affianced husband possessed one another before marriage, it was considered a terrible disgrace; such haste and precipitancy would be cause enough for dismissing both from the Acolytes.

Elis's lovely face showed both relief and a residual disturbance. "I could not have believed it of you," she said, then added softly, "I know it to be untrue, but I have heard whispers in the courts—forgive me, Domaris, I know you detest such gossip, but—but they believe it is Rajasta's child!"

Domaris's mouth worked soundlessly for a moment before she covered her face with her hands and rocked to and fro in misery. "Oh, Elis," she wept, "how could they!" *That*, then, was the reason for the cold looks and the whispers behind her back. Of course! Such a thing would have been shame unutterable and unspeakable; of all the forbidden relationships in the Temple, the spiritual incest with one's Initiator was the most unthinkable. The bond of Priest and disciple was fixed as immutably as the paths of the stars. "How can they think such a thing?" Domaris sobbed, desolately. "My son's name, and the name of his father, have been acknowledged before the Vested Five, and the entire Temple!"

Elis turned furiously crimson, shamed at the turn their conversation had taken. "I know," she whispered, "but—he who acknowledges a child is not always the true father. . . . Chedan acknowledged my Lissa, when we had never shared a single couch. I have heard it said—that—it is only because Rajasta is Guardian that he has not been scourged from the Temple, because he seduced you—"

Domaris's sobs became hysterical.

Elis regarded her cousin, frightened. "You must not cry like that, Domaris! You will make yourself ill, and injure your child!"

Domaris made an effort to control herself, and said helplessly, "How can they be so cruel?"

"I—I—" Elis's hands twisted nervously, fluttering like caged wild birds. "I should not have told you, it is only filthy gossip, and—"

"No! If there is more, tell me! It is best I should hear it from you." Domaris wiped her eyes and said, "I know you love me, Elis. I would rather hear it all from you."

It took a little while, but at last Elis relented. "Arvath it was who said this—that Micon was Rajasta's friend, and would

take on himself the burden—that it was a deception so transparent that it was rotten. He said Micon was only a wreck of a
man, and—and could not have fathered your child—'' She
stopped again, appalled, for Domaris's face was white even to
the lips, except for two spots of hectic crimson which seemed
painted on her cheeks.

"Let him say that to me," said Domaris in a low and terrible
voice. "Let him say that honestly to my face, instead of sneak-
ing behind me like the craven filth he is if he can think such
rottenness! Of all the filthy, foul, disgusting—'' She stopped
herself, but she was shaking.

"Domaris, Domaris, he meant it not, I am sure," Elis protested, frightened.

Domaris bent her head, feeling her anger die, and something
else take its place. She knew Arvath's sudden, reckless jeal-
ousies—and he had had some provocation. Domaris hid her
face in her hands, feeling soiled by the touch of tongues, as if
she had been stripped naked and pelted with manure. She
could hardly breathe under the weight of shame. What she had
. . . discovered, with Micon, was sacred! This, *this* was defile-
ment, disgrace.

Elis looked at her in helpless, pained compassion. "I did
wrong to tell you, I knew I should not."

"No, you did right," said Domaris steadily. Slowly she
began once more to recover her self-control. "See? I will not
let it trouble me." She would confess it to Rajasta, of course;
he could help her bear it, help her to learn to live with this
shameful thought—but no word or breath of this should ever
reach Micon's ears. Dry-eyed now, she looked into Elis's eyes
and said softly, "But warn Arvath to guard his tongue; the
penalty for slander is not light!"

"So I have reminded him already," Elis murmured; then
looked away from Domaris, biting her lip. "But—if he is too
cruel—or if he makes a scene which embarrasses you—ask one
question of him." She paused, drawing breath, as if afraid of
what she was about to say. "Ask Arvath why he left me to
throw myself on Chedan's mercy, to face the Vested Five
alone, lest my Lissa be born one of the *no people*."

In shocked silence, Domaris slowly took Elis's hand and
pressed it. So *Arvath* was Lissa's father! That explained many
things; his insane jealousy was rooted deep in guilt. Only the
fact that everyone knew for a certainty that Chedan had not

truly fathered Elis's child had allowed him to honorably
acknowledge the child—and even so, it could not have been an
easy decision for him to have made. And that Arvath had let
this happen!

"Elis, I never guessed!"

Elis smiled ever so slightly. "I made sure you would not,"
she said coolly.

"You should have told me," Domaris murmured distractedly. "Perhaps I could have—"

Elis stood up to move restlessly about the room. "No, you
could have done nothing. There was no need to involve you.
Actually, I'm almost sorry I told you now! After all, you will
have to marry the—the worthless fool, someday!" There was
wrath and shadowy regret in Elis's eyes, and Domaris said no
more. Elis had confided in her, she had given Domaris a
powerful weapon which might, one day, serve to protect her
child against Arvath's jealousy—but that gave Domaris no
right to pry.

Nevertheless, she could not help wishing that she had known
of this before. At one time, she had had influence enough with
Arvath that she could have persuaded him to accept his responsibility. Elis had humiliated herself to give her child caste
—and Chedan had not been pleasant about the matter, for
they had risked much.

Domaris knew herself well enough to realize that only the
greatest extremity could bring her to use this powerful weapon
against Arvath's malice. But her new understanding of his underlying cowardice helped her to regain her perspective in the
matter.

They talked of other things, until Elis clapped her hands
softly and Simila brought Lissa to her. The child was now past
two, and beginning to talk; in fact, she chattered and babbled
incessantly, and at last Elis gave her a tiny exasperated shake.
"Hush, mistress tongueloose," she admonished, and told
Domaris acidly, "What a nuisance she is!"

Domaris was not fooled, however, noting the tenderness
with which Elis handled the tiny girl. A vagrant thought came
to trouble her: did Elis still love Arvath? After all that had
happened, it seemed extremely unlikely—but there was,
beyond any imaginable denial, an unbreakable bond between
them . . . and always would be.

Smiling, Domaris held out her arms to Lissa. "She grows

more like you every day, Elis," she murmured, taking the little
girl up and holding the small, wriggling, giggling body to her
breast.

"I hope she is a finer woman," Elis retorted, half speaking
to herself.

"She could not be more understanding," said Domaris, and
released the heavy child, smiling tiredly. Leaning back, with a
gesture now familiar, Domaris pressed one hand against her
body.

"Ah, Domaris!" With an excess of tenderness, Elis caught
Lissa to her. *"Now* you know!"

And Domaris bowed her head before the dawning knowledge.

V

All through the quiet hours of the night Rajasta sat beside
Micon, rarely leaving his side for more than the briefest
moment. The Atlantean slept fitfully, twitching and muttering
in his native tongue as if the pains that sleep could ease were
only replaced with other pains, deeper and less susceptible of
treatment, a residue of anguish that gnawed its way deeper
into Micon's tortured spirit with every passing moment. The
pallor of false dawn was stealing across the sky when Micon
moved slightly and said in a low, hoarse voice, "Rajasta—"

The Priest of Light bent close to him. "I am here, my
brother."

Micon struggled to raise himself, but could not summon the
strength. "What hour is it?"

"Shortly before dawn. Lie still, my brother, and rest!"

"I must speak—" Micon's voice, husky and weak as it was,
had a resoluteness which Rajasta recognized, and would brook
no argument. "As you love me, Rajasta, stop me not. Bring
Deoris to me."

"Deoris?" For a moment Rajasta wondered if his friend's
reason had snapped. "At this hour? Why?"

"Because I ask it!" Micon's voice conceded nothing.
Rajasta, looking at the stubborn mouth, felt no desire to
argue. He went, after encouraging Micon to lie back, and
hoard his strength.

Deoris returned with him after a little delay, bewildered and disbelieving, dressed after a fashion; but Micon's first words banished her drowsy confusion, for he motioned her close and said, without preliminaries, "I need your help, little sister. Will you do something for me?"

Hardly hesitating, Deoris replied at once, "Whatever you wish."

Micon had managed to raise himself a little on one elbow, and now turned his face full toward her, with that expression which gave the effect of keen sight. His face seemed remote and stern as he asked, "Are you a virgin?"

Rajasta started. "Micon," he began.

"There is more here than you know!" Micon said, with unusual force. "Forgive me if I shock you, *but I must know;* I have my reasons, be sure of that!"

Before the Atlantean's unexpected vehemence, Rajasta retreated. For her part, Deoris could not have been more surprised if everyone in the room had turned into marble statuary, or removed their heads to play a game of ball with them.

"I am, Lord," she said, shyness and curiosity mixing in her tone.

"The Gods be praised," said Micon, pulling himself more upright on his bed. "Rajasta, go you to my travel chest; within you will find a bag of crimson silk, and a bowl of silver. Fill that bowl with clear water from a spring. Spill no drop upon the earth, and be sure that you return before the sun touches you."

Rajasta stared at him stiffly a moment, surprised and highly displeased, for he guessed Micon's intention; but he went to the chest, found the bowl, and departed, his mouth tightly clenched with disapproval; *for no one else,* he told himself, *would I do this thing!*

They awaited the Priest of Light's return in nearly complete silence, for though Deoris at first pressed him to tell her his intentions, Micon would only say that she would soon know, and that if she did not trust him, she was not bound to do as he asked.

At last Rajasta returned, and Micon directed, in a low voice, "Place it here, on this little table—good. Now, take from the chest that buckle of woven leather, and give it to Deoris—Deoris, take it from his hand, but touch not his fingers!" Once this had been done, and Micon had in his own hands the bag of crimson silk, the Atlantean went on, "Now, Deoris, kneel at my side; Rajasta, go you and stand afar from us—*let not even your shadow touch Deoris!*"

Micon's mutilated fingers were unsteady as he fumbled with the knot, unfastening the red silk. There was a short pause, and then, holding his hands so that Rajasta could not see what was between them, he said quietly, "Deoris—look at what I have in my hands."

Rajasta, watching in stiff disapproval, caught only a momentary but almost blinding flash of something bright and many-coloured. Deoris sat motionless, no longer fidgeting, her hands quiet on the hand-woven leather buckle—a clumsily-made thing, obviously the work of an amateur in leatherwork. Gently, Micon said, "Look into the water, Deoris. . . ."

The room was very still. Deoris's pale blue dress fluttered a little in the dawn breeze. Rajasta continued to fight back an unwonted anger; he disliked and distrusted such magic—such games were barely permissible when practiced by the Grey-robes, but for a Priest of Light to dabble in such manipulations! He knew he had no right to prevent this, but much as he loved Micon, in that moment, had the Atlantean been a whole man, Rajasta might have struck him and walked out, taking Deoris with him. The Guardian's severe code, however, allowed no such interference; he merely tightened his shoulders and looked forbidding—which, of course, had no effect whatever upon the Atlantean Prince.

"Deoris," Micon said softly, "what do you see?"

The girl's voice sounded childish, unmodulated. "I see a boy, dark and quick . . . dark-skinned, dark-haired, in a red tunic . . . barefoot . . . his eyes are grey—no, they are yellow. He is weaving something in his hands . . . it is the buckle I am holding."

"Good," Micon said quietly, "you have the Sight. I recognize your vision. Now put down the buckle, and look into the water again . . . *where is he now, Deoris?*"

There was a long silence, during which Rajasta gritted his teeth and counted slowly to himself the passing seconds, keeping silence by force of will.

Deoris sat still, looking into the basin of silvery water, surprised and a little scared. She had expected some kind of magical blankness; instead, Micon was just talking in an ordinary voice, and she—she was seeing pictures. They were like daydreams; was that what he wanted? Uncertain, she hesitated, and Micon said, with a little impatience, "Tell me what you see!"

Haltingly, she said, "I see a little room, walled in stone . . . a cell—no, just a little grey room with a stone floor and stone half way to the ceiling. He—he lies on a blanket, asleep . . ."

"Where is he? *Is he in chains?*"

Deoris made a startled movement. The pictures dissolved, ran before her eyes. Only rippling water filled the bowl. Micon breathed hard and forced his impatience under control. "Please, look and tell me where he is now," he asked gently.

"He is not in chains. He is asleep. He is in the—he is turning. His face—ah!" Deoris's voice broke off in a strangled cry. "Riveda's chela! The madman, the apostate—oh, send him away, send him—" The words jerked to a stop and she sat frozen, her face a mask of horror. Micon collapsed weakly, fighting to raise himself again.

Rajasta could hold himself aloof no longer. His pent-up emotion suddenly exploded into violence; he strode forward, wrenched the bowl from Deoris's hands and flung its contents from the window, hurling the bowl itself into a corner of the room, where it fell with a harsh musical sound. Deoris slid to the floor, sobbing noiselessly but in great convulsive spasms that wrenched her whole body in, and Rajasta, stooping over her, said curtly, "Stop that!"

"Gently, Rajasta," Micon muttered. "She will need—"

"I know what she will need!" Rajasta straightened, glanced at Micon, and decided that Deoris's need was more imperative. He lifted the girl to her feet, but she drooped on his arm. Rajasta, grimly angry, signalled to his slave and commanded, "Summon the Priest Cadamiri, at once!"

It was not more than a minute or two before the white-robed form of a Priest of Light, spare and erect, came with disciplined step from a nearby room; Cadamiri had been readying himself for the Ceremony of Dawn. Tall and gaunt, the Priest Cadamiri was still young: but his severe face was lined and ascetic. His stern eyes immediately took in the scene: the fainting child, the fallen silver bowl, Rajasta's grim face.

Rajasta, in a voice so low that even Micon's sharp ears could not hear, said, "Take Deoris to her rooms, and tend her."

Cadamiri raised a questioning eyebrow as he took the

swooning girl from Rajasta's arms. "Is it permitted to ask—?"

Rajasta glanced toward Micon, then said slowly, "Under great need, she was sent out over the Closed Places. You will know how to bring her back to herself."

Cadamiri hefted the sagging, half-lifeless weight of Deoris, and turned to carry her from the room, but Rajasta halted him. "Speak not of this! I have sanctioned it. Above all— say no word to the Priestess Domaris! Speak no falsehood to her, but see that she learns not the truth. Refer her to me if she presses you."

Cadamiri nodded and went, Deoris cradled in his arms like a small child—but Rajasta heard him mutter sternly, "What need could be great enough to sanction *this?*"

And to himself, Rajasta murmured, "I wish I knew!" Turning back to the racked figure of the Atlantean, he stood a moment, thoughtful. Micon's desire to learn the fate of his brother Reio-ta was understandable, but to put Deoris at hazard thus!

"I know what you are thinking," Micon said, tiredly. "You ask yourself why, if I had this method at my disposal, I did not use it earlier—or under more closely guarded auspices."

"For once," said Rajasta, his tone still curt, biting back anger, "you misread my thoughts. I am in fact wondering why you dabble in such things at all!"

Micon eased himself back against his cushions, sighing. "I make no excuses, Rajasta. I had to know. And—and your methods had failed. Do not fear for Deoris. I know," he said, waving a hand weakly as Rajasta began to speak again, "I know, there is some danger; but no more than she was in before, no more than you or Domaris are in—no more than my own unborn child, or any other who is near to me. Trust me, Rajasta. I know full well what I did—better than you, or you would not feel as you do."

"Trust you?" Rajasta repeated. "Yes, I trust you; else I would not have permitted this at all. Yet it was not for such a purpose that I became your disciple! I will honor my vow to you—but you must make compact with me, too, for as Guardian I can permit no more of this—this *sorcery!* Yes, you are right, we were all in danger merely by keeping you among us—but now you have given that danger a clearer focus! You have learned what you sought to know, and so I will forgive it; but had I known beforehand exactly what you intended—"

Micon laughed suddenly, unexpectedly. "Rajasta, Rajasta," he said, calming himself, "you say you trust me, and yet at the same time that you do not! But you say nothing of Riveda!"

Chapter Twelve

LIGHT'S HOSTAGE

I

Only the comparatively few high Initiates of the Priesthood of Light were admitted to this ceremony, and their white mantles made a ghostly gleaming in the shadowed chamber. The seven Guardians of the Temple were gathered together, but the sacred regalia upon their breasts was shrouded in swathes of silvery veilings, and all save Rajasta were hooded, their mantles drawn so closely over their heads that it was impossible to ascertain whether men or women stood there. As Guardian of the Outer Gate, Rajasta alone wore his blazoning clear to see on his breast, the symbol gleaming visible about his brow.

Laying his hand on Micon's arm, Rajasta said softly, "She comes."

Micon's haggard face became radiant, and Rajasta felt—not for the first time—the stab of an almost painful hope, as Micon asked eagerly, "How looks she?"

"Most beautiful," Rajasta returned, and his eyes dwelt on his Acolyte. "Robed in stainless white, and crowned with that flaming hair—as if in living light."

Indeed, Domaris had never seemed more beautiful. The shimmering robes lent her a grace and dignity that was new and yet wholly her own, and her coming motherhood, perfectly noticeable, was not yet a disfigurement. Her loveliness seemed such a visible radiance that Rajasta murmured softly, "Aye, Micon: light-crowned in truth."

The Atlantean sighed. "If I might—only once—behold her," he said, and Rajasta touched his arm in sympathy; but there was no time for further speech, for Domaris had advanced, and knelt before the high seat of the Guardians.

At the foot of the altar the eldest of the Guardians, Ragamon, now aged and grey but still erect with a serene dignity, stood with his hands outstretched to bless the kneeling woman. "Isarma, Priestess of Light, Acolyte to the Holy Temple; Isarma, daughter of Talkannon; vowed to the Light and to the Life that is Light, do you swear by the Father of Light and the Mother of Life, ever to uphold the powers of Life and of Light?" The old Guardian's voice, thin now, almost quavering, still held a vibrant power that clanged around the hewn rock of the chamber, and his narrowed eyes were clear and sharp as they studied the uplifted face of the white-clad woman. "Do you, Isarma, swear that, fearing nothing, you will guard the Light, and the Temple of Light, and the Life of the Temple?"

"I do so swear," she said, and stretched her hands toward the altar—and at that moment a single ray of sunlight lanced the gloom, kindling the pulsing golden light upon the altar. Even Rajasta was always impressed by this part of the rite— although he knew that a simple lever, operated by Cadamiri, had but caused some water to run through a pipe, altering the pipe's balance of weight and setting in motion a system of pulleys that opened a tiny aperture exactly overhead. It was a deception, but a sensible one: those who took their vows honestly were reassured by that beam of sunlight, while those who knelt and swore falsely were chastened, even terrified; more than once this little deception had saved the Guardians from undesirable infiltrations.

Domaris, her face aglow and reverent, laid her hands over her heart. "By the Light, by the Life, I so swear," she said again.

"Be watchful, vigilant and just," charged the ancient. "Swear it now not by yourself alone, not by the light within you and above you, but also by that Life you bear; pledge you now, as your surety and hostage, the child you carry in your womb; this lest you hold your task lightly."

Domaris rose to her feet. Her face was pallid and solemn, but her voice did not hesitate. "I do pledge the child of my body as hostage," she said, and both hands curved themselves about her body, then stretched again toward the altar, with a gesture of supplication, as if offering something to the light that played there.

Micon stirred a little, unquietly. "I like not that," he murmured.

"It is customary, that pledge," Rajasta reassured him, softly.

"I know, but—" Micon shrank, as if with pain, and was silent.

The old Guardian spoke again. "Then, my daughter, these be thine." At his signal, a mantle of white was laid about the woman's shoulders; a golden rod and a gold-hilted dagger were placed in her folded hands. "Use these justly. My mantle, my rod, my dagger, pass to you; punish, spare, strike or reward, but above all, Guard; for the Darkness eats ever at the Light." Ragamon stepped forward to touch her two hands. "My burden upon thee." He touched her bowed shoulders, and they straightened. "Upon thee, the seal of Silence." He drew up the hood of the mantle over her head. "Thou art Guardian," he said, and with a final gesture of blessing, vacated the raised space, leaving Domaris alone in the central place before the altar. "Fare thee well."

Chapter Thirteen

THE CHELA

I

The garden was dry now; leaves crackled underfoot, and blew about aimlessly with the night wind. Micon paced, slowly and silently, along the flagstoned walk. As he halted near the fountain, a lurking shadow sprang up noiselessly before him.

"Micon!" It was a racking whisper; then the shadow darted forward and Micon heard the sound of heavy breathing.

"Reio-ta—it is you?"

The shadow bowed his head, then sank humbly to his knees. "Micon . . . my Prince!"

"My brother," said Micon, and waited.

The chela's smooth face was old in the moonlight; no one could have known that he was younger than Micon.

"They betrayed me!" the chela said, raspily. "They swore you would go free—and unhurt! Micon—" His voice broke in agony. "Do not condemn me! I did not submit to them from cowardice!"

Micon spoke with the weariness of dead ages. "It is not for me to condemn you. Others will do that, and harshly."

"I—I could not bear—it was not for myself! It was only to stop your torture, to save you—"

For the first time, Micon's controlled voice held seeds of wrath. "Did I *ask* for life at your hands? Would I buy my freedom at such a price? That one who knows—what *you* know—might turn it to a—spiritual whoredom? *And you dare to say it was for my sake?"* His voice trembled. "I might have —forgiven it, had you broken under torture!"

The chela started back a little. "My Prince—my brother— forgive me!" he begged.

Micon's mouth was a stern line in the pallid light. "My forgiveness cannot lighten your ultimate fate. Nor could my curses add to it. I bear you no malice, Reio-ta. I could wish you no worse fate than you have brought upon yourself. May you reap no worse than you have sown. . . ."

"I—" The chela inched closer once more, still half crouching before Micon. "I would strive to hold it worthily, our power . . ."

Micon stood, straight, stiff and very still. "That task is not for you, not now." He paused, holding himself immobile, and in the silence the fountain gushed and spattered echoingly behind them. "Brother, fear not: *you shall betray our house not twice!"*

The figure at Micon's feet groaned, and turned his face away, hiding it in his hands.

Inflexibly, Micon went on, "That much I may prevent! Nay —say no more of it! You cannot, you know you cannot use our powers while I live—and I hold death from me, until I *know* you cannot so debase our line! Unless you kill me here and now, my son will inherit the power I hold!"

Reio-ta's grovelling figure sank lower still, until the prematurely old face rested against Micon's sandalled feet. "My Prince—I knew not of this—"

Micon smiled faintly. "This?" he repeated. "I forgive you this—and that I see not. But your apostasy I cannot forgive, for it is a cause that you, yourself, set in motion, and its effect *will* reach you; you will be ever incomplete. Thus far, and not further, can you go. My brother—" His voice softened. "I love you still, but our ways part here. Now go—before you rob me of what poor strength remains to me. Go—or end my life now, take the power and try to hold it. *But you will not be able to!* You are not ready to master the storm-wrack, the deep forces of earth and sky—and now you shall never be! Go!"

Reio-ta groaned in anguished sorrow, clasping Micon's knees. "I cannot bear—"

"Go!" said Micon again, sternly, steadily. "Go—while I

may yet hold back your destiny, as I hold back my own. Make what restitution you may."

"I cannot bear my guilt . . ." The voice of the chela was broken now, and sadder than tears. "Say one kind word to me —that I may know you remember that we were once brothers. . . ."

"You *are* my brother," Micon acknowledged gently. "I have said that I love you still. I do not abandon you utterly. But this must be our parting." He bent and laid a wasted hand upon the chela's head.

Crying out sharply, Reio-ta cringed away. "Micon! Your pain—burns!"

Slowly and with effort, Micon straightened and withdrew. "Go quickly," he commanded, and added, as if against his own will, in a voice of raw torture, *"I can bear no more!"*

The chela sprang to his feet and stood a moment, gazing haggardly at the other, as if imprinting Micon's features upon his memory for all time; then turned and ran, with stumbling feet, from his brother's presence.

The blind Initiate remained, motionless, for many minutes. The wind had risen, and dry leaves skittered on the path and all about him; he did not notice. Weakly, as if forcing his steps through quicksand, he turned at last and went toward the fountain, where he sank down upon the dampened stone rim, fighting the hurricane clamor of the pain that he refused to give mental lease. Finally, his strength all but gone, he lay huddled on the flagstones amid the windblown leaves, victoriously master of himself, but so spent that he could not move.

In response to some inner uneasiness, Rajasta came—and the face of the Guardian was a terrible thing to see as he gathered Micon up into his strong arms, and bore him away.

The next day, the whole force of the Temple gathered for the search. Riveda, suspected of connivance, was taken into custody for many hours, while they sought throughout the Temple precincts, and even in the city below, for the unknown chela who had once been Reio-ta of Ahtarrath.

But he had disappeared—and the Night of the Nadir was one day closer to them all.

Chapter Fourteen

THE UNREVEALED GOD

I

About three months after Deoris had been received into the Temple of Caratra, Riveda encountered her one evening in the gardens. The last rays of the setting sun turned the young Priestess into a fairy shape of mystery, and Riveda studied her slim, blue-garbed form and grave, delicate young face with a new interest as he carefully phrased his request. "Who would forbid you, if I should invite you to visit the Grey Temple with me, this evening?"

Deoris felt her pulses twitch. To visit the Grey Temple—in the company of their highest Adept! Riveda did her honor indeed! Still she asked, warily, "Why?"

The man laughed. "Why not? There is a ceremony this evening. It is beautiful—there will be some singing. Many of our ceremonials are secret, but to this one I may invite you."

"I will come," Deoris said. She spoke demurely, but inwardly she danced with excitement: Karahama's guarded confidences had awakened her curiosity, not only about the Grey-robes, but about Riveda himself.

They walked silently under the blossoming stars. Riveda's hand was light on her shoulder, but Deoris was intensely aware of the touch, and it made her too shy to speak until they neared the great windowless loom of the Temple. As Riveda held aside the heavy bronze doors for her to pass, Deoris shrank in amazed terror from the bent wraith that slipped past them—the chela!

Riveda's hand tightened on her arm until Deoris almost cried out. "Say nothing of this to Micon, child," he warned sternly. "Rajasta has been told that he lives; but it would kill Micon to be confronted with him again!"

Deoris bent her head and promised. Since that night when Cadamiri had carried her, senseless, from Micon's rooms, her awareness of Micon had been almost as complete as that of Domaris; the Atlantean's undercurrents of emotion and thought were clear to her, except where they concerned herself. Her broadened perceptions had gone almost unnoticed, except for her swift mastery of work far beyond her supposed skill in the Temple; not even Domaris had guessed at Deoris's wakening awareness. Domaris was now wholly absorbed in Micon, and in their coming child. And the waiting, Deoris knew—and there was still more than a month to wait—was an unbearable torment to both, a joy and yet an insufferable pain.

The bronze doors clamored shut. They stood in a narrow corridor, dimly dark, that stretched away between rows of closed stone doors. The haggard, haunted figure of the chela was nowhere to be seen.

Their footsteps were soundless, muffled in the dead air, and Deoris, moving in the silence, felt some electric tension in the man beside her, a coiled strength that was almost sensible to her nerves. At the end of the corridor was an arched door bound about with iron. Riveda knocked, using a curious pattern of taps, and from nowhere a shrill, high, bodiless voice challenged in unfamiliar syllables. Riveda spoke equally cryptic words in response; an invisible bell sounded in midair, and the door swung inward.

They passed into—greyness.

There was no lack of light, but warmth or color there was none; the illumination was serene and cold, a mere shimmer, a pallor, an absence of darkness rather than a positive light. The room was immense, lost above their heads in a grey dimness like a heavy fog, or solidified smoke. Beneath their feet, the floor was grey stone, cold and sprinkled with chips of crystal and mica; the walls, too, had a translucent glitter, like winter moonlight. The forms that moved tenuously, like wraiths of mist in the wan radiance, were grey as well; tenebrous shadows, cloaked and cowled and mantled in sorcerer's grey— and there were women among them, women who moved rest- lessly like chained flames, robed in shrouding veils of saffron color, dull and lightless. Deoris glanced guardedly at the women, in the moment before Riveda's strong hands turned her gently about so that she faced—

A Man.

He might have been man or carven idol, corpse or auto- maton. He *was*. That was all. He existed, with a curious sort of finality. He sat on the raised dais at one end of the huge Hall, on a great throne-like chair, a grey bird of carven stone poised above his head. His hands lay crossed on his breast. Deoris found herself wondering whether He were really there, or if she dreamed Him there. Involuntarily, she whispered, "Where sits the Man with Crossed Hands. . . ."

Riveda bent and whispered, "Remain here. Speak to no one." Straightening, he walked away. Deoris, watching him wistfully, thought that his straight figure, grey-robed and cowled in grey though he was, had a kind of sharpness, as if he were in focus whereas the others were shadowy, like dreams within a dream. Then she saw a face she knew.

Standing tautly poised, half-hidden by one of the crystal pillars, a young girl watched Deoris shyly; a child, tall but slight, her slim body still straight between the saffron veils, her small pointed face lifted a little and shadowed by the trans- lucent light. Frost-pale hair lay whitely around her shoulders, and the suppressed glitter of the Northern lights dwelt in her intent, colorless eyes. The diaphanous gauze about her body fluttered lightly in an invisible breeze; she seemed weightless, a wraith of frost, a shimmer of snowflakes in the chilly air.

But Deoris had seen her outside this eerie place, and knew she was real; this silver-haired girl slipped sometimes like a ghost in or out of Karahama's rooms. Karahama never spoke of the child, but Deoris knew that this was the nameless girl, the child of the *no people*, born to the then-still-outcast Karahama. Her mother, it was said, called her Demira, but she had no real name. By law, she did not exist at all.

No man, however willing, could have acknowledged Demira as his daughter; no man could have claimed or adopted her. Even Karahama had only a debatable legal existence—but Karahama, as the child of a free Temple woman, had a certain acknowledged, if illegitimate, status. Demira, under the strict laws of the Priest's Caste, was not even illegitimate. She was nothing. She was covered by no law, protected by no statute, recorded in no Temple writing; she was not even a slave. She quite simply *did not exist*. Only here, among the lawless *saji*, could she have found shelter and sustenance.

The stern code of the Temple forbade Deoris, Priest's daughter and Priestess, to recognize the nameless girl in any way—but although they had never exchanged a single word, Deoris knew that Demira was her own near kinswoman, and the child's strange, fantastic beauty excited Deoris's pity and interest. She now raised her eyes and smiled timidly at the outcaste girl, and Demira smiled back—a quick, furtive smile.

Riveda returned, his eyes abstracted and vague, and Demira slipped behind a pillar, out of sight.

II

The Temple was crowded now, with men in grey robes and the saffron-shrouded *saji*, some of whom held curious stringed instruments, rattles and gongs. There were also many chelas in grey kilts, their upper bodies bare except for curious amulets; none were very old, and most of them were approximately Deoris's own age. Some were only little boys of five or six. Looking about the room, Deoris counted only five persons in the full grey robe and cowl of Adeptship—and realized, startled, that one of these was a woman; the only woman there, except Deoris herself, who was not wearing the *saji* veils.

Gradually, the Magicians and Adepts formed a roughly circular figure, taking great pains about their exact positions. The *saji* with their musical instruments, and the smaller chelas, had withdrawn toward the translucent walls. From their ranged ranks came the softest of pipings, a whimper of flutes, the echo of a gong touched with a steel-clad fingertip.

Before each Magician stood either a chela or one of the *saji*; sometimes three or four clustered before one of the Adepts or one of the oldest Magicians—but the chelas were in the majority, only four or five of those in the inner ring being women. One of these was Demira, her veils thrown back so that her silver hair glittered like moonlight on the sea.

Riveda motioned Reio-ta to take his place in the forming Ring, then paused and asked, "Deoris, have you the courage to stand for me in the Chela's Ring tonight?"

"Why, I—" Domaris stuttered with astonishment. "I know nothing of it, how could I—?"

Riveda's stern mouth held the shadow of a smile. "No knowledge is necessary. In fact the less you know of it, the better. Try to think of nothing—and let it come to you." He signalled Reio-ta to guide her, and, with a final look of appeal, Deoris went.

Flutes and gongs broke suddenly into a dissonant, harsh chord, as if tuning, readying. Adepts and Magicians cocked their heads, listening, testing something invisible and intangible. Deoris, the chord elusive in her skull, felt herself drawn into the Ring between Reio-ta and Demira. A spasm of panic closed her throat; Demira's small steely fingers clutched hers like torturer's implements. In a moment she must scream with horror. . . .

The flattened impact of Riveda's hand struck her clenched fingers, and her frenzied grasp loosened and fell free. He shook his head at her briefly and, without a word, motioned her out of the Ring. He did not do it as if the failure meant anything to him; he seemed absolutely abstracted as he beckoned to a *saji* girl with a face like a seagull to take her place.

Two or three other chelas had been dismissed from the Ring; others were being placed and replaced. Twice more the soft but dissonant chords sounded, and each time positions and patterns were altered. The third time, Riveda held up his hand, looking angry and annoyed, and stepped from his place, glaring around the Chela's Ring. His eyes fell upon Demira, and roughly, with a smothered monosyllable, he grasped the girl's shoulder and pushed her violently away. She reeled and almost fell—at which the woman Adept stepped out of line and caught the staggering child. She held Demira for a minute; then, carefully, her wrinkled hands encircling the child's thin wrist, she re-guided her into the Ring, placing her with a challenging glance at Riveda.

Riveda scowled darkly. The woman Adept shrugged, and gently moved Demira once more, and then again, changing her position until suddenly Riveda nodded, immediately taking his eyes from Demira and apparently forgetting her existence.

Again the dissonant whimper of flutes and strings and gongs

sounded. This time there was no interruption. Deoris stood watching, faintly bewildered. The chelas answered the music with a brief chanting, beautifully timed but so alien to Deoris's experience that it seemed meaningless. Accustomed to the exalted mysticism of the Temple of Light, and the sparse simplicity of their rituals, this protracted litany of intonation and gesture, music and chant and response, was incomprehensible.

This is silly, Deoris decided, *it doesn't mean anything at all.* Or did it? The face of the woman Adept was thin and lined and worn, although she seemed young, otherwise; Riveda's aspect, in the pitiless light, gave the impression almost of cruelty, while Demira's fantastic, frosty beauty seemed unreal, illusive, with something hard and vicious marring the infantile features. All at once, Deoris could understand why, to some, the ceremonies of the Grey Temple might seem tinged with evil.

The chanting deepened, quickened, pulsed in strange monodies and throbbing cadences. A single whining, wailing dissonance was reiterated; the muffled piping came behind her like a smothered sob; a shaken drum rattled weirdly.

The Man with Crossed Hands was watching her.

Neither then nor ever did Deoris know whether the Man with Crossed Hands was idol, corpse, or living man, demon, god, or image. Nor was she able—then or ever—to determine how much of what she saw was illusion . . .

The eyes of the Man were grey. Grey as the sea; grey as the frosty light. She sank deep into their compelling, compassionate gaze, was swallowed up and drowned there.

The bird above his chair flapped grey stone wings and flew, with a harsh screech, into a place of grey sands. And then Deoris was running after the bird, among needled rocks and the shadows of their spires, under skies split by the raucous screaming of seagulls.

Far away, the booming of surf rode the winds; Deoris was near the sea, in a place between dawn and sunrise, coldly grey, without color in sands or sea or clouds. Small shells crunched beneath her sandals, and she smelled the rank stench of salt water and seaweed and marshy reeds and rushes. To her left, a cluster of small conical houses with pointed grey-white roofs sent a pang of horror through Deoris's breast.

The Idiot's Village! The awful stab of recognition was so

sharp a shock that she thrust aside a briefly flickering certainty that she had never seen this place before.

There was a deathly silence around and between and over the screeching of the seagulls. Two or three children, large-headed and white-haired with red eyes and mouths that drooled above swollen pot-bellied torsos squatted, listless, between the houses, mewling and muttering to one another. Deoris's parched lips could not utter the screams that scraped in her throat. She turned to flee, but her foot twisted beneath her and she fell. Struggling to rise, she caught sight of two men and a woman coming out of the nearest of the chinked pebble-houses; like the children, they were red-eyed and thick-lipped and naked. One of the men tottered with age; the other groped, his red eyes caked blots of filth and blood; the woman moved with a clumsy waddling, hugely swollen by pregnancy into an animal, primal ugliness.

Deoris crouched on the sands in wildly unreasoning horror. The half-human idiots were mewling more loudly now, grimacing at her; their fists made scrabbling noises in the colorless sands. Scrambling fearfully to her feet, Deoris looked madly around for a way of escape. To one side, a high wall of needled rock bristled her away; to the other, a quicksand marsh of reeds and rushes stretched on to the horizon. Before her the idiots were clustering, staring, blubbering. She was hemmed in.

But, how did I come here? Was there a boat?

She spun around, and saw only the empty, rolling sea. Far, far in the distance, mountains loomed up out of the water, and long streaks of reddening clouds, like bloody fingers, scraped the skies raw.

And when the sun rises . . . when the sun rises . . . The vagrant thought slipped away. More of the huge-headed villagers were crowding out of the houses. Deoris began to run, in terror-stricken panic.

Ahead of her, lancing through the greyness and the bloody outstretched streaks of sullen light, a sudden spark flared into a glowing golden gleam. *Sunlight!* She ran even faster, her footsteps a thudding echo of her heart; behind her the groping pad-pad-pad of the pursuit was like a merciless incoming tide.

A stone sailed past her ears. Her feet splashed in the surf as she turned, whirling like a cornered animal. Someone rose up before her, red hideous eyes gleaming emptily, lips drawn back over blackened and broken teeth in a bestial snarl. Frantically, struck the clutching hands away, kicked and twisted and struggled free—heard the creature shrieking its mindless howling cries as she stumbled, ran on, stumbled again—and fell.

The light on the sea exploded in a burst of sunshine, and she stretched her hands toward it, sobbing, crying out no more coherently than the idiots behind her. A stone struck her shoulder; another grazed her skull. She struggled to rise, scratching at the wet sands, clawing to free herself from groping, scrabbling hands. Someone was screaming, a high, wild ululation of anguish. Something hit her hard in the face. Her brain exploded in fire and she sank down . . . and down . . . and down . . . as the sun burst in her face and she died.

III

Someone was crying.

Light dazzled her eyes. A sharp-sweet, dizzying smell stung her nostrils.

Elis's face swam out of the darkness, and Deoris choked weakly, pushed away the hand that held the strong aromatic to her nostrils.

"Don't, I can't breathe—Elis!" she gasped.

The hands on her shoulders loosened slightly, laid her gently back in a heap of pillows. She was lying on a couch in Elis's room in the House of the Twelve, and Elis was bending over her. Behind Elis, Elara was standing, wiping her eyes, her face looking drawn and worried.

"I must go now to the lady Domaris," Elara said shakily.

"Yes, go," Elis said without looking up.

Deoris struggled to sit up, but pain exploded blindingly in her head and she fell back. "What happened?" she murmured weakly. "How did I get here? Elis, what *happened?*"

To Deoris's horror, Elis, rather than answering, began to cry, wiping her eyes with her veil.

"Elis—" Deoris's voice quavered, little-girlish. "*Please* tell me. I was—in the Idiot's Village, and they threw stones—" Deoris touched her cheek, her skull. Though she fancied she felt a stinging sensation, there were no lacerations, no swellings. "Oh, my head!"

"You're raving again!" Elis grabbed Deoris's shoulders and shook her, hard. It brought a sudden flash of horror; then the vague half-memory closed down again as Elis snapped, "Don't you even remember what you did?"

"Oh, Elis, stop! Please don't, it hurts my head so," Deoris moaned. "Can't you tell me what happened? How did I get here?"

"You don't remember!" Shock and disbelief were in Elis's voice. As Deoris struggled to sit up again, Elis supported her cousin with an arm around her shoulders. Still touching her head, Deoris looked toward the window. It was late afternoon, the sun just beginning to lengthen the shadows. *Yet it had been before moonrise when she went with Riveda—*

"I don't remember anything," Deoris said shakily. "Where is Domaris?"

Elis's mouth, which had softened, became set and angry again. "In the House of Birth."

"Now?"

"They were afraid—" A strained fury tightened Elis's voice; she swallowed hard and said, "Deoris, I swear that if Domaris loses her child because of this, I will—"

"Elis, let me come in," someone outside the door said; but before any reply could be made, Micon entered, leaning heavily on Riveda's arm. Unsteadily, the Atlantean moved to the bedside. "Deoris," he said, "can you tell me—"

Hysterical laughter mixed with sobs in Deoris's throat. "What can I tell *you?*" she cried. *"Doesn't anybody know what's happened to me!"*

Micon sighed deeply, slumping noticeably where he stood. "I feared this," he said, with a great bitterness. "She knows nothing, remembers nothing. Child—my dear child! You must never allow yourself to be—used—like that again!"

Riveda looked tense and weary, and his grey robe was crumpled and darkly stained. "Micon of Ahtarrath, I swear—"

Abruptly, Micon pulled away from the support of Riveda's arm. "I am not yet ready for you to swear!"

At this, Deoris somehow got to her feet and stood swaying, sobbing with pain and fright and frustration. Micon, with that unerring sense that served him so well instead of sight, reached toward her clumsily—but Riveda drew the girl into his own arms with a savage protectiveness. Gradually her trembling stilled, and she leaned against him motionless, her cheek resting against the rough material of his robe.

"You shall not blame *her!*" Riveda said harshly. "Domaris is safe—"

"Nay," said Micon, conciliatingly, "I meant not to blame, but only—"

"I know well that you hate me, Lord of Ahtarrath," Riveda interrupted, "though I—"

"I hate no one!" Micon broke in, sharply. "Do you insinuate—"

"Once for all, Lord Micon," Riveda snapped, "I do not *insinuate!*" With a great gentleness that contrasted strangely with his harsh words, Riveda helped Deoris to return to the couch. "Hate me if you will, Atlantean," the Grey-robe said, "you and your Priestess leman—and that unborn—"

"Have a care!" said Micon, ominously.

Riveda laughed, scornful—but his next words died in his throat, for out of the clear and cloudless sky outside the window came the rolling rumble of impossible thunder as Micon's fists clenched. Elis, forgotten, cowered in the corner, while Deoris began to shiver uncontrollably. Micon and Riveda faced each other, Adepts of vastly different disciplines, and the tension between them was like an invisible, but tangible, force, quivering in the room.

Yet it lasted only a moment. Riveda swallowed, and said, "My words were strong. I spoke in anger. But what have I done to merit your insults, Micon of Ahtarrath? My beliefs are not yours—none could fail to see that—but you know my creed as I know yours! By the Unrevealed God, would *I* harm a childing woman?"

"Am I then to believe," Micon asked savagely, "that a Priestess of Caratra would—*of her own will*—harm the sister she adores?"

Deoris's hands went to her mouth in a wordless shriek and she ran to Elis, clinging to her cousin and sobbing in nightmarish disbelief.

"I invited the child," Riveda stated, coldly, "to witness a ceremony in the Grey Temple. Believe, if you will, that it was with malice and forethought—that I invoked Dark Powers. But I give you my word, the pledged word of an Adept, that I meant no more than courtesy! A courtesy it is my privilege to extend to any regularly pledged Priest or Priestess."

Save for the muted snuffling of Deoris, still huddled against Elis, the room was quite silent. The late afternoon light had vanished, as if night had come, while the skies continued to fill with sudden, heavy clouds. The two women dared not even so much as look at the wrangling Adepts.

Yet at last the awful tensions in the room abated somewhat; the very stones of the walls seemed to sigh in relief as Micon half-turned away from Riveda, who, had any been watching, could have been seen to blink several times, and wipe a cold sweat from his forehead.

"During the ceremony," the Grey-robe resumed, in a quiet voice, "Deoris became giddy and fell to the floor; one of the girls took her into the open air. Afterward, it did not seem serious. She spoke to me quite normally. I conducted her to the gates of the House of the Twelve. That is all that I know of this. All." Riveda spread his hands, then looked around at Deoris and asked her gently, "Do you truly remember nothing?"

Deoris shuddered as the terror she had been thought closed in again, squeezing her heart with icy talons. "I was watching the—the Man with Crossed Hands," she whispered. "The—the bird on his throne flew! And then I was in the Idiot's Village—"

"Deoris!" Micon's cry was a strained and hoarse shout. The Atlantean drew a deep breath that was almost a sob. "What mean you by—the Idiot's Village?"

"Why, I—" Deoris's eyes grew wide, and with growing horror, she whispered, "I don't know, I never—I never heard of—"

"Gods! Gods!" Micon's haggard face was suddenly like that of a very old man, and he staggered where he stood; gone now was the inner strength that had called on the powers of Ahtarrath, as he stumbled and groped his way into a nearby chair. "I feared that! And it has come!" He bent his head, covered his face with gaunt and twisted hands.

Deoris, at seeing Micon's sudden weakness, had left Elis and rushed to the Atlantean's side. Half-kneeling before him, she pleaded, "Micon, tell me! *What did I do?*"

"Pray that you never remember!" Micon said, his voice muffled behind his hands. "But by the mercy of the Gods, Domaris is unhurt!"

"But—" Deoris found herself oddly unable to speak that

name which had so upset Micon, and so instead said only, "But that place—what—how could I have—?" Her voice broke down utterly.

Micon, regaining control of himself, stretched one trembling hand to the crown of her head and drew the sobbing girl to him. "An old sin," he murmured, in a quavery old man's voice, "an all-but-forgotten shame of the House of Ahtarrath . . . *enough!* This attack was not aimed at you, Deoris, but at—at one of the Ahtarrath yet unborn. Do not torture yourself, child."

Silent, Riveda stood, unmoving as stone, his arms crossed tight upon his chest, his lips tightly set and his bright blue eyes half-closed. Elis sat shivering on the couch, staring at the floor, alone with her thoughts.

"Go to Domaris, my darling," said Micon softly; and after a moment, Deoris wiped away her tears, kissed the Atlantean's hand reverently, and went. Elis rose and followed her from the room on tiptoe. Behind them was silence.

Riveda broke the stillness, saying roughly, "I will never rest easy until I know who has done this!"

Micon dragged himself heavily to his feet. "What I said was the truth; this was an attack on me, through my son. I personally am not now worth attacking."

Riveda chuckled—a low-pitched rumble of cynical amusement. "I wish I had known that a few minutes ago, when the very thunders of heaven came to your defense!" The Greyrobe paused, then asked, softly, "Or is it that you do not trust me?"

Micon answered sharply, "You are in part to blame; though you took Deoris into danger unknowing, nonetheless—"

Riveda's fury exploded, spilled over. "*I* to blame? What of you? Had you managed to pocket your damnable pride long enough to testify against these devils, they would have been flogged to death long ago, and this could not have happened! Lord of Ahtarrath, I intend to cleanse my Order! Not now for your sake, nor even to preserve my own reputation—that has never been so good! But the health of my Order requires—" He suddenly realized he was shouting, and lowered his voice. "He who allows sorcery is worse than he who commits it. Men may sin from ignorance or folly—but what of a wise man, pledged to cleave to Light, whose charity is so great that he refuses even to protect the innocent, for fear of injuring the

guilty? If that is the path of Light, I say, let Darkness fall!''
Riveda, looking down at the collapsed Micon, felt his last
anger fading. He put his hand on the Atlantean's thin shoulder
and said gravely, ''Prince of Ahtarrath, I swear that I will find
who has done this, though it cost me my own life!''

Micon said, in a voice whose very shrillness revealed the
edge of exhaustion, ''Seek not too far, Riveda! Already you
are too deeply involved in this. Look to yourself, lest it cost
you more than your life!''

Riveda emitted a little snort of ugly, mirthless laughter.
''Keep your dooms and prophecies, Prince Micon! I have no
less love for life than any other—but it is my task to find the
guilty, and take steps to prevent another such—incident.
Deoris, too, must be guarded—and it is my right to guard her,
even as it is yours to guard Domaris.''

Micon said, in a quick, low voice, ''What mean you?''

Riveda shrugged. ''Nothing, perhaps. It may be your
prophecy carries its own contagion, and I see my own karma
reflected in yours.'' He stared at Micon, his eyes wide and
bleak and blue. ''I don't know quite why I said that. But you
will not bid me spare punishment to those responsible!''

Micon sighed, and his emaciated hands twitched slightly.
''No, I will not,'' he murmured. ''That, too, is karma!''

Chapter Fifteen

THE SIN THAT QUICKENS

I

Only in extreme emergency or death were men allowed within the boundaries of the Temple of Caratra; however, the circumstances were unusual, and after certain delays Mother Ysouda conducted Micon to the rooftop court where Domaris had been taken, for coolness, once they knew that her child would not be prematurely born.

"You must not stay long," the old Priestess cautioned, and left them alone.

Micon waited until her receding footsteps were lost on the stairs, then said with a mirthful sternness that mocked its own anxiety, "So, you have terrified us all for nothing, my Lady!"

Domaris smiled wanly. "Blame your son, Micon, not his mother! Already he thinks himself lord of his surroundings!"

"Well, and is he not?" Micon seated himself beside her and asked, "Has Deoris been to you?"

She looked away. "Yes. . . ."

Micon's hand closed gently on hers and he said lovingly, "Heart-of-flame, be not resentful. Our child is safe—and Deoris is as innocent as you, beloved!"

"I know—but your son is very precious to me!" Domaris whispered; then, with implacable vehemence: "That—damned —Riveda!"

"Domaris!" In surprise and displeasure, Micon covered her lips with his hand. She kissed the palm, and he smiled, then went on gently, "Riveda knew nothing of this. His only fault was that he suspected no evil." He touched her eyes, lightly, with his gaunt fingers. "You must not cry, beloved—" Then, half-hesitant, his hand lingered. "May I—?"

"Of course." Divining his wish, Domaris took his hand lightly in hers, guiding it gently across her swollen body. Suddenly, all of Micon's senses coalesced; past and present fell together in a single coherent moment of sensation so intense that it seemed almost as if he saw, as if every sense combined to bring the meaning of life home to him. He had never been so keenly alive as in that moment when he smelled the sharp-sweet odor of drugs, the elusive perfume of Domaris's hair, and the clean fragrance of linens; the air was moist with the cool and salty sting of the sea, and he heard the distant boom of surf and the gurgle of the fountain, the muted sounds of women's voices in distant rooms. Under his hand he felt the fine textures of silk and linen, the pulsing warmth of the woman-body, and then, through the refined sensitivity of his fingers, he felt a sharp little push, a sudden slight bulging, elusive as a butterfly beneath his hand.

With a quick movement, Domaris sat up and stretched her arms to Micon, holding herself to him in an embrace so light that she barely touched the man. She had learned caution, where a careless touch or caress could mean agony for the man she loved—and Domaris, young and passionately in love, had not easily learned that lesson! But for once Micon forgot caution. His arms tightened about her convulsively. Once, once only he should have had the right to see this woman he loved with every atom, every nerve of his whole being. . . .

The moment passed, and he admonished gently, "Lie still, beloved. They made me promise not to disturb you." He loosed her, and she lay back, watching him with a smile so resigned that Domaris herself did not know it was sorrowful. "And yet," said Micon, his voice troubled, "we have been too cowardly to speak of many things . . . . There is your duty to Arvath. You are bound by law to—to what, exactly?"

"Before marriage," Domaris murmured, "we are free. So runs the law. After marriage—it is required that we remain constant. And if I should fail, or refuse, to give Arvath a son—"

"Which you must not," said Micon with great gentleness.

"I shall not refuse," Domaris assured him. "But if I should fail, I would be dishonoured, disgraced . . ."

"This is my karma," Micon said sorrowfully, "that I may never see my son, that I may not live to guide him. I sinned against that same law, Domaris."

"Sin?" Domaris's voice betrayed her shock. *"You?"*

He bent his head in shamed avowal. "I desired the things of the spirit, and so I am—Initiate. But I was too proud to recall that I was a man, too, and so under the law." The blind face brooded, distantly. "In my pride I chose to live as an ascetic and deny my body, under the false name of worthy austerity—"

Domaris whispered, "That is necessary to such accomplishment—"

"You have not heard all, beloved. . . ." Micon drew a shaky breath. "Before I entered the Priesthood, Mikantor required me to take a wife, and raise up a son to my house and my name." The stern mouth trembled a little, and his rigid self-control faltered. "As my father commanded, so I allowed myself to be wedded by the law. She was a young girl, pure and lovely, a princess; but I was—I was blind to her as I am—" Micon's voice broke altogether, and he covered his face with his hands. At last he spoke, in a suffocated voice. "And so it is my fate that I may never look on your face—you that I love more than life and more than death! I was blind to her, I told her coldly and—and cruelly, Domaris—that I was vowed a Priest, and—and she left my marriage-bed as virgin as she came to me. And in that, I humiliated her and sinned, against my father and against myself and against our whole House! Domaris—knowing this—can you still love me?"

Domaris had turned deathly white; what Micon had confessed was regarded as a crime. But she only whispered, "Thou hast paid the price, thrice over, Micon. And—and it brought thee to me. And I love thee!"

"I do not regret that." Micon's lips pressed softly against her hand. "But—can you understand this? Had I had a son, I could have died, and my brother been spared his apostasy!" The dark face was haunted and haggard. "Thus I carry the blame for his sin; and other evil shall follow—for evil plants evil, and reaps and harvests a hundredfold, and sows evil yet again . . ." He paused and said, "Deoris too may need protection. Riveda is contaminate with the Black-robes."

At her quick gasp of horror, he added quickly, "No, what you are thinking is not true. He is no Black-robe, he despises them; but he is intelligent, and seeks knowledge, and he is not too fastidious where he acquires it. . . . Never underrate the power of intellectual curiosity, Domaris! It leads to more trouble than any other human motive! If Riveda *were* malicious, or deliberately cruel, he would be less dangerous! But he serves only one motive: the driving force of a powerful mind which has never been really challenged. He is entirely devoid of any personal ambition. He seeks and serves knowledge for its own sake. Not for service, not for self-perfection. If he were a more selfish man, I would feel easier about him. And—and Deoris loves him, Domaris."

"*Deoris?* Loves that detestable old—?"

Micon sighed. "Riveda is not so old. Nor does Deoris love him as—as you and I understand love. If it were only that, I would feel no concern. Love is not to be compelled. He is not the man I should have chosen for her, but I am not her guardian." He sensed something of the woman's confusion and added quietly, "No, this is something other. And it disturbs me. Deoris is barely old enough to feel *that* kind of love, or to know it exists. Nor—" He paused. "I hardly know how to say this . . . She is not a girl who will grow easily to know passion. She must ripen slowly. If she should be too soon awakened, I would fear for her greatly! And she loves Riveda! She adores him—although I do not think she knows it herself. To give Riveda his due, I do not believe he has fostered it. But understand me: he could violate her past the foulest prostitution and leave her virgin—or he could keep her in innocence, though she bore him a dozen children!"

Domaris, troubled and even a little dazed by Micon's unusual vehemence, bit her lip and said, "I *don't* understand!"

Reluctantly, Micon said, "You know of the *saji*—"

"Ah, no!" It was a cry of horror. "Riveda would not dare!"

"I trust not. But Deoris may not be wise in loving." He forced a weary smile. "*You* were not wise, to be sure! But—" Again he sighed. "Well, Deoris must follow her karma, as we follow ours." Hearing Domaris's sigh, an echo of his own, Micon accused himself. "I have tired you!"

"No—but he is heavy now, and—your son hurts me."

"I am sorry—if only I could bear it for you!"

Domaris laughed a little, and her hands, feather-soft, stole into his. "You are Prince of Ahtarrath," she said gaily, "and I am your most obedient handmaiden and slave. But this one privilege you cannot have! I know my rights, my Prince!"

The grave sternness of his face relaxed again, and a delighted grin took its place as he bent to kiss her. "That would indeed be magic of an extraordinary sort," he admitted. "We of Ahtarrath have certain powers over nature, it is true. But alas, all my powers could not encompass even such a little miracle!"

Domaris relaxed; the moment of danger was past. Micon would not break again.

But the Night of the Nadir was almost upon them.

Chapter Sixteen

THE NIGHT OF
THE NADIR

I

These months have not been kind to Micon, Rajasta thought, sad and puzzled by the Atlantean's continuing failure to heal to any significant degree.

The Initiate stood before the window now, his gaunt and narrow body barely diminishing the evening light. With a nervousness of motion that was becoming less and less foreign to him, Micon fingered the little statuette of Nar-inabi, the Star-Shaper.

"Where got you this, Rajasta?"

"You recognize it?"

The blind man bent his head, half-turning away from Rajasta. "I cannot say that—now. But I—know the craftsmanship. It was made in Ahtarrath, and I think it could belong only to my brother, or to me." He hesitated. "Such works as this are—extremely costly. This type of stone is very rare." He half-smiled. "Still, I suppose I am not the only Prince of Ahtarrath ever to travel, or have something stolen. Where did you find it?"

Rajasta did not reply. He had found it in this very building, in the servants' quarters. He told himself that this did not necessarily implicate any of the residents, but the implications dismayed and sickened him, for it was by the same token impossible, now, to eliminate any of them as suspects. Riveda might be truly as innocent as he claimed, and the true guilt lie elsewhere, perhaps among the very Guardians themselves—Cadamiri, or Ragamon the Elder, even Talkannon himself! These suspicions shook Rajasta's world to the very foundations.

A haunting sadness drifted across Micon's face as, with a lingeringly gentle touch, he set the exquisitely carven, opalescent figurine carefully on a little table by the window. "My poor brother," he whispered, almost inaudibly—and Rajasta, hearing, could not be quite sure that Micon referred to Reiota.

Realizing that he had to say something, the Priest of Light took refuge in pleasantries. "Already it is the Nadir-night, Micon, and you need have no fear; your son will surely not be born tonight. I have just come from Domaris; she and those who tend her assure me of that. She will sleep soundly in her own rooms," Rajasta went on, "without awakening and without fear of any omens or portents. I have asked Cadamiri to give her a sleeping drug. . . ."

Yet, as he had spoken, the Priest of Light had stumbled slightly over the name of Cadamiri, as his new-found apprehension conflicted with his desire to assure Micon. The Atlantean, sensing this without knowing the precise reason for Rajasta's nervousness, grew rigid with tension.

"The Nadir-night?" Micon half-whispered. "Already? I had lost count of the days!"

A fitful gust of wind stirred in the room, bringing a faint echo; a chant, in a strange wailing minor key, weirdly cadenced and prolonged. Rajasta's brows lifted and he inclined his head to listen, but Micon turned and went, not swiftly but with a concentrated intention, to the window again. There was deep trouble on his features, and the Priest came to stand beside him.

"Micon?" he said, with a questioning unhappiness.

"I know that chant!" the Atlantean gasped. "And what it forebodes—" He raised his thin hands and laid them gropingly on Rajasta's shoulders. "Stay thou with me, Rajasta! I—" His voice faltered. *"I am afraid!"*

The older man stared at him in ill-concealed horror, glad Micon could not see him. Rajasta had been with Micon through times of what seemed the ultimate of human extremity —yet never had the Initiate betrayed fear like this!

"I will not leave you, my brother," he promised—and the chant sounded again, ragged phrases borne eerily on the wind as the sun sank into the dusk. The Priest felt Micon grow tense, the wracked hands clutching on Rajasta's shoulders, the noble face ashen and trembling, a shivering that gradually crept over the man's entire body until every nerve seemed to quiver with a strained effort. . . . And then, despite the visible dread in Micon's bearing and features, the Atlantean released his hold on Rajasta and turned again to the window, to stare sightlessly at the gathering darkness, his face listening avidly.

"My brother lives," Micon said at last, and his words fell like drum-beats of doom, slow-paced in the falling night. "Would that he did not! None of the line of Ahtarrath chants thus, unless—unless—" His voice trailed away again, giving way to that listening stillness.

Suddenly Micon turned, letting his forehead fall against the older man's shoulder, clutching at him in the grip of emotions so intense that they found a mirror in Rajasta's mind, and both men trembled with unreasoning fear; nameless horrors flickered in their thoughts.

Only the wind had steadied: the broken cadences were more sustained now, rising and falling with a nightmarish, demanding, monotonous, aching insistence that kept somehow a perfect rhythm with the pounding of blood in their ears.

"They call on *my power!*" Micon gasped brokenly. "This is black betrayal! Rajasta!" He raised his head, and the unseeing features held a desperation that only increased the terror of the moment. *"How shall I survive this night?* And I must! I must! If they succeed—if that which they invoke—be summoned—only my single life stands between it and all of mankind!" He paused, gasping for breath, shivering uncontrollably. "If that link be made—then even I cannot be sure I can stay the evil!" He stood, half-swaying, at once twisted and yet utterly erect, clinging to Rajasta; his words fell like dropped stones. "Only three times in all our history has Ahtarrath summoned thus! And thrice that power has been harnessed but hardly."

Rajasta gently raised his own hands to echo Micon's, so that they stood with their hands upon each other's shoulders. "Micon!" said Rajasta sharply. *"What must we do?"*

The Atlantean's clutching hands relaxed a little, tightened, and then fell to his sides. "You would help me?" he said, in a broken, almost childish voice. "It means—"

"Do not tell me what it means," said Rajasta, his own voice quaking a little. *"But I will help you."*

Micon drew a shaky breath; the least bit of color returned to his face. "Yes," he murmured, and then, his voice becoming stronger, "yes, have not much time."

II

Groping in the chest where he kept his private treasures, Micon took out a flexible cloak of some metallic fabric and drew it about his shoulders. Next he removed a sword wrapped in sheer, filmy cloth, which he set down close beside him. Muttering to himself in his native tongue, Micon rummaged in the chest for no little while until he at last brought out a small bronze gong, which he handed to Rajasta with the admonition that it must not touch the floor or walls.

All the time the awful chant rose and fell, rose and fell, with eerie wailing overtones and sobbing, savage cadences; a diapason of sonic minors that beat on the brain with bone-shaking reiteration. Rajasta stood holding the gong, concentrating his attention fully on Micon as he bent over the chest again, shutting his mind and ears to that sound.

The Atlantean's angry mutterings turned to a sigh of relief, and he brought forth a final object—a little brazier of bronze, curiously worked with embossed figures that bulged and intertwined in a fashion that confused the eye into thinking they moved. After a moment Rajasta recognized them for what they were, a representation of fire-elementals.

With the sparse economy of movement so characteristically his, Micon rose to his feet, the wrapped sword in one hand. "Rajasta," he said, "give me the gong." When this was done, the Atlantean went on, "Move the brazier to the center of the room, and build thou a fire—pine and cypress and ultar." His words were clipped and brief, as if he recited a lesson learned well.

Rajasta, ignoring the second thoughts that already besieged him, set about the task resolutely. Micon went to the window again, and placed the sword upon the little table next to the figurine of Nar-inabi. Unwrapping the cloth, he exposed the decorated blade and the bejewelled hilt of the ceremonial weapon, and grasped it firmly again, to stand facing the window in a strained, listening attitude; Rajasta could almost see the Initiate gathering strength to himself; in sudden sympathy, he laid his hand on Micon's arm.

Micon stirred, impatiently. "Is the fire ready?"

Rebuked, the Priest bent to the brazier; kindling the slivers of fragrant wood, scattering the grains of incense over the thin blaze. Clouds of misty white smoke billowed upward; the smouldering woods were tiny sullen eyes glaring through the smoke.

Far away the chant rose and fell, rose and fell, gathering strength and volume. The thin column of fire rolled narrowly upward through the smoke, and subsided.

"It is ready," Rajasta said—and the chanting swelled, a rising flood of sound; and around the sound crept silence, as if the very pulses of the living were hushed and slow and heavy.

Almost majestic of aspect, quite changed from the Micon Rajasta knew so well, the Atlantean Initiate moved slowly to the room's centre, placed the very tip of the ceremonial blade upon the brazier's metal rim, and half-circled so that again he faced the window. The sword's point still touching the brazier, Micon raised the gong, and held it before him at arm's length a moment; the smoking incense rose to writhe about the gong, as metal filings to a magnet.

"Rajasta!" Micon said, commandingly. "Stand by me, your arm across my shoulders." He winced as the Priest of Light complied. "Gently, my brother! Good. And now—" He drew a deep breath. "We wait."

The keening wail deepened, a rushing crescendo of sonic vibrations that ranged away and above the audible tones. Then—silence.

They waited. The sudden quiet lengthened, dripped and shadowed, crept back and welled up, suggesting the starless vastnesses of the universe, drowning all sounds in a dead, immense weight of stillness that crushed them like the folds of burial robes.

Rajasta could feel Micon's body, straight and stiff and real beneath the metallic cloak, and it was somehow the only real thing in all that empty deadened stillness. With a rasping whisper a wind blew through the window, and the lights grew dim; the air about them quivered, and a prickling came and crawled over Rajasta's skin. He felt, rather than saw, a misty shivering in the gloom, sensed faint distortions in the outlines of the familiar room.

The trained resonance of the Initiate's voice rang through the weight of the silence: "I have not summoned! By the Gong—" Moving suddenly, he struck the gong a sharp, hard blow with the sword's pommel; the brazen clamor sounded clashingly through the deadness. "By the Sword—" Again Micon raised the sword and held it outstretched, the point toward the window. "And by the Word on the Sword—by iron and bronze and fire—" He plunged the sword down, into the flame, and there was a crackling and sputtering of sparks.

Then the Word came slowly from Micon's throat, almost visible, in long tremolos of slow vibration that echoed and re-echoed through octave over octave, thrilling and reverberating, sounding on . . . and on . . . and on, into some unimaginable infinity of time and space, quivering through universe after universe, into a stirring and a quickening that had neither place nor moment, but encompassed beginning and end and all between.

The shimmering distortion swirled and sparkled, faster and faster as if the masonry walls spun around and closed in upon them. Once more Micon raised the sword and sounded the gong with its pommel; again he thrust the blade's point into the brazier. There came a dull, distant roaring as the fire flared and tongued its way up the embedded blade. The distortions continued to twist around them, closer but less dizzyingly swift now; no longer did the room seem about to collapse.

Red and sullen orange, the hot light glowed in a streak across the Initiate's dark face. Slowly, slowly, the shimmerings wrapped themselves around the sword-blade, and for a moment lingered, a blue-white corona pulsing, before flowing down the blade into the flickering fire—which, with a hiss and a whisper, extinguished itself. The floor beneath them quaked and rattled. Then all was quiet.

Micon let himself lean against Rajasta, shivering, the aura of power and majesty quite gone from him. The sword remained, still upright in the burnt-out coals of the brazier. Rajasta was about to speak when there was a final, ear-splitting boom from far away.

"Fear not," Micon whispered, harshly. "The power returns through those who sought to use it, unsanctioned. Our work is —ended, now. And I—" He sagged suddenly and went limp, a dead weight in the Priest's arms.

Rajasta lifted the Atlantean bodily and carried him to the bed. He laid Micon down, gently loosed and removed the leather thong about the Initiate's wrist, from which the gong had hung suspended. Setting the instrument aside, Rajasta dampened a bit of cloth he found nearby and bathed the beaded sweat from the unconscious man's face. Micon stirred and moaned.

Rajasta frowned sternly, his lips pursed with worry. The Atlantean had a white and death-like pallor, a waxen quality that boded no good. *This*, Rajasta reflected, *is exactly what I do not like about magic! It weakens the strong, enervates the weak! It would be a fine thing,* he thought angrily, *if Micon drove away one danger, only to succumb to this!*

The Atlantean groaned again, and Rajasta rose up, to stride to the door with a sudden decision. Summoning a slave, the Priest said only, "Send for the Healer Riveda."

III

For Domaris, drugged but tense with half-waking, formless shadows and horrors, the Nadir-night was a confused nightmare. It was almost a relief to struggle to awareness and find imperative physical pain substituted for dreams of dread; her child's birth, she suddenly realized, was imminent.

On a fatalistic impulse, she sent no word to Micon or Rajasta. Deoris was nowhere to be found, and only Elara knew when she went, alone and afoot as the custom required, to the House of Birth.

And then there was the long waiting, more tiresome at first than painful. She submitted to the minor irritations of the preliminary stages with good grace, for Domaris was too well-disciplined to waste her strength in resentment: answering questions, giving all sorts of intimate information, being handled and examined like some animal (*like a kittening cat,* she told herself, trying to be amused instead of annoyed) kept her mind off her discomfort.

She was not exactly afraid: in common with all Temple women, she had served in Caratra's Temple many times, and the processes of birth held no mysteries for her. But her life had been one of radiant health, and this was almost her first experience with pain and its completely personal quality.

Moreover, and worse, she felt sorry for the little girl they had left with her during this first time of waiting. It was all too obviously the child's first attendance at a confinement, and she acted frightened. This did not add to Domaris's assurance, for she hated blundering of any sort, and if she had one deep-rooted fear, it was of being placed in unskilled hands when she could not help herself. And yet, irrationally, her annoyance grew, rather than lessening, when little Cetris told her, by way of reassurance, that the Priestess Karahama had chosen to attend her confinement.

Karahama! thought Domaris. *That daughter-to-the-winds!*

It seemed a long time, although it was barely past noon, when Cetris sent for the Priestess. To Domaris's complete astonishment, Deoris came into the room with her. It was the first time since the ceremony that Domaris had seen her sister robed as a Priestess of Caratra, and for a moment she hardly recognized the little white face beneath the blue veil. It seemed to her that Deoris's face was the most welcome thing she had ever seen in her life.

She turned toward her little sister—they had kept her on her feet—and held out her arms. But Deoris stood, stricken, in the doorway, making no move to come near her.

Domaris's knuckles were white as she clenched her hands together. "Deoris!" she pleaded. With frozenly reluctant steps, Deoris went to her sister's side and stood beside Domaris, while Karahama took Cetris to a far corner and questioned her in an undertone.

Deoris felt sick, seeing the familiar agony seize on Domaris. Domaris! Her sister, always to Deoris a little more than human. The realization shook something which lay buried in Deoris's heart; somehow, she had thought it would have to be different with Domaris. Ordinary things could not touch *her!* All that—the pain and the danger and the blood—it couldn't happen to Domaris!

And yet it could, it would. It was happening now, before her eyes.

Karahama dismissed Cetris—the little girls of twelve and thirteen were allotted only these simple tasks of waiting, of fetching and carrying and running errands—and came to Domaris, looking down at her with a reassuring smile. "You may rest now," she remarked, good-humouredly, and Domaris sank gratefully down on the couch. Deoris, steadying her with quick, strong hands, felt that Domaris was trembling, and sensed—with a terrible sensitivity—the effort Domaris was making not to struggle, or cry out.

Domaris made herself smile at Deoris and whisper, "Don't look like that, you silly child!" Domaris felt quite bewildered: what was the matter with Deoris? She had seen Deoris's work, had made a point of informing herself, for personal reasons, about her sister's progress. She knew that Deoris was already permitted to work without supervision, even to go unattended into the city to deliver the wives of such commoners or merchant women as might request the attendance of a Priestess; a token of skill which not even Elis had won as yet.

Karahama, noticing the smile and the rigid control, nodded with satisfaction. *Good! This Domaris has courage!* She felt kindly disposed toward her more fortunate half-sister, and now, bending above her, said pleasantly, "You will find the waiting easier now, I think. Deoris, the rule has not yet been broken—only bent a little." Karahama smiled at her own tiny joke as she added in dismissal, "You may go now."

Domaris heard the sentence with her heart sinking. "Oh, please let her stay with me!" she begged.

Deoris added her own plea: "I will be good!"

Karahama only smiled tolerantly and reminded them of the law: both women must surely know that in Caratra's House it was forbidden for a woman's sibling sister to attend the birth of her child. "Moreover," Karahama added, with a deferential movement of her head, "as an Initiate of Light, Domaris must be attended only by her equals."

"How interesting," Domaris murmured dryly, "that my own sister is not my equal."

Karahama said, with a little tightening of her mouth, "The rule does not refer to equality of birth. True, you are both daughters to the Arch-Priest—but you are Acolyte to the Guardian of the Gate, and an Initiate-Priestess. You must be attended by Priestesses of equivalent achievement."

"Has not the Healer-Priest Riveda, as well as yourself, pronounced Deoris capable?" Domaris argued, persisting despite the inner knowledge that it would serve no purpose.

Karahama deferentially repeated that the law was the law, and that if an exception was made now, exception would pile upon exception until the law crumbled away completely. Deoris, afraid to disobey, bent miserably to kiss her sister goodbye. Domaris's lips thinned in anger; this bastard half-sister presumed to lecture them on law, and speak of equals—either of birth or achievement! But a sudden wrench of pain stopped the protests on her tongue; she endured the pain for a moment, then cried out, clutching at Deoris's hands, twisting in sudden torment. Deoris could not have freed herself if she had tried, and Karahama, watching not unsympathetically for all her icy reserve, made no motion to interfere.

At last the spasm passed, and Domaris raised her face; sweat glistened on her forehead and her upper lip. Her voice had a knife's edge: "As an Initiate of Light," she said, throwing Karahama's words back at her, "I have the right to suspend that law! Deoris stays! Because *I wish it!*" She added the indomitable formula—"As I have said it."

It was the first time Domaris had used her new rank to command. A queer little glow thrilled through her, to be drowned in the recurring pain. An ironical reflection stirred in the back of her mind: she had power over pain for others, but she was powerless to save herself any of this. Men's laws she might suspend almost as she willed; but she might not abrogate Nature so much as a fraction for her own sake, whatever her power, for she must experience fully, to her own completion. She endured.

Deoris's small hands were marked red when Domaris released them, and the older girl raised them remorsefully to her lips and kissed them. "Do I ask too much, puss?"

Deoris shook her head numbly. She couldn't refuse anything Domaris asked—but in her heart she wished that Domaris had not asked this, wished that Domaris had not the power to set aside those laws. She felt lost, too young, totally unfitted to take this responsibility.

Karahama, indignant at this irrefutable snubbing of herself and her authority, departed. Domaris's pleasure at this development was short-lived, for Karahama returned minutes later with two novice pupils.

Domaris raised herself, her face livid with fury. "This is intolerable!" she protested, her wrath driving out pain for a moment. Temple women were supposed to be exempt from being the objects of lessons; Domaris, as a Priestess of Light, had the right to choose her own attendants, and she certainly was not subject to this—this humiliation!

Karahama paid not the slightest attention, but went on

calmly lecturing to her pupils, indirectly implying that women in labor sometimes developed odd notions. . . . Domaris, smouldering with resentment, submitted. She was angry still, but there were intervals now, more and more often, when she was unable to express herself—and it is not effective to vent one's wrath in broken phrases. The most humiliating fact was that with each paroxysm she lost the thread of her invective.

Karahama's retaliation was not entirely heartless, however. Before long, she concluded her remarks, and began to dismiss her pupils.

Domaris summoned enough concentrated coherence to command, "You too may go! You have said yourself that I must be attended by my equals—so—leave me!"

It was biting dismissal: it repaid, in full and in kind, the indignity offered to Domaris. Spoken to an equal, without witnesses, it would have been cruel and insulting enough; said to Karahama, before her pupils, a blow in the face would have been less offensive.

Karahama drew herself erect, half inclined to protest; then, forcing a smile, only shrugged. Deoris *was* capable, after all; and Domaris was not in the slightest danger. Karahama could only demean herself further by argument. "So be it," she said tersely, and went.

Domaris, conscious that she violated the spirit if not the letter of the law, was almost moved to call her back—but still, not to have Deoris with her! Domaris was not perfect; she was very human, and very angry. Also, she was torn again by a hateful wave of pain that seemed to tear her protesting body in a dozen different directions. She forgot Karahama's existence. "Micon!" she moaned, writhing, "Micon!"

Deoris quickly bent over her, speaking soothing words, holding her, quieting the restless rebellion with a skillful touch. "Micon will come, if you ask it, Domaris," she said, when her sister had calmed a little. "Do you want that?"

Domaris dug her hands convulsively into the bedding. Now at last she understood this—which was not law but merely custom—which decreed that a woman should bear her child apart and without the knowledge of the father. "No," she whispered, "no, I will be quiet." Micon should not, must not know the price of his son! If he were in better health—but Mother Caratra! Was it like this for everyone?

Although she tried to keep her mind on the detailed instructions Deoris was giving, her thoughts slid away again and again into tortured memories. *Micon*, she thought, *Micon! He has endured more than this! He did not cry out! At last I begin to understand him!* She laughed then, more than a little hysterical, at the thought that, once, she had prayed to the Gods that she might share some of his torments. *Let no one say the Gods do not answer our prayers! And yes, yes! I would endure gladly worse than this for him!* Here her thoughts slid off into incoherence again. *The rack must be like this, a body broken apart on a wheel of pain . . . and so I share what he endured, to free him of all pain forever! Do I give birth, or death? Both, both!*

Grim, terrible laughter shook her with hysterical frenzies until mere movement became agony unbearable. She heard Deoris protesting angrily, felt hands restraining her, but none of Deoris's coaxing and threatening could quiet her hysteria now. She went on and on, laughing deliriously until it became more than laughter and she sobbed rackingly, unconscious to all except pain and its sudden cessation. She lay weeping in absolute exhaustion, unknowing, uncaring what was going on.

"Domaris." The strained, taut voice of her sister finally penetrated her subsiding sobs. "Domaris, darling, please try to stop crying, *please*. It's over. Don't you want to see your baby?"

Limp and worn with the aftermath of hysteria, Domaris could hardly believe her ears. Languidly she opened her eyes. Deoris looked down, with a weary smile, and turned to pick up the child—a boy, small and perfectly formed, with a reddish down that covered lightly the small round head, face tightly-screwed and contorted, squalling lustily at the need to live and breathe apart from his mother.

Domaris's eyes had slipped shut again. Deoris sighed, and set about wrapping the baby in linen cloths. *Why should such an indefinite scrap of flesh be allowed to cause such awful pain?* she asked herself, not for the first time. Something was gone irrevocably from her feeling for her sister. Domaris never knew quite how close Deoris came to hating her then, for having put her through this. . . .

When Domaris's eyes opened again, reason dwelt behind them, though they looked dark and haunted. She moved an exploring hand. "My baby," she whispered fearfully.

Deoris, afraid her sister would break into that terrible

sobbing again, held the swaddled infant where Domaris could see him. "Can't you hear?" she asked gently. "He screams loud enough for twins!"

Domaris tried to raise herself, but fell back with weariness. She begged hungrily, "Oh, Deoris, give him to me!"

Deoris smiled at the unfailing miracle and bent to lay the baby boy on his mother's arm. Domaris's face was ecstatic and shining as she snuggled the squirming bundle close—then, with sudden apprehension, she fumbled at the cloths about him. Deoris bent and prevented her, smiling at this, too—further proof that Domaris was no different from any other woman. "He is perfect," she assured. "Must I count every finger and toe for you?"

With her free hand, Domaris touched her sister's face. "Little Deoris," she said softly, and stopped. She would never have wanted to endure that without Deoris at her side, but there was no way to tell her sister that. She only murmured, so very low that Deoris could, if she chose, pretend not to hear: "Thank you, Deoris!" Then, laying her head wearily beside the baby, "Poor mite! I wonder if he is as tired as I am?" Her eyes flickered open again. "Deoris! Say nothing of this to Micon! I must myself lay our son in his arms. That is my duty—" Her lips contracted, but she went on, steadily, "and my very great privilege."

"He shall not hear it from me," Deoris promised, and lifted the baby from his mother's reluctant arms.

Domaris almost slept, dreaming, although she was conscious of cool water on her hot face and bruised body. Docilely, she ate and drank what was put to her lips, and knew, sleepily, that Deoris—or someone—smoothed her tangled hair, covered her with clean fresh garments that smelled of spices, and tucked her between smooth fragrant linens. Twilight and silence were cool in the room; she heard soft steps, muted voices. She slept, woke again, slept.

Once, she became conscious that the baby had been laid in her arms again, and she cuddled him close, for the moment altogether happy. "My little son," she whispered tenderly, contentedly; then, smiling to herself, Domaris gave him the name he would bear until he was a man. "My little Micail!"

IV

The door swung open silently. The tall and forbidding form of Mother Ysouda stood at the threshold. She beckoned to Deoris, who motioned to her not to speak aloud; the two tiptoed into the corridor.

"She sleeps again?" Mother Ysouda murmured. "The Priest Rajasta waits for you in the Men's Court, Deoris. Go at once and change your garments, and I will care for Domaris." She turned to enter the room, then halted and looked down at her foster daughter and asked in a whisper, "What happened, girl? How came Domaris to anger Karahama so fearfully? Were there angry words between them?"

Timidly, with much prompting, Deoris related what had happened.

Mother Ysouda shook her grey head. "That is not like Domaris!" Her withered face drew down in a scowl.

"What will Karahama do?" Deoris asked apprehensively.

Mother Ysouda stiffened, conscious that she had spoken too freely to a mere junior Priestess. "You will not be punished for obeying the command of an Initiate-Priestess," she said, with austere dignity, "but it is not for you to question Karahama. Karahama is a Priestess of the Mother, and it would indeed be unbecoming in her to harbor resentment. If Domaris spoke thoughtlessly in her extremity, doubtless Karahama knows it was the anger of a moment of pain and will not be offended. Now go, Deoris. The Guardian waits."

The words were rebuke and dismissal, but Deoris pondered them, deeply troubled, while she changed her garments—the robes she wore within the shrine of the Mother must not be profaned by the eyes of any male. Deoris could guess at much that Mother Ysouda had not wanted to say: Karahama was not of the Priest's Caste, and her reactions could not accurately be predicted.

In the Men's Court, a few minutes later, Rajasta turned from his pacing to hasten toward Deoris.

"Is all well with Domaris?" he asked. "They say she has a son."

"A fine healthy son," Deoris answered, surprised to see the

calm Rajasta betraying such anxiety. "And all is well with Domaris."

Rajasta smiled with relief and approval. Deoris seemed no longer a spoilt and petulant child, but a woman, competent and assured within her own sphere. He had always considered himself the mentor of Deoris as well as of Domaris, and, though a little disappointed that she had left the path of the Priesthood of Light and thus placed herself beyond his reach as a future Acolyte or Initiate, he had approved her choice. He had often inquired about her since she had been admitted to the service of Caratra, and it pleased him greatly that the Priestesses praised her skill.

With genuine paternal affection he said, "You grow swiftly in wisdom, little daughter. They tell me you delivered the child. I had believed that was contrary to some law. . . ."

Deoris covered her eyes with one hand. "Domaris's rank places her above that law."

Rajasta's eyes darkened. "That is true, but—did she ask, or command?"

"She—commanded."

Rajasta was disturbed. While a Priestess of Light had the privilege of choosing her own attendants, that law had been made to allow leniency under certain unusual conditions. In wilfully invoking it for her own comfort, Domaris had done wrong.

Deoris, sensing his mood, defended her sister: "*They* violated the law! A Priest's daughter is exempt from having pupils or novices beside her, and Ka—" She broke off, blushing. In the heat of the moment, she had forgotten that she spoke to a man. Moreover, it was unthinkable to argue with Rajasta; yet she felt impelled to add, stubbornly, "If anyone did wrong, it was Karahama!"

Rajasta checked her with a gesture. "I am Guardian of the Gate," he reminded her, "not of the Inner Courts!" More gently, he said, "You are very young to have been so trusted, my child. Command or no command—no one would have dared leave the Arch-Priest's daughter in incompetent hands."

Shyly, Deoris murmured, "Riveda told me—" She stopped, remembering that Rajasta did not much like the Adept.

The Priest said only, "Lord Riveda is wise; what did he tell thee?"

"That—when I lived before—" She flushed, and hurried.

on, "I had known all the healing arts, he said, and had used them evilly. He said that—in this life, I should atone for that. . . ."

Rajasta considered, heavy-hearted, recollecting the destiny written in the stars for this child. "It may be so, Deoris," he said, noncommittally. "But beware of becoming proud; the dangers of old lives tend to recur. Now tell me: did it go hard for Domaris?"

"Somewhat," Deoris said, hesitantly. "But she is strong, and all should have been easy. Yet there was much pain that I could not ease. I fear—" She lowered her eyes briefly, then met Rajasta's gaze bravely as she went on, "I am no High Priestess in this life, but I very much fear that another child might endanger her greatly."

Rajasta's mouth became a tight line. Domaris had indeed done ill, and the effect of her wilfulness was already upon her. Such a recommendation, from one of Deoris's skill, was a grave warning—but her rank in the Temple was not equivalent to her worth, and she had, as yet, no authority to make such a recommendation. Had Domaris been properly attended by a Priestess of high rank, even one of lesser skill, her word, when properly sworn and attested, would have meant that Domaris would never again be allowed to risk her life; a living mother to a living child was held, in the Temple of Light, as worth more than the hope of a second child. Now Domaris must bear the effect of the cause she had herself set in motion.

"It is not your business to recommend," he said, as gently as possible. "But for now, we need not speak of that. Micon—"

"Oh, I almost forgot!" Deoris exclaimed. "We are not to tell him, Domaris wants to—" She broke off, seeing the immense sadness that crossed Rajasta's face.

"You must think of something to tell him, little daughter. He is gravely ill, and must not be allowed to worry about her."

Deoris suddenly found herself unable to speak, and her eyes stared wide.

Brokenly, Rajasta said, "Yes, it is the end. At last—I think it is the end."

Chapter Seventeen

DESTINY AND DOOM

I

Micail was three days old when Domaris rose and dressed herself with a meticulous care unusual with her. She used the perfume Micon loved, the scent from his homeland—his first gift to her. Her face was still, but not calm, and although Domaris kept from crying as Elara made her lovely for this ordeal, the servant woman herself burst into tears as she put the wriggling, clean-scented bundle into his mother's arms.

"Don't!" Domaris begged, and the woman fled. Domaris held her son close, thinking drearily, *Child, I bore you to give your father death*.

Remorsefully she bent her face over the summer softness of his. Grief was a part of her love for this child, a deep bitter thing twisting into her happiness. She had waited three days, and still she was not sure that either her body or her mind would carry her through this final duty to the man she loved. Lingering, still delaying, she scanned the miniature indeterminate features of Micail, seeking some strong resemblance to his father, and a sob twisted her throat as she kissed the reddish down on his silken forehead.

At last, raising her face proudly, she moved to the door and went forth, Micail in her arms. Her step was steady; her reluctant feet did not betray her dread.

Guilt lay deep on her. Those three days were, she felt, a selfishness that had held a tortured man to life. Even now she moved only under the compulsion of sworn duty, and her thoughts were barbed whips of self-scorn. Micail whimpered protestingly and she realized that she was clutching him far too tightly to her breast.

She walked on, slowly, seeing with half her eyes the freshening riot of color in the gardens; though she pulled the swaddlings automatically closer about her child's head, Domaris saw only Micon's dark haggard face, felt only the bitterness of her own pain.

The way was not long, but to Domaris it was the length to the world's end. With every step, she left the last of her youth a little further behind. Yet after a time, an indefinite period, the confusion of thought and feeling gradually cleared and she found herself entering Micon's rooms. She swayed a little with the full realization: *Now there is no return.* Dimly she knew that for her there had never been.

Her eyes swept the room in unconscious appeal, and the desperation in her young face brought choking grief to Deoris's throat. Rajasta's eyes became even more compassionate, and even Riveda's stern mouth lost some of its grimness. This last Domaris saw, and it gave her a new strength born of anger.

Proudly she drew herself erect, clasping the child. Her eyes resting on Micon's wasted face; she put the others out of her mind. This was the moment of her giving; now she could give more than herself, could surrender—and by her own act—her hopes of any personal future. Silently she moved to stand beside him, and the change which but a few days had wrought in him smote her like a blow.

Until this moment, Domaris had allowed herself to cling to some faint hope that Micon might still be spared to her, if only a little longer. . . . Now she saw the truth.

Long she looked upon him, and every feature of Micon's darkly noble frame etched itself forever across her life with the bitter acid of agony.

Finally Micon's sightless eyes opened, and it seemed that at last he saw, with something clearer than sight, for—although Domaris had not spoken, and her coming had been greeted with silence—he spoke directly to her. "My lady of Light," he whispered, and there was that in his voice which defied naming. "Let me hold—our son!"

Domaris knelt, and Rajasta moved to unobtrusively support Micon as the Atlantean drew himself upright. Domaris laid the child in the thin outstretched arms, and murmured words in themselves unimportant, but to the dying man, of devastating significance: "Our son, beloved—our perfect little son."

Micon's attenuated fingers ran lightly, tenderly across the little face. His own face, like a delicate waxen death-mask, bent over the child; tears gathered and dropped from the blind eyes, and he sighed, with an infinite wistfulness. "If I might— only once—behold my son!"

A harsh sound like a sob broke the silence, and Domaris raised wondering eyes. Rajasta was as silent as a statue, and Deoris's throat could never have produced that sound . . .

"My beloved—" Micon's voice steadied somewhat. "One task remains. Rajasta—" The Atlantean's ravaged face turned to the Priest. "It is yours to guide and guard my son." So saying, he allowed Rajasta to take the baby in his hands, and quickly Domaris cradled Micon's head against her breast. Weakly smiling, he drew away from her. "No," he said with great tenderness, "I am weary, my love. Let me end this now. Begrudge not your greatest gift."

He rose slowly to his feet, and Riveda, shadow-swift, was there to put his strong arm under Micon's. With a little knowing smile, Micon accepted the Grey-robe's support. Deoris reached to clasp her sister's icy hand in her tiny warm one, but Domaris was not even aware of the touch.

Micon leaned his face over the child, who lay docile in Rajasta's arms, and with his racked hands, lightly touched the closed eyes.

"See—what I give you to see, Son of Ahtarrath!"

The twisted fingers touched the minute, curled ears as the Initiate's trained voice rang through the room: "Hear—what I give you to hear!"

He drew his hands lightly over the downy temples. "Know the power I know and bestow upon you, child of Ahtarrath's heritage!"

He touched the rosy seeking mouth, which sucked at his finger and spat it forth again. "Speak with the powers of the storm and the winds—of sun and rain, water and air, earth and fire! Speak only with justice, and with love."

The Atlantean's hand now rested over the baby's heart. "Beat only to the call of duty, to the powers of love! Thus I, by the Power I bear—" Micon's voice thinned suddenly. "By the—the Power I bear, I seal and sign you to—to that Power . . ."

Micon's face had become a drained and ghastly white. Word by word and motion by motion, he had loosed the superb forces which alone had held him from dissolution. With what seemed a tremendous effort, he traced a sign across the baby's brow; then leaned heavily on Riveda.

Domaris, with hungry tenderness, rushed to his side, but Micon, for a moment, paid her no heed as he gasped, "I knew this would—I knew—Lord Riveda, you must finish—finish the binding! I am—" Micon drew a long, labored breath. "Seek not to play me false!" And his words were punctuated by a distant clap of thunder.

Grim, unspeaking, Riveda let Domaris take Micon's weight, freeing him for the task. The Grey-robe knew well why he, and not Rajasta or some other, had been chosen to do this thing. The apparent sign of the Atlantean's trust was, in fact, the exact opposite: by binding Riveda's karma with that of the child, even in this so small way, Micon sought to ensure that Riveda, at least, would not dare attack the child, and the Power the baby represented. . . .

Riveda's ice-blue eyes burned beneath his brows as, with a brusque voice and manner, he took up the interrupted ritual: "To you, son of Ahtarrath, Royal Hunter, Heir-to-the-Word-of-Thunder, the Power passes. Sealed by the Light—" The Adept undid, with his strong skillful hands, the swaddlings about the child, and exposed him, with a peculiarly ceremonious gesture, to the flooding sunlight. The rays seemed to kiss the downy skin, and Micail stretched with a little cooing gurgle of content.

The solemnity of the Magician's face did not lighten, but his eyes now smiled as he returned the child to Rajasta's hands, and raised his arms as for invocation. "Father to son, from age to age," Riveda said, "the Power passes; known to the true-begotten. So it was, and so it is, and so it shall ever be. Hail Ahtarrath—and to Ahtarrath, farewell!"

Micail stared with placid, sleepy gravity at the circle of faces which ringed him in—but not for long. The ceremony ended now, Rajasta hastily placed the baby in Deoris's arms, and took Micon from Domaris's embrace, laying him gently down. Still the Atlantean's hands groped weakly for Domaris, and she came and held him close again; the naked grief in her eyes was a crucifixion.

Deoris, the baby clasped to her breast, sobbed noiselessly, her face half-buried in Rajasta's mantle; the Priest of Light stood with his arm around her, but his eyes were fixed upon Micon. Riveda, his arms crossed on his chest, stared somberly upon the scene, and his massive shadow blotted the sunlight from the room.

The Prince was still, so still that the watchers, too, held their breath. . . . At last he stirred, faintly. "Lady—clothed with Light," he whispered. "Forgive me." He waited, and drops of sweat glistened on his forehead. *"Domaris."* The word was a prayer.

It seemed that Domaris would never speak, that speech had been dammed at its fountainhead, that all the world would go silent to the end of eternity. At last her white lips parted, and her voice was clear and triumphant in the stillness. "It is well, my beloved. Go in peace."

The waxen face was immobile, but the lips stirred in the ghost of Micon's old radiant smile. "Love of mine," he whispered, and then more softly still, "Heart—of flame—" and a breath and a sigh moved in the silence and faded.

Domaris bent forward . . . and her arms, with a strange, pathetic little gesture, fell to her sides, empty.

Riveda moved softly to the bedside, and looked into the serene face, closing the dead eyes. "It is over," the Adept said, almost tenderly and with regret. "What courage, what strength—and what waste!"

Domaris rose, dry-eyed, and turned toward Riveda. "That, my Lord, is a matter of opinion," she said slowly. "It is our triumph! Deoris—give me my son." She took Micail in her arms, and her face shone, unearthly, in the sublimity of her sorrow. "Behold our child—and our future. Can you show me the like, Lord Riveda?"

"Your triumph, Lady, indeed," Riveda acknowledged, and bent in deep reverence.

Deoris came and would have taken the baby once more, but Domaris clung to him, her hands trembling as she caressed her little son. Then, with a last, impassioned look at the dark still face that had been Micon's, she turned away, and the men heard her whispered, helpless prayer: "Help me—O Thou Which Art!"

Deoris led her sister, resistless, away.

II

That night was cold. The full moon, rising early, flooded the sky with a brilliance that blotted out the stars. Low on the horizon, sullen flames glowed at the sea-wall, and ghost-lights, blue and dancing, flitted and streamed in the north.

Riveda, for the first and last time in his life robed in the stainless white of the Priest's Caste, paced with stately step backward and forward before Micon's apartments. He had not the faintest idea why he, rather than Rajasta or one of the other Guardians, had been chosen for this vigil—and he was no longer so certain why Micon had suffered his aid at the last! Had trust or distrust been the major factor in Micon's final acceptance of him?

It was clear that the Atlantean had, in part at least, feared him. But why? He was no Black-robe! The twists and turns of it presented a riddle far beyond his reading—and Riveda did not like the feeling of ignorance. Yet without protest or pride he had divested himself tonight of the grey robe he had worn for so many years, and clothed himself in the ritual robes of Light. He felt curiously transformed, as if with the robes he had also slipped on something of the character of these punctilious Priests.

Nonetheless he felt a deeply personal grief, and a sense of defeat. In Micon's last hours, his weakness had moved Riveda as his strength could never have done. A grudged and sullenly yielded respect had given way to deep and sincere affection.

It was seldom, indeed, that Riveda allowed events to disturb him. He did not believe in destiny—but he knew that threads ran through time and the lives of men, and that one could become entangled in them. *Karma*. It was, Riveda thought grimly, like the avalanches of his own Northern mountains. A single stone rattled loose by a careless step, and all the powers of the world and nature could not check an inch of its motion. Riveda shuddered. He felt a curious certainty that Micon's death had brought destiny and doom on them all. He didn't like the thought. Riveda preferred to believe that he could master destiny, pick a path through the pitfalls of karma, by his will and strength alone.

He continued his pacing, head down. The Order of Magicians, known here as Grey-robes, was ancient, and elsewhere held a more honored name. In Atlantis were many Adepts and Initiates of this Order, among whom Riveda held high place. And now Riveda knew something no one else had guessed, and felt it was legitimately his own.

Once, in mad raving, a word and a gesture had slipped unaware from his chela, Reio-ta. Riveda had noted both, meaningless as they had seemed at the moment. Later, he had seen the same gesture pass between Rajasta and Cadamiri when they thought themselves unobserved; and Micon, in the delirium of agony which had preceded the quiet of his last hours, had muttered Atlantean phrases—one a duplicate of Reio-ta's. Riveda's brain had stored all these things for future reference. Knowledge, to him, was something to be acquired; a thing hidden was something to be sought all the more assiduously.

Tomorrow, Micon's body was to be burned, the ashes returned to his homeland. That task he, Riveda, should undertake. Who had a better right than the Priest who had consecrated Micon's son to the power of Ahtarrath?

III

At daybreak, Riveda ceremoniously drew back the curtains, letting sunlight flood in and fill the apartment where Micon lay. Dawn was a living sea of ruby and rose and livid fire; the light lay like dancing flames on the dark dead face of the Initiate, and Riveda, frowning, felt that Micon's death had ended nothing.

This began in fire, Riveda thought, *it will end in fire . . . but will it be only the fire of Micon's funeral? Or are there higher flames rising in the future. . . ?* He frowned, shaking his head. *What nonsense am I dreaming? Today, fire will burn what the Black-robes left of Micon, Prince of Ahtarrath . . . and yet, in his own way, he has defeated all the elements.*

With the sun's rise, white-robed Priests came and took Micon up tenderly, bearing him down the winding pathway into the face of the morning. Rajasta, his face drawn with grief, walked before the bier; Riveda, with silent step and bent head, walked after. Behind them, a long procession of white-

mantled Priests and Priestesses in silver fillets and blue cloaks
followed in tribute to the stranger, the Initiate who had died in
their midst . . . and after these stole a dim grey shadow,
bowed like an old man shaken with palsied sobbing, grey cloak
huddled over his face, his hands hidden within a patched and
threadbare robe. But no man saw how Reio-ta Lantor of
Ahtarrath followed his Prince and brother to the flames.

Also unseen, high on the summit of the great pyramid, a
woman stood, tall and sublime, her face crimsoned with the
sunrise and the morning sky ablaze with the fire of her hair. In
her arms a child lay cradled, and as the procession faded to
black shadows against the radiant light in the east, Domaris
held her child high against the rising sun. In a steady voice, she
began to intone the morning hymn:

> *O beautiful upon the Horizon of the East,*
> *Lift up the light unto day, O eastern Star;*
> *Day-star, awaken, arise!*
> *Joy and giver of light, awake,*
> *Lord and giver of life,*
> *Lift up thy light, O Star of Day,*
> *Day-star, awaken, arise!*

Far below, the flames danced and spiralled up from the
pyre, and the world was drowned in flame and sunlight.